LUCIAN

A JAMES THOMAS NOVEL

BROOKE SIVENDRA

1

JAMES THOMAS

"I've got a plan."

Worry lines etched into his brother's forehead as the words left James' lips.

James continued. "We're going to dangle Eric like a piece of meat in front of a starving lion, because that's what Biskup is. He's hungry, he's desperate for that code, and his pride is wounded. Eric betraying him would've humiliated him, and a man like Alexandr Biskup will never let that go unpunished. He can't; he's too proud, too ego-driven. If he finds out that Eric is still alive, he'll have no choice but to hunt him because he needs to show the underground that no one crosses him and gets away with it."

Deacon's eyes were hard and unrelenting. James had expected as much. It was a risky plan, but the payoff would be huge. It could save James' life. And Mak's.

"That's all good and well," Deacon said, "but how do we get close enough to dangle Eric and not get mauled to death ourselves?"

"By using our best weapon," James said, setting his eyes upon Samuel, who looked nervously between the two brothers. "Samuel can drip-feed the intel at an agonizingly slow pace, which will give me time to recover," James said, the throbbing ache of his upper arm a constant reminder of the fresh bullet wound. "All Biskup needs to know at this stage is that Eric is alive. We need his trust—as far as that extends in this business—before we show our faces."

"And what happens if we get to that point and we still have no idea where Eric is?" Cami asked.

"The intel should be enough to convince him that we can find him. We'll then plead for time," James said, and Deacon shook his head. James pressed on. "There's an advantage to the alliance between Saratani and the Russians, and that is that if we can't find Eric, we can target Sokolov. They might just lead us to each other."

"This master plan of yours is wrought with traps," Deacon said. "At every corner there is an if—"

"I'm going to die, Deacon," James interjected, his voice slightly raised. "I can't outrun this alliance and you know it. Maybe I can for a month, maybe for a year, but eventually they *will* find me. And I refuse to go down like that. I will die trying before I give up on this life, so don't ask me to do that."

"I'm not asking that of you," Deacon said. "But there has to be a better way. If we gain Biskup's trust, and then can't find Eric, he'll have another example to set and we'll be it. We'll be further complicating an already dire situation."

"We're beyond dire, Deacon. This is the only hope we have."

James locked eyes with his brother and James saw more pain in them than he ever had, and he then realized he'd misunderstood Deacon's hesitance. His brother had lost Nicole—the great love of his life—and now he thought he was going to lose his brother, too. But James knew if they didn't try, Deacon would lose him anyway. Sitting idle wasn't going to get them anywhere, and it was a bigger risk than taking action—any form of action.

Deacon puffed up with resignation. "One condition, James, and this is not negotiable." When James nodded, Deacon continued. "You do not do this alone. If we're working with Biskup, Mak should be safe, at least with her multiple security teams. I go with you, and we do this together. And you stop making the calls like you did in

Amman. If we don't agree, we don't do anything until we find another solution. Do we have a deal?"

Deacon's eyes pierced through his chest, his words like a dagger to the heart, because James knew for the first time in his life that he was going to lie to his brother.

James nodded. "Agreed."

His heart pounded as Deacon continued to eyeball him. Only when Deacon looked to Samuel did James think he'd fooled him. Although, he also wondered if Deacon was just believing what he wanted to because he knew James—he knew him better than anyone—and he knew James would give his life for Deacon's even if that meant deceiving him at some point.

Heaviness clung to the cells of his lungs and the air in the room felt thick, adding to the tension James already felt with his brother. It was an awful feeling, one James couldn't shake, and one he knew he wouldn't completely be able to until this situation was over. Even then, James seriously wondered whether Deacon would be able to fully support his relationship with Mak. James thought that would only come when Deacon had forgiven himself for Nicole's death. That was something James couldn't help him with, but he could resolve the tension this case was causing by killing off Sokolov and capturing Eric. Frankly, that day couldn't come soon enough.

And, if Deacon was now on board with his plan, James didn't want to waste another minute—not when Mak was waiting for him downstairs.

"I think today is a good day to turn on the tap," James said, angling his body toward Samuel. "What's the best way—"

An alert on Samuel's computer caused his head to snap up and James felt his heart skip a beat. It skipped two when Samuel's gaze met his.

"Biskup is in New York," Samuel said, seeming to push the words from his throat.

"What? Where?" James' blood ran cold.

The large screens on the wall flickered, projecting an image of Alexandr Biskup standing outside Mak's office building.

"Oh, God," Deacon said, his eyes doubling in size. "Maybe he's so pissed about all of his men that we've killed that he's making his presence known. This is not a good start to our friendship." Deacon shook his head.

"No, it's not," James said, watching as Biskup lit up a cigarette and chatted to the man standing next to him. They both wore navy-blue suits, but other than that they looked nothing alike. "Find out who he is," James said, nodding toward the acquaintance.

James noted the time, monitoring how long the men spent there. It had been several minutes before Biskup reached his hand into the inner pocket of his jacket and withdrew an envelope. He held it up, as if making a show of it, and then tucked it under his arm. The men walked off casually, but James' eyes never left that envelope. When they passed by a bus shelter, Biskup deposited the envelope in the bin beside it. Immediately afterward, a car pulled up and they got in. Even though Samuel was tracking them, James knew that without men on the ground, they'd lose them. James, however, was in no state to go running through the streets after him. Deacon was, and James needed him to get that envelope even though retrieving it could be like an obstacle course tricked with snags.

"I don't have surveillance in there," Samuel said, referencing the car park Biskup's entourage had driven into.

"Forget about Biskup for the time being," James said, knowing full well it was useless to exhaust resources trying to track him.

"That envelope could be a trap," Deacon said, voicing the thoughts in James' mind. "We need to find a way to access that bin without exposing ourselves... Where can we get a garbage truck?"

They all looked to Samuel, who quickly put his head down once again.

"I've got the address for the city's sanitation depot where the trucks are stored. I assume you want to steal one?"

A wide smile grew on Deacon's face. "I wasn't planning on asking to borrow one."

James grinned, despite the looming sense of threat surrounding Biskup's presence.

Samuel ignored Deacon's smart remark. "I've also got the pick-up schedule for the route the bin is located on. It was emptied this morning, so it's due to be picked up again tomorrow morning—which Biskup would know. Whether it's a trap or not, he'll have someone watching that bin."

James nodded. "So we need to create a situation that provides protection from every angle while we pick up that envelope. The truck itself will provide a portion of cover, but we need more than that."

"Tom can drive," Deacon said. "And I'll do the pickup. We need snipers in place, and teams of people in the street to avoid any of Biskup's potential men getting a clear view and being tempted to take a shot."

James nodded—he was confident in the plan because of one major factor. "I think Biskup wants us to get that envelope. I agree he'll have men watching, but I don't think he's intending to kill us— not today, at least. He wants to communicate, so let's find out what he has to say."

Deacon drew his cell phone. "Tom, grab your kit. I've got a driving job for you. I'll meet you in the car park in five minutes." He hung up, pushing his chair back as he stood. He looked to James. "You don't look great. You should eat something while we go and pick up this truck."

James nodded, his body aching. He was starving, and he was feeling faint again.

"I'll organize the teams to go out on the street," Cami said, standing to leave.

James stood, too. "Samuel, call me when everyone is ready," he said, before turning to Deacon. "Be careful hot-wiring that truck, brother."

Deacon chuckled. "It might be the first garbage truck I've stolen, but it's certainly not the first vehicle," he said as they walked out.

James went to his apartment and quickly bathed, being mindful to keep his bandage dry. He dressed, sprayed some cologne and brushed his teeth before making his way back to Mak.

She was sitting at the dining table when he entered, typing on her phone. Her eyes flickered up to him, more questioning than ever.

"I'm sorry," James said. "Client situation." It was becoming a repetitive excuse, and one he knew she wasn't buying.

She put her phone down. James closed his eyes, inhaling her intoxicating scent. He moaned softly as she parted her lips.

"I can't get enough of you," he whispered.

"So stop leaving me every five seconds," she joked, but he wondered how much truth there was behind her words.

"I would never leave you if I had a choice," he said, pulling out a chair and sitting down beside her.

Mak looked at the takeaway container of food and stood up. "It's probably cold. I'll heat it for you." She placed a hand on his shoulder and kissed his forehead before moving toward the kitchen. The heat of her lips lingered on his skin.

James swiveled on the chair, his eyes following her. "You don't have to wait on me, Mak. It's just a flesh wound."

"I'm convinced it's a more serious wound than you're letting on," she said, tipping the contents of the container into a ceramic bowl. She put it in the microwave.

James didn't particularly want to respond, so he sat mute.

She rested her hip against the cabinet opposite the microwave, looking at him now. "Regardless, I would like to be able to do something for you every once in a while. You do so much for me—you handle everything—and I can't do anything to help you in return. Heating your food and getting your meds from the kitchen isn't quite cutting it, but I suppose it's better than nothing."

"Come here," he said.

Her eyes flickered to the microwave before she moved in his direction. As she neared him, he wrapped one arm around her waist and drew her down on his lap, straddling him.

"You do more for me than you'll ever know," James said. He tucked a loose strand of hair behind her ear. "I have more resources available to me than I should, and more money than I could ever need. But what you give me can't be bought. You give me purpose, you give me hope for a future I had never even dreamed was possible. You make me happy, Mak—something I've never really been before. I wasn't ever unhappy as such, but I guess I didn't know what I was missing because I'd never had it."

His eyes locked with Mak's. "I never understood Deacon and Nicole's relationship, nor did I understand Jayce and Zahra's. I didn't get why they couldn't walk away when there were so many reasons to. But I get it now."

James felt like a rubber band was squeezing his chest, but there was nothing painful about it.

"I lied to you last night," James said, feeling her body tense. The microwave beeped but James held her in place. "It's a lie that we tell everyone because it makes things easier. But I want you to know me —as much as you can. And then maybe you'll understand why you're so important to me."

Her pupils dilated and he knew it was a response to fear—fear of the truth that followed the lie. James didn't know how she was going to take the news, but he knew it was the right time to tell her. The impact of keeping such a secret would only get worse the longer he lived the lie.

"You asked me whether I have any other siblings, and the answer is that I don't know. I don't know if I have *a* sibling."

Her forehead creased.

"Deacon is not my biological brother, Mak, but in every sense I think of him that way."

Her lips parted, her jaw dropped, and she instinctively leaned backward. He didn't let her go.

"I'm sorry, but I felt I couldn't tell you. I don't even know how Deacon is going to react to me telling you now. No one knows except Samuel and Cami."

"I..." Mak started, but the words didn't follow.

"I know. And I understand if you're angry. We tell that lie because it stops the questions—it stops people from asking about our partnership, how it came about and how we know each other. It minimizes the number of stories we need to keep straight."

"The number of lies, you mean?" Mak said.

James nodded. "Yeah. But that lie has become a truth, because I do think of Deacon as my brother. He's family, just like Samuel and Cami are."

Mak shook her head, looking past him. "So everything you've told me about your family is a lie, then?"

"No," James said, angling her head so that she was forced to look at him. "Regarding Deacon's family, he does look like his mother. She is a beautiful woman, and if you ever met her you would recognize them as family immediately. Regarding my family, I don't know them. I was raised in orphanages and never, not once, did a family member come forward. Samuel was able to find some information about my father—possibly, if the information is correct—but that's it."

Her pursed lips smoothed out and her body softened in his arms. He didn't tell her the orphanage story because he wanted pity, though; he just wanted her to know him.

"Where is he?" Mak asked with a softer voice.

"He's dead. Murdered, it seems. I wouldn't believe it was him except for one thing: the eyes." He met her gaze. "I celebrate my birthday on the fifth of January—a date we made up because I don't know my birth date. I was left, without any papers or form of identification, on the doorstep of an orphanage. I'm not just a mystery to you, or to this world, I'm a mystery unto myself as well. But I don't want you to feel bad for me—I certainly don't. I'm telling you this because I want you to know what you mean to me. I wasn't given a family, Mak, but somehow I managed to make one for myself. And I never thought I'd have a partner to share this life with, but then I met you. I don't need anything from you except for your love and support. That's all I want. That's all I need."

Her eyes glistened but no tears fell.

James' heart was pounding in his chest, walloping against his rib cage. His body burned with desire, and with hesitation. Everything she'd done had led him to believe she felt the same way—but this was new territory for him, and he wasn't sure how good at it he was.

She wrapped her arms around his neck and brought their lips

together. There was no tongue, no hunger, no neediness, but there was something even more beautiful. When she drew back, he cupped her cheek, knowing what he wanted to say to her, but not knowing if she was ready to hear it. However, he'd already been hit by one bullet —and with no guarantee he'd survive the next, he didn't want to die without her knowing.

His eyes locked with Mak's, and James felt like someone had a hand around his heart, squeezing it. He brushed his thumb over her cheek.

"I love you, Mak," he whispered. "I had no idea how beautiful falling in love would feel."

A tear dripped from the corner of her eye as she brushed her lips over his. "I wish I had met you earlier—I wish that you were the man I had married."

James wished that too, more than she could understand.

She looked deep into his eyes, behind the mask he wore. "I love you, too, James."

James squeezed her body against his chest and parted his lips. Her tongue wrapped around his. James groaned, every cell in his body raw and tingling. Her kiss was all-consuming, but he yearned for more.

He slid his hands underneath her sweater and glided over her skin. His body felt so electric that for a moment he forgot about his injury, until he reached his arm up and a spear of pain shot through his neck. He winced involuntarily and Mak pulled back.

"I'm okay," James said.

She tilted her head to the side, giving him a once over.

"You're not okay. You're pale, and it's the afternoon and you still haven't eaten." She leaned back, and then said, "Eat first, and then we can finish that. I'm not going anywhere, James Thomas. We have plenty of time."

James smiled, but her words hung above him like dark clouds.

I'm not so sure, Mak. But I'll fight until the end.

2

JAMES THOMAS

His lap was cold, and he missed the heat of her body immediately. Mak retrieved his lunch from the microwave, placing a towel underneath the bowl, and carried it over to him. She sat beside him.

"Thank you," James said, still smiling from their conversation.

She looked at him, her eyes creasing as her lips tilted up. "Eat," she said.

He lifted the fork with his left hand, and noticed she was watching him. "Yes?"

"I thought you would struggle to eat, being right-handed and all," she said, leaning back and crossing one leg over the other.

James shrugged. "I've trained myself to be both left and right handed," he said, and then added by way of explanation, "I need to be able to shoot with my left hand." And that had never been more true than it had been when James had been shooting at her husband a few days ago.

"Oh. I see," she said, giving him an odd grin. "You're a man of many talents, Mr. Thomas."

James scoffed. "You don't need to seduce me, Mak. I'm way past seduction. I'm like an animal now that can't get enough. See, you complain about me going away, but if I were here every day, you might change your mind." He gave her a smoldering look and she bit her lip.

"I hope I get to find out one day," Mak said, and James nodded, but he already knew today wasn't that day. As soon as his phone rang, he'd have to go back to Samuel's office. Deacon didn't need him for such a mission, but James still didn't think it would be appropriate to be making love to his girlfriend while his brother was risking his life to retrieve an envelope, a message, from Biskup—not to mention that James' mind was burning to know what was inside.

The thought occurred to him that he needed to tell Mak about moving apartments, given that he had confirmation his team would finish the additional upgrades tomorrow morning, but he was reluctant to do that until he knew what Biskup wanted—especially since he'd shown up outside her building. James wouldn't move Mak until they had confirmation that he'd left the country, along with his supports.

"A penny for your thoughts," Mak said.

"This pasta is so good," James said, spinning a lie that he didn't touch his conscience.

She rolled her eyes and James grinned but didn't comment. He looked at his watch, figuring he had about an hour until Deacon would be back with the truck. He ate the last forkful of pasta and washed it down with a glass of juice that Mak had retrieved for him while he'd been eating.

"While I do have you for five minutes," Mak started, "what has happened with the case I passed up?"

James pushed his bowl away, giving her his full attention. "Samuel has fed the information to the man's lawyers. They've got the intel, so on that end of things it's just a matter of waiting until the appeal goes through."

"And do you know who has been assigned the case?" Mak crossed her arms over her chest.

James gave her the name.

She wiggled her lips back and forth and then frowned. "He won't raise the accusations."

James had already come to the same conclusion. Deacon and Samuel had reviewed her colleague's case history, and nothing indicated he would. He was a good lawyer, but he didn't take on the kind of cases Mak was known to. James thought her boss gave her that case for a reason—because he'd known Mak was brave enough to voice the accusations.

James couldn't tell her everything was going to work out, to have faith in her colleague—because James knew this story wasn't going to have the ending Mak wanted. James wondered, in time, how she would feel over passing up the case. Would she resent him for asking her to do it? Would she feel like she betrayed herself? James didn't want to be responsible for that, but they also couldn't deal with another security case—not now.

"I don't know, Mak," James finally said, unable to offer her a more comforting answer.

Silence dwelled between them but it was quickly broken by James' phone.

Samuel: Come upstairs.

Already? James checked his watch again, thinking he'd made a mistake. He hadn't. Deacon couldn't possibly be back yet, which meant there was another problem.

"I'm sorry," James said with remorseful eyes. "I'll be back as soon as I can."

She gave a small smile.

He kissed her temple, letting his lips linger for a moment before he turned to leave.

With each step James took toward Samuel's office his worry grew. He needed this alliance. He did not need another complication.

Depending on the message inside the envelope, this could be the perfect beginning for their partnership. A partnership that James knew would give him enough power to defeat Saratani and the Russians. It still wouldn't be easy, and he could definitely still lose, but his odds would be greatly improved.

And it served one other purpose—his primary focus even before his own survival: it would take the heat off Mak. She wouldn't be entirely out of danger, but as long as James could keep a truce with Biskup, he wouldn't try and take her. James wouldn't let his guard down, though, because like they all knew, Biskup could betray them at any point. But for a man with a wounded ego, finding Eric himself would be a more attractive offer than retrieving the code from Eric's estranged wife. And although James didn't know Biskup personally, he thought at some point the man would've had to have questioned whether she actually had the code. Now it was James' responsibility to convince him that she didn't—and not get killed in the process.

Samuel looked up when he entered, and an image of the man that James had seen on the street with Biskup flashed up on the screen.

"Meet Maksym Kovalenko," Samuel said, his cheeks puffing as he sighed and shook his head. "He is very bad news."

James sat down.

"Well, bad doesn't cut it," Samuel continued. "Kovalenko is the worst of the worst. He's a rogue contractor, and given his past history, he is loyal to none. However, reports suggest he's been with Biskup for several years, so whatever arrangement they have—it's currently working for them both."

"If he's been with Biskup that long, then he would've been around when Eric was. And that means Eric has outsmarted them both," James said, thinking aloud. "What's black-marked this guy's record?"

"What hasn't? He's known to all of the major databases, which is why it didn't take me long to get intel. I've had it since you walked out the door but I thought I'd put together a full profile before I dragged you back up here. Drug, weapon and human trafficking appear to be his business dealings of choice. But it's not that I'm concerned about; it's his...violent nature. These"—a series of photographs loaded on the screens—"are assumed to be his handiwork."

James scrunched up his nose. It was almost impossible to recognize the bloody lumps in the photographs as bodies, but the odd toenail or protruding bone gave it away.

"It is suggested he likes to rape, mutilate, and then burn his victims alive. I don't know if he has a particular hate for women, or if it's just a coincidence, but all of these are women." Samuel tilted his head toward the images and drew his lips to the side.

"It's making me very nervous that he's here in New York," James said. Mak was not even leaving this building until he had confirmation Kovalenko had left America.

"Me too, hence why I called you up. I'm sure you'll agree that Biskup wanted us to identify him, but the question is, why? Other than showing he's a threat to Mak, I'm not sure what else would be gained by that, and perhaps we won't know until we pick up the envelope."

James was silent, but his mind was racing. For every opponent, he always tried to put himself in their shoes—in this case Alexandr Biskup's shoes. What was he aiming to achieve? Was it a loaded-threat tactic? Was it a power play? Was he sending an early forecast of Mak's future if she didn't communicate the code?

"I think he's intending to show us her fate—if she doesn't play ball. It's a brazen move coming to New York so publically... What's Maksym's record with the agencies?" James asked.

"He's been arrested on suspicion once—probably the only time they got close enough to him—and in the car he managed to get his hands loose. He bit the neck of the man next to him, ripping his jugular out, before proceeding to eliminate everyone in the car. It was eighteen months ago."

Samuel continued. "One more concerning thing... Reports suggest he's a sniper. Self-trained, but trained nonetheless."

James squeezed the bridge of his nose. In an hour, tops, Deacon was going to be exposed and James knew there was little he could do about it. Deacon wouldn't come in, nor would he let James take his place. His brother would get that envelope, regardless of the risks, because he knew how badly they needed it.

"It may not be a hit, James. Biskup may actually want us to get that envelope," Samuel said.

"And it might be—exactly as Deacon had first thought." James groaned. "Where is Deacon now? How far away are they?"

A map loaded onto the screen and a green circle began moving along the grid. Samuel was using Deacon's tracker to locate him.

"Forty-five minutes, max," Samuel said. "What are you going to do?"

"He's not going to come in," James said, and Samuel muttered in agreement. "So we've got to protect him." James drew his cell phone and dialed Cami's number.

"Hey," she answered.

"How many have you got ready?" James asked.

"Thirty-three. We're putting on protective gear now," Cami said. "What's up?"

"The man that was with Biskup is a sniper, amongst other things."

"Oh, shit," she said.

"Exactly. And you know Deacon, and he's not going to let me do this—especially not when I'm injured. Get your gear on and then I want everyone in Samuel's office as soon as possible."

'Got it," she said, hanging up.

James chewed on his cheek as he looked at the surveillance image of the bin. His eyes flickered to the surrounding buildings, any of which could provide a clear shot for a trained sniper.

"Can you please show me a three-hundred-and-sixty-degree view?" James asked, his eyes glued to the screen as the camera began to rotate.

"That's as good as we can get," Samuel said.

James bit his lip, wondering if Biskup knew that, too.

What game are you playing?

"The truck isn't enough, nor will our teams on the street be enough. Kovalenko is ruthless; he might put bullets into as many of them as he needs to get the main target—Deacon. The truck will provide protection, but we need more of that. We need tall protection."

Samuel raised an eyebrow. "Such as?"

"Two buses," James said, nodding as he formulated his plan. "They need to go up on the sidewalk, create a box, as such."

"You're going to drive two buses up onto a New York sidewalk? That's going to create hysteria, and bring the police."

"Exactly—it will create confusion for everybody except us, provided it's timed perfectly. We just need to be out of there before the police arrive, which should be doable."

Samuel repeated the word *should*, his dislike evident.

The more James thought through the plan, the more confident he was. The best way to obstruct a sniper was always to create bedlam. "Let's tell Deacon," James said, inserting his earwig.

Samuel nodded and then pressed his ear, enabling two-way communication.

"Deacon?" James said.

"Copy."

"We've got a situation. The man accompanying Biskup this morning is a sniper, a damn good one by all accounts—" James hadn't even finished before Deacon interjected.

"Don't even think about it—you're not going out there."

"I wasn't going to suggest that," James said. The only reason he wasn't going to was because he knew it wouldn't get him anywhere. "We're putting in additional resources to provide some tall cover." James proceeded to detail the plan to Deacon, and took the ensuing silence as an indication that his brother was thinking it through.

"Good plan," Deacon said. *"You need to have Zack and Joshi driving those buses, though. And tell them if they run over a pedestrian, we'll kill them ourselves."*

James smiled. "Will do. We're going to need some additional time to get this set up. Be on standby."

"Okay, brother."

James pressed his ear lobe and then turned to the door as Cami opened it, leading the team in.

"All right," James said, standing up and moving toward the whiteboard. "Move in and pay attention. We've got an additional situation to deal with." James drew up the plan on the whiteboard, naming the drivers and indicating where everyone should be and what their roles were. "Any questions?"

They all shook their heads.

James advised them to go down to the prep room and wait until the buses had been picked up.

"I'm going to suit up," James said, ignoring Samuel's hard eyes.

"What do you think you're going to do?"

"Nothing—hopefully. Can you please find a vacant room I can use above the bus shelter? If all goes well, I'll watch from there. If things don't go well, I need to be as close as possible."

Samuel gave a resigned nod.

James went to his apartment and retrieved his kit and bulletproof gear from his closet. He was pulling his sweater over his head—a somewhat difficult task—when Samuel called, giving him instructions. James double-checked his weapon and his earwig, then took the elevator down to the basement to pick up some additional weaponry. When he had what he wanted, he climbed into his car, throwing his bag on the passenger seat, and turned the key in the ignition.

While he drove toward Mak's office apartment, he ran through the plan again—looking for potential pitfalls, of which there were many. Regardless, when James arrived at his destination, he was as confident in it as he was going to get.

"James—what are you doing?" Deacon's voice came through his earwig.

"Getting the best view in the house," James responded.

"Make sure you stay there," Deacon said, and James told him he intended to. And that was the truth—unless something disastrous happened, he intended to stay put.

James entered the code Samuel had given him into the access pad, and the front door of the building opened. He took the elevator up to level ten, and stalked toward apartment twenty-three. James looked over his shoulder, and then drew his scalpel, jimmying the lock. It opened and he quickly moved inside, closing the door behind him. He put his bag down on the windowsill, and began unpacking its contents.

He set up a rifle with a telescopic sight at the window and

brought his eye to the lens. He looked from window to window, building to building. He didn't see Kovalenko, but that didn't mean he wasn't there. He could be in the same building as James.

"James, everyone is in place. We're three blocks out," Deacon said.

"How is the truck?" James asked, grinning as his brother responded.

"It stinks! You can't believe how pungent it is in here," Deacon said. In order to move as efficiently as possible, James knew his brother was standing on the back loading dock of the truck—a truck that almost certainly hadn't been washed since its last round.

James chuckled. "Cami, check in."

"Copy. In place and ready."

"All right. Deacon, call the shots," James said. The timing had to be perfect, and only Deacon could ensure that from his position.

James kept his eye on the buildings, continuing to survey each window. He kept his breathing steady as he listened to his brother lead the team, calling time intervals and positions. When they were one block out, James' eyes moved like roving darts. And as the truck pulled up, James saw it—the silhouette of two men standing in a window.

His heart pulsed a little faster but his hands were steady as he adjusted the lens. *Biskup and Kovalenko.*

"Samuel," James said. "Three o'clock."

"Copy. I've got a surveillance view of the building, but I can't see much."

"Maksym's not set up for a sniper shot," James said. "The plan remains the same."

"Copy," Deacon said as James continued to watch the men in the window. The men that had been causing hell for them, and for his girlfriend. It was ironic that he would end up needing them on his team.

"Three, two, one," Deacon said, and even though James knew where every single one of his staff were, and which direction they would move in—chaos erupted. James could hear the sound of screeching tires and squealing voices even from his position. The

buses lurched up onto the sidewalk, creating the perfect shield. Cami's teams moved in, jamming up the traffic flow, and people began to push each other out of the way as their survival instincts kicked in.

Deacon jumped from the truck and zipped toward the bin. He had it unlatched and was running back to the truck. He made a hurdle-like stride, launching up onto the platform.

With his brother back in the truck, and the envelope secured, James returned his focus to the two men. Biskup appeared to be looking down on the events below with a small grin on his lips. James wondered why the man was smiling, but didn't have time to ponder on it—because when he looked at Kovalenko, the man looked straight back at him, smiled, and waved.

James' jaw locked tight; but when Kovalenko backed away, and held his hands up in surrender, he knew that the envelope hadn't been a setup.

"Deacon, where's that envelope?" James asked.

"I'm searching... I've got it... Oh, shit. It says: Makaela. You have something I want. Something I need. Something that is very valuable. I'm giving you one last chance to give it to me, otherwise the last time you'll hear your mother's voice will be when she's screaming for mercy. You have twenty-four hours. Call me: 212-589-0095."

A pit of unease coiled in his stomach, but James drew his cell phone. "Samuel, we need to get security teams on all of Mak's family, immediately. And get ready to send that phone number the image of Eric on the balcony," James said and dialed the number that Deacon had called out. James looked through the lens again, but the men were gone.

The phone rang three times.

"Hello."

"It's Biskup," Samuel confirmed.

"She doesn't have the code," James said. "But someone else does. Someone who deceived you. Someone I think you would very much want to find."

"Who are you?"

"I'm going to tell you soon, but first I'm going to show you something. Check your messages," James said.

A pause followed.

"Interesting," Biskup said, and there was an edge to his voice that hadn't been there a few seconds ago.

"Isn't it? It was taken two weeks ago, in Amman, Jordan."

The phone was silent. James continued. "I'll give you more, but first you're going to prove to me that I can trust you. If anything happens to Makaela's mother, or any member of her family, you'll get nothing. Is that understood?"

"You have my word."

James smiled grimly. "In twenty-four hours you'll receive the next piece of information. I suggest you go back to your hotel, put your feet up, and relax until then."

"I might even book in to the spa," Biskup said.

"You do that," James said, ending the call.

He ducked below the window, unsure of where the men were.

It was time to leave.

3

MAK ASHWOOD

The bet had been placed, and Mak was determined to win—even if that meant training on her own. Cami had teased her—challenged her—that she couldn't hit five target points in succession. Telling Mak that she couldn't do something only made her more determined, and Cami knew that. Mak didn't care, though; game or not, it gave her something else to do in this building.

Mak reloaded and raised her weapon. Her hands were steady and her breath calm—just as she'd been taught. Her eyes zoomed in on the target, focusing her shot, and she pulled the trigger five times. Mak exhaled, putting the weapon down and pressing the button that would bring the target forward.

Mak jumped as James spoke from behind her. "Do you have any idea how sexy you look?"

He wrapped one arm around her waist, drawing her into his hard body.

"Don't scare me like that! I might've shot you!"

James chuckled. "I made sure your weapon was down first."

He kissed the hollow behind her ear and Mak shivered.

"I didn't hear you come in," Mak said. "How long were you watching?"

"Long enough to be totally aroused," he said, pushing his erection against her ass.

The target stopped in front of them. *Three out of five.*

"You're improving... Remind me not to piss you off," he joked.

"I'm trying to win a bet," Mak said, turning in his arms.

His eyes sparkled as he grinned at her. "I did hear about that, and you might actually pull it off."

"You hear about everything, don't you?"

He gave an arrogant smirk. "Everything," he said, before brushing his lips over hers. Mak closed her eyes, her focus obliterated.

"When do I get my own weapon?" Mak asked in a husky whisper.

He drew her bottom lip between his teeth. "If you keep shooting like that—soon."

His hand slipped from her waist, clutching her ass. She rose up onto the balls of her feet and wrapped her arms around his neck. "How is the client situation?"

"Looking more promising than it has in a while..." James said between kisses. "Come upstairs with me."

His voice was deep and throaty and arousal pearled low in her hips.

"I would love to," she said, and then swept her tongue over his. He moaned and his hand gripped tighter, clutching her. She parted her lips, giving him full access to her mouth, and he took it.

"Let's go before I can't stop," he said breathlessly as he pulled back. "Put your weapon away quick."

Mak did exactly as she was told, and James Thomas was the only one she didn't mind taking orders from—sometimes, at least. She could feel the heat of his eyes on her. Eyes fueled by lust, and eyes that were also making sure she was cleaning and storing her weapon properly. James Thomas was always vigilant.

When she was done, a sexy smirk formed on his lips and he took her hand once more. He was controlled as they walked out of the range and toward the elevator, but once those doors shut, he kissed her—hard.

"I'm aching for you," he groaned, pressing her up against the wall.

"You can have me, any way you want," Mak said, raising one eyebrow.

James smirked again, his thumb flipping her bottom lip. "You might regret that."

The threat was loaded with seduction but not for a second did Mak think she would regret it.

"I'll take my chances," she said with a throaty voice.

The elevator sounded and Mak looked at the floor number. "My apartment?"

James grinned. "I don't want to be quiet." He tugged her hand, leading the way.

"You're injured, James," Mak said as he closed the door behind them and pressed her up against it.

"I'm feeling like a million bucks right now," he said, his tongue running up her neck. "And I'll feel even better once I'm inside you."

Mak closed her eyes, succumbing to the moment. Her breasts were full and heavy and her panties were wet. Which James soon discovered.

"Oh, Mak," he groaned as his fingers pushed the silky fabric aside. Her body shuddered as he rubbed her.

She undid the button of his jeans—a move she was getting very good at—while he quickly pulled a condom from his pocket. She freed his erection from his briefs and slid her small hands up and down, reveling in the groans slipping from his lips.

He tilted his head back, but when he swayed, Mak held his waist. "Sit on the couch," she said, giving him the orders now. He diligently obeyed, but not before stepping out of his jeans and slipping off his shoes.

When he sat down, Mak helped him to take off his T-shirt, and then he rested back against the cushions, a grin on his lips.

Mak let her eyes run over him, greedily taking her time, building the anticipation. And then, slowly, she removed each item of her clothing, finishing with her bra, which she let drop from above her head.

Mak squealed as James took her wrists and spun her around. His hand grabbed her hip and lowered her onto his lap. She heard the telltale ripping noise of the condom package, and then a few seconds later he growled in her ear, "Sit on me."

Mak tilted her head back as she lifted her hips, guiding his cock into her. She inhaled sharply as he stretched her, and then, using her tiptoes, began to rock back and forth.

"You feel so good," he said, their bodies moving in unison. He sucked on her earlobe and she dug her nails into his forearm as she rested her head back on the cushion.

His fingers travelled north, and when he twisted her nipple she winced—a wince of pure pleasure. James groaned in response and it made her heart flutter. She loved being able to reduce him to a hungry, needy man.

Mak was glad that they didn't have to be quiet, that they didn't have to rush, and that they could enjoy the moment.

"Lean forward," he whispered.

She used his knees to balance herself as she lifted her hips up and down. James gave another guttural groan. He put one hand on the small of her back, guiding her as his hips rose and fell in perfect rhythm to hers.

Mak felt the heaviness in her pelvis spread through her body like lava, but she didn't want to come—not yet. She wanted more time with James, more moments of pure, erotic bliss. But, when she began to tremble, he drew her back in, his fingers once more slipping between her wet folds.

"I'm going to come if you do that," she panted, desperately fighting her climax. "I don't want to come... I don't want this to stop."

"Think of this as round one, because I'm not nearly done with you," he said, his fingers moving faster. Her insides clenched and James swore.

"Let go... I want to feel you," he said, sucking on the delicate skin of her neck.

Mak submitted and a wave of ecstasy rocked her body. She screamed, tightening around him, and James gripped her inner thigh, slamming his hips into hers as he found his own climax.

His body went lax and he moaned softly, nibbling on her shoulder. "That was worth waiting for."

Mak giggled, drawing his arm over her belly and holding it there. "You're always worth it, James. Always."

~

Incoming call: Maya.

Mak rolled over, retrieving her cell phone from the bedside table. James' eyelids fluttered open, and then closed again. They'd spent the afternoon in bed once they'd moved from the couch, and Mak thought James probably needed to eat and take more meds again but he seemed to be in no hurry to get up. He draped one arm across her waist and sighed.

"Hello," Mak said, her voice groggy with sleep.

"What are you doing? Are you asleep? It's six in the evening," Maya said.

"Afternoon nap," Mak said, resting her head back down on the pillow.

"Is James home?"

"Yes, he got back last night." It was strange to think he hadn't even been home for twenty-four hours. They'd done a lot of love-making in that time, Mak thought with an impetuous smirk.

Maya scoffed. "Now I get it. Anyway, what are you guys doing this evening? Zahra is cooking at their apartment and I'm heading over there now. They asked if you wanted to join us? Well, James too, I'm sure, given that he's back. I know you're not allowed to leave the building and all, but Jayce thought given it's their apartment, and because he's got security there that you might be allowed to."

"Thank you for the offer, and thank Zahra and Jayce for me, but I can't at the moment," Mak said knowing full well taking the risk of a security breach wasn't worth it.

James opened his eyes. She knew he hadn't missed a single bit of the conversation. "What is it?" he asked.

"Maya, can you hold on for a second?" Mak said before putting the call on mute. "Zahra and Jayce are cooking dinner, and they asked if we wanted to go."

James looked thoughtful. "Tell her you'll call her back," he said.

"We can go?" Mak said, raising one eyebrow.

"No, we can't go there; but they could come over here. I'll call Jayce—just tell Maya you'll call her back."

Mak returned the phone to her ear just in time to hear a car horn sounding angrily in the background.

"Maya, just give me a minute and I'll call you back," Mak said and hung up.

James held out his hand and she passed him the phone.

"Jayce, it's James Thomas... No, this is Mak's number. So, Maya invited us for dinner at your apartment..." James grinned and shook his head as he looked at the ceiling. "All right, all right... We can't come, but I'm more than happy to host dinner in my apartment. Or on the rooftop. Provided Zahra is cooking, of course." James chuckled. "Okay. Wait until Maya gets there and then I'll have cars ready to bring you over. See you soon."

James smiled. "We should get dressed."

4

JAMES THOMAS

James looked to his brother as Deacon sat at his kitchen table. *His life should've been so different,* James thought. A pang of unwarranted guilt hit him as he thought about the current state of their lives, and he wondered whether the same thoughts had crossed Deacon's mind.

"Are you sure you don't want to join us?" James asked one last time.

Deacon shook his head. "No, but thanks. I'll go and sit with the security teams at Mak's parents and monitor that closely."

James nodded. They'd deployed security teams—ghosts—to cover all of Mak's family members, with additional resources allocated to her parents. His men were in the shadows, but they were close enough to act if needed. It was a strategy that provided protection without them needing to explain Mak's case—something James didn't want to do. It would only cause them to worry, and there was absolutely nothing they could do to help. Maya had been oblivious to the men following her today, and that was exactly how James wanted it to stay.

He didn't, however, think that his brother needed to sit with the security men at Mak's parents. James' gut feeling was that nothing was going to happen tonight, because Biskup had been lured in. *I wouldn't risk it*, James thought—not when the reward was so great.

And James knew Deacon agreed with him, which reinforced his assumption that his brother was just using it as an excuse to get out of dinner, and that pang of guilt tugged at James once more.

James had never wanted to be in a relationship, but he'd found himself in one, completely happy and more content than he could've ever imagined. In a way he didn't feel like he deserved it, because it had never been a dream of his. It had been his brother's dream— that's all he'd wanted with Nicole—and that dream had been ripped away from him so suddenly, so violently, so tragically. Life wasn't fair, nor was it just.

"Okay, I'm going to go and see Samuel before I head out," Deacon said, excusing himself.

His apartment was silent for a few minutes, and James looked over his surroundings. He had never thought he'd be hosting a dinner. But then, he had never dared to believe his life would pan out the way it had—good and bad.

Mak arrived a few minutes later dressed in a pair of casual jeans that hugged her ass. James' eyes lingered on them as she walked toward the kitchen before following her. He wrapped his arms around her, bringing her back flush against his chest.

She held his forearms and tilted her head back, looking at him. "You set the table?"

James grinned. "I thought that seemed appropriate, but dinner parties are not my thing."

Mak beamed a dazzling smile. "Thank you for offering to have everyone here."

"I want you to have a normal life, Mak—as much as possible right now. One day we'll be able to go to their apartment for dinner, but not right now."

She nodded. "I've never seen their apartment."

"It's quite amazing, design-wise. And the quality is excellent. Jayce once said he'd build us the next Thomas Security, and at the time I laughed. However, that day might actually come, and I would consider it. Jayce has extremely high expectations—of everything—so I know he'd do a good job."

"You're going to build another Thomas Security?" Mak asked, seemingly surprised.

James shrugged his shoulders. "Not for some time, but we may outgrow this building at some point."

Mak nodded, but James hadn't told her the real reason he could consider it: if she moved in with him, he'd want a larger apartment for them. His place wasn't small, but it only had one bedroom. James would also need to come up with a solution to the current sound-proofing issue while still maintaining its purpose.

His doorbell sounded and, with a grin on his lips, he asked her, "Are you ready?"

Her eyes darted side-to-side. "Ready for what?"

James chuckled. *Ready for Jayce.* James shuffled Mak toward the front door, letting her go only to open it.

"Hey, guys!" Maya said, cradling a bottle of wine in her arms.

James welcomed her in and then looked into Jayce's twinkling eyes.

"It's good to see you both...together," Jayce said. Zahra shook her head, but she was wearing a smile to match her fiancé's.

James chuckled. "I've already warned her."

Mak looked between them all, clearly amused.

"You have no idea how much I love this, Mak," Jayce said, stepping in. "James with a girlfriend...hosting dinner... This is fantastic."

Jayce shook James' hand and he refrained from wincing, but when Zahra went to hug James he gently held her back.

"Slight injury," he said apologetically, and then leaned in to kiss her cheek instead.

Jayce's eyes flickered to Mak and then back to James, but he knew better than to say anything.

"Are you okay?" Zahra asked, appearing to be genuinely concerned.

"I'm fine. Just need a few weeks to heal," James said, giving her a reassuring smile.

With the greetings done, James showed everyone to the kitchen and Zahra took the lead, unpacking everything they'd brought and putting everyone to work. Jayce poured the drinks, one of which James politely declined.

Incoming call: Samuel.

James felt the heat of Mak's eyes, and Jayce's. "I'll be back in a minute," James said, moving in the direction of his bedroom.

He closed the door behind him. "Hello," James said.

"Sorry to interrupt. We've got a potential problem..."

"Mak's parents?" James asked.

"No. Eric and Sokolov... I think. I just had an alert on Angela's house in Paris. James, someone's there."

James' eyes widened. *Why?* They couldn't have found her body— or the baby's. James had made sure of it.

"What are they doing?" James asked.

"I don't know—that's the problem. I got the alert because I lost access to the security system you installed, but not before I got a shot of two men entering together. I've been able to identify one of them— he's Russian and linked to Sokolov."

James sat down on the edge of his bed. Why were they there? What did they want? Was there a chance they'd found out about his baby?

"Can you reaccess it?" James asked, ignoring the sick feeling balling in his stomach.

"No. They've cut the wires. I would need someone on the ground there."

James didn't know what they were doing, but he knew he didn't like it.

If Eric wasn't the link to the higher groups—and also the key to solving Mak's security case—James would've loved to have put a bullet in him. It was a shame he had to keep him alive.

"Why do you think they're there?" James asked.

"Honestly, I don't know. I would guess that they found out she was informing on you—although, if that's the reason, I'm surprised it took them that long," Samuel said, mirroring the thoughts in James' mind.

Samuel continued. "I've set up additional alerts, and I'm watching via CCTV. There's not much else we can do, I don't think. Other than pray whatever they're looking for they don't find."

James had murdered his own child, so he didn't think for a second God, or the universe, was going to give him a break on this one.

"Whatever this is—it isn't good, Samuel."

"No. I agree."

James advised Samuel to call if he got any updates, but he wasn't hopeful he would. James ended the call.

What are you doing, Eric?

What are you looking for?

James rubbed his palms over his face, taking a deep, steadying breath. Sitting in his bedroom wasn't going to help—it would only raise questions—so he followed the sounds back to the kitchen.

The music was on, the drinks had been poured and Mak was helping to prepare dinner when he returned. Her eyes cast questions his way, but he silenced them with a smile—for now.

"Are you sure you don't want a small one?" Jayce asked, holding up a whiskey glass.

"No, thanks," James said, pouring himself a soda. "Zahra, can I do anything to help?"

"We've got it all under control," she said with assurance.

Jayce finished fixing himself a drink, and then they sat down on the couches given that their help appeared to not be needed.

"What happened?" Jayce asked, nodding toward James' arm.

"Flesh wound," he said. "Didn't quite dodge one."

Jayce understood. "How did she take it?"

"Not thrilled," James said.

Jayce nodded, looking thoughtful. "When Kyoji lived with me, I'd always worry that I'd wake up and find out he wasn't coming home—that he would never walk through the door again. You get used to it—the risk—to a point, but the fear never truly goes away. She'll have to live with that."

"I know. And she knows. I wish I could make it easier, I wish I could promise her I wasn't going to get hurt, but I can't," James said. "Nothing about this relationship is particularly easy."

"The easy ones aren't worth having, are they?" Jayce said with a sympathetic grin.

"No, they're not... How are the wedding plans coming along?" James asked to change the conversation.

Jayce scoffed, stealing a glance at Zahra. "She's still a bit pissed that we're now having a winter wedding, but otherwise good." Jayce's gaze diverted to the windows, a view of the sky indicating that winter had indeed arrived. "I would get married tomorrow if I could, but she's not so keen on a Vegas wedding." He chuckled, looking back to James with a sly grin. "And what about you? You look smitten, Thomas. Are you going to get married one day?"

James grinned, took a sip of his soda, and then shrugged his shoulders. "I don't know. I didn't think this relationship was possible, so let's just see where things go."

"Maybe you'll surprise us all and have a minivan full of kids," Jayce said, and James knew he was teasing him, but the mention of children immediately took his mind back to Paris. The image of the ultrasound flashed in his mind. Something that brought most people immense joy had sent fear—and regret—ripping through him as he'd realized what he'd done.

"What's wrong?" Jayce asked, and James immediately shook his head, blocking out the memories that haunted him.

"Nothing. I don't need a crystal ball to tell you that a minivan full of kids is not in my future," James said.

Jayce chuckled, nodding. "Looks like they're ready for us," he said, standing up.

James carried his glass and put it down on the dining table.

"Everything okay?" Mak asked as she stopped in front of him.

He draped an arm over her shoulder and drew her in. "Yes," he said, and he meant it, because everything would be okay while she was beside him.

He kissed her cheek, not caring who was watching them, and whispered in her ear, "I love you."

~

James sat down opposite Samuel. "No news is good news, I assume?"

Dinner had been entertaining—though probably more so for him than it had been for Mak. It was the first time he'd found himself on a couple's date, and he had to admit that although unusual, he enjoyed it. He'd even managed to push aside thought of Paris for a few hours; but, like all nightmares, the reprieve was brief.

"No, nothing yet, and I'm watching all activity on the dark net closely," Samuel said, folding his arms on the table.

Angela was listed as a missing person—a missing *agent*, according to the CIA database. She'd been retired when they had their casual fling, but had evidently taken up the opportunity to freelance for them as an informant—for a reason James would likely never know.

"They won't find her, or him," James said confidently, and Samuel nodded in agreement.

After James had confirmed the baby was his, he'd gone back to the temporary grave he'd placed Angela in and retrieved her body. And then, for a reason still unknown to him now, he'd cut out the fetus from her womb. He buried them separately, his grave marked by a geographical location that James would never forget. He didn't know why then, and he didn't know why now, he just knew that if he wanted to visit the grave in the future, he'd know where it was.

Angela's body wouldn't yet be decomposed enough to conceal her dissected abdomen—it would take years to decay to that level. He thought back to where she was resting now, though, and his confidence was renewed. They wouldn't find her. And nor would they find evidence of her pregnancy—at least he hoped they wouldn't. He, and Samuel, had destroyed everything they had known about, but there was still a risk she'd told someone, or she had medical records that they hadn't uncovered. The medical record risk was unlikely—given Samuel's craft—but James couldn't rule it out completely.

"The last update on your file in the CIA database is a report she gave," Samuel said, shrugging. "They might be clutching at straws... much like we are. It could be nothing."

"Or it could be something," James said.

What are you looking for, Eric?

"Why wouldn't he have searched her house earlier? They haven't just started hunting me, so they've had plenty of time, and opportunity, to do it. Why now?"

"I don't know, but I don't like it," Deacon said from behind him as he walked into Samuel's office. He sat down beside James. "Something isn't right about this."

James rolled his lips over one another. He agreed, but couldn't come up with a viable explanation.

"How was dinner?" Deacon asked.

"Strange, but good," James said, watching his brother's reaction. He felt that flare of tension again.

Deacon nodded but didn't continue the conversation.

"Oh, by the way," James said, knowing it was as good a time as ever to break the news, "I told Mak we're not biological brothers."

Deacon rolled his eyes, and James thought he would've had a stronger response if not for the fact that Deacon had told Nicole—without James knowing—so he didn't have a leg to stand on.

"So, what are we going to do next with Biskup?" Deacon asked, clearly ready for another change of topic.

Two sets of eyes landed on James. He grinned. "I think we should show him the pictures, with dates, of Nikolas Junez' trip to Manchester."

Deacon gave a sly grin, nodding slowly. "Good plan."

5

JAMES THOMAS

Alexandr Biskup was playing by the rules, and so James was ready to reward him. He dialed the number they'd been given yesterday.

"I was beginning to think you were reneging on your promise," Biskup said. "That would've been a shame, for all involved."

"When I make a promise, I keep it. I told you to wait twenty-four hours, and it is exactly that to the minute. I'm going to send you something now—something you're not going to like, but something you need to see..." James paused. "Are you still interested?"

"Very," Biskup replied—one word loaded with intrigue.

James nodded at Samuel, and when he nodded in return, James continued. "Check your messages."

James wished he had a view of Biskup. He wanted to see his reaction, to see how powerful the betrayal was. If Biskup hadn't cared so much about this woman—the woman Eric had beaten and strangled to death—then this wasn't going to be as powerful a move as James was betting on. But, the more he knew about Eric, the more sure he was about one thing: he liked to torment people, and he chose her for a reason—she was Biskup's main girl.

The silence was excruciating, and James looked at Samuel and Deacon, who were sitting as still as palace guards, eagerly anticipating Biskup's reaction. Twenty seconds passed before he responded.

"You have my full attention," Biskup said finally, and James heard the tightness in his voice. Even a man with a heart like Biskup's had a soft spot and could be wounded. And Eric knew it—he'd known where to hit him. Eric was the master of games.

"So, it seems we have a common enemy. Makaela Ashwood does not have the code—I promise you that. She had no idea of her husband's business dealings—in fact she had no idea what he even did for a living. She knew nothing about the man she was married to because Eric made sure of that. He's manipulative, and he's deceiving —and now you know that better than anyone," James said.

"What do you want?" Biskup asked.

"I'm very good at finding people—as you can see. And I'm willing to help you find Eric—I'll even go to the frontline and do the dirty work myself. On one condition."

Biskup's scoff echoed in the room as the conversation played over the speaker system, but James ignored it. "You, and your good friend Kovalenko, are going to leave New York tonight. In fact, you're going to leave America tonight. Call your pilot, and tell him to fire up the engines, because you're on your way," James said, changing his tone to indicate the severity of the instruction.

"And, you're going to take with you every support that you have dedicated to kidnapping Makaela. I need to know that I can trust you, and you're going to have to prove it to me. If you have anyone watching her, I will find them and, like the others, they won't live to see another sunrise. I want you to give me your word now that she is safe from your men—from you—and I'll send you a bonus gift."

"Ooh, I do like the sound of that," Biskup said. "You know, I never thought she'd be such a problem. But then I never expected to encounter you—whoever you are."

"You could look at it as bad luck," James responded. "Or, you could look at it as a blessing because I'm going to give you something much better—I'm going to give you Eric, served up on a platter for you to do with as you please."

"Why do you need me?" Biskup asked, clearly no fool.

"Eric has resources, and I need backup. That's all I'm willing to say at this stage. But, it would be remiss of me not to mention that if you do agree to this deal, and then you go against your word, I will hunt you and I will find you. And when I do, I will slaughter every single member of your family—children included. Your son... I see he's growing up and following in his daddy's shoes. He's thirteen, right? If you go against me, he won't live to see his fourteenth birthday, and I will not give him an easy death. But not only that—you'll have a front-row seat to the entire affair."

"You've made your point." His voice was terse.

"A threat is only a threat until it's acted upon. And, if you forget all about Makaela Ashwood, then I'll have absolutely no reason to act on it, will I?"

When Biskup didn't respond, James continued. "The choice is yours—so what is it?"

The silence dragged on, but James thought it was only for effect: Biskup had made up his mind. The thought of finding Eric—alive—was too alluring.

"I'll call my pilot now," Biskup said in an almost singsong voice.

Deacon shook his head and rolled his eyes.

"You do that. Make your arrival in Prague known, and then I'll send you that bonus gift I mentioned," James said, noting the time on his watch.

"And what if I'm not going to Prague?"

"As long as you're not in America, I don't give a fuck where you go —just make it known," James said.

Biskup chuckled. "You have a deal. Oh, and by the way, you never gave me your name..."

"James," he said, ending the call. He put his phone down on the table.

"What bonus are you intending to send him?" Samuel said, raising one eyebrow.

Samuel hadn't been able to regain access to the camera system in Angela's house, but he had been able to get a CCTV image of Eric and Sokolov one block away. They had been there—together. "The surveillance photo from Paris," James said.

Now Deacon raised an eyebrow. "Is it a good idea for us to reveal that so early into this very tentative relationship?"

James wasn't entirely sure, but he knew one thing. "Biskup has to be prepared to take on the Russians. If he's not, there's absolutely no point in setting this up. Going to war with Eric means going to war with his friends. It's going to be ugly, and I want him to know that up front."

Deacon rubbed his jaw, looking thoughtful.

"Biskup has to know that we're skilled, have access to intel that he doesn't—that no one does—and that we're capable of actually finding Eric. If he doesn't have confidence in any one single part of that equation, this won't work."

"I agree," Deacon said. "I'm just not sure it's going to work regardless."

James sighed. "I'm not either, but it's the best chance we've got. It's time to hedge our bets, and I'm banking on Biskup's brutal men to get us to Eric."

Deacon scoffed. "That part isn't a gamble, at least. We know what his men are like—they'll do anything required. Anything."

"Exactly," James said. "If Eric hasn't been afraid up until this point, he should be now. He started this, and we'll finish it," James said, locking eyes with his brother.

❧

"Where are we going?" Mak asked.

James rolled his eyes. "I told you, it's a surprise."

"I'm not good with surprises," she said. "Haven't you worked that out by now?"

"This is a different kind of surprise—a good surprise...at least I hope it is," James said, and then diverted his eyes to the front of the car. "It's a good surprise, right, Deacon?"

"I think so," he said, his answer teasing.

"What are you two up to?" Mak asked, looking between them.

James flashed her a beaming grin. "We've been busy working on something," he said, angling his head to look out of the window. "What do you think?"

Mak looked around her. "Am I missing something?"

Deacon drove into the underground car park and Mak's eyebrows knitted together. "Where are we?"

"At your new apartment," James said, watching her face widen with delight.

"What? I'm moving out? How is this possible?"

James chose his next words very carefully. "We were able to send confirmation that Eric is alive to Alexandr Biskup... He's very grateful for the gift, and his attention—and efforts—are now focused elsewhere."

Mak's eyes narrowed. "Have you talked to him? Why would you believe him? What are you not telling me?"

"That's three questions too many. Nothing about your security provisions have changed except that you'll be in a different building. I'm not relaxing your security, I'm just trying to give you some part of your life back—your own space."

"I appreciate that—I honestly do," she said, looking into his eyes. "But you're not answering my questions."

"Yes, contact has been made with Biskup. We gave him some intel, and he's promised to stay away from you. We'll continue to give him intel as we receive it, and that should keep him at bay. But, at the same time, we're not letting our guard down."

Mak looked between the two brothers. "I feel like I'm getting the abbreviated version. I'd rather the full story."

"That's more than you should even know," James said, and Deacon muttered in agreement before getting out of the car. James waited for the security team to assemble and then they ushered Mak into the elevator.

The mixed emotions he'd had about moving her continued to plague him. A large part of him didn't want her to move out—he liked her being in the same building as him. But, the risk of Eric watching her was too great now. They couldn't take the chance—if Eric found Thomas Security, their entire operation and the lives of everyone in that building would be at risk.

James gave her hand a little squeeze as they rode the elevator up. He hoped she liked the apartment, yet he couldn't imagine how she wouldn't. It was very nice. And it was very safe. It was a win-win situation that had taken some serious negotiation on his behalf, and a hefty persuasion fee, because the owners hadn't initially been inclined to move out. *But everyone has a price.*

When they arrived at her floor, Deacon led them out and toward the apartment. Mak immediately noticed the setup.

"Where are the other apartments? Is this the penthouse?" she asked, blinking as she looked around her.

"Close to the top, but no—this is not the penthouse suite," James said. That wasn't a lie, but this building was created for security-conscious buyers, and, therefore, floors five to eleven housed only two apartments each with completely separate entrances and foyers. Mak hadn't realized, likely because they'd entered from the basement, that there were two sets of elevators that serviced the building to accommodate the design.

She looked at him, her face concealing whatever she was thinking. "So where are the other apartments?"

James cleared his throat. "One other apartment is located on the other side of the lifts. You both have private entrances."

Her jaw dropped. "Now I don't believe you about the rent. I have no doubt that you know exactly how much I earn, and what is in my bank account"—she raised one eyebrow—"and you know that I can't afford it."

Deacon looked between them.

"I told you that I negotiated a good rate. You should be excited about this apartment."

"I don't like being lied to." Mak put her hands on her hips.

"Mak, I can't move you into an apartment that isn't secure. You either move into this apartment, or you don't move at all and you continue to live in Thomas Security. They are your two options," James said.

"Stop side-stepping. Did you, or did you not, lie to me about the price of the rent?"

"The rent I discussed with you previously was for a different apartment," he said and her eyes flared. "That apartment is no longer available, but this is. It's more expensive, but it's even better—in terms of security—and there is no price too high for your safety. I need to be able to go away and know that you're safe."

"Aren't you full of secrets today," she said, and he almost flinched under the glare of her eyes.

James stole another sideways look at his brother. James couldn't tell if Deacon was worried or amused by the conversation.

"I didn't tell you because it's the only option we have and I didn't want you to immediately shut it down," he said, continuing when she opened her mouth to speak. "You will pay the amount of rent you agreed to pay, and I will cover the difference. Can we at least look at the apartment?"

Deacon took the cue, and unlocked the door while Mak continued to glower at James. He was not winning any brownie points over this apartment at this point.

"Let's see what you think," Deacon said, holding the door wide.

Mak clenched her jaw and turned on her heels. She walked into the apartment, and then stopped. She spun back to him.

"My stuff is already here?"

He shrugged his shoulders. "We like to be efficient. It's just boxes, they can always be returned to your other apartment."

She muttered under her breath and turned away from him. Her head moved in a motion that indicated she was surveying the apartment and then she walked off in the direction of the hallway. James didn't follow her in but stopped in the kitchen.

Deacon looked at him, a half-cocked smile on his lips. "That went well."

James shook his head—he didn't think he'd heard the worst of it yet. And might not until they were alone. They were yet to have a fight, but this looked to be their first.

She breezed past him, not even glancing in his direction, as she went to look in the rooms that came off the main living space. She straightened as she peered into one of the rooms.

"What is this?" she asked.

James thought her tone was more inquisitive than furious, but he guessed she was just temporarily distracted.

"That room, and the adjoining one, aren't technically for you. That room is a security control center, and the room next door will be a bedroom for security—should they need it. It's a precaution, but given we had the space available we wanted to use it well."

She nodded, took one last look around the room, and then closed the door.

She walked toward them. "I wish I could be more excited about this apartment—it's very impressive."

"You should be excited. It's what you need, Mak. I didn't do this for any other reason than your security."

Deacon cleared his throat. "I'll wait outside."

James' eyes didn't leave Mak's, but he waited until he heard the door close.

"I want to give you some form of your life back, Mak. That's all I'm trying to do. If I have to pay extra to do that, I have absolutely no issue doing so."

"You should have discussed this with me. This shouldn't have been a surprise, James."

"This is a security decision, Mak, just as much as it is a decision for you about where you want to live. I can't—and won't—take any risk that I don't need to when it comes to your safety."

"I get that, but it's the way you dealt with it. You should've been up front about it, and the costs, and then I wouldn't feel so blindsided. Have you not noticed I have major trust issues right now? I don't need anyone else sparking questions of doubt in my mind."

James took a deep breath. "Okay. I'm sorry I didn't tell you, but I honestly thought you would refuse the apartment if you knew and demand that I find something else—which I'm not going to do. This is the best apartment for you and I'm not willing to compromise."

Mak opened her mouth to speak, but was interrupted by his cell phone.

Incoming call: Samuel.

"Hold that thought," James said to Mak, who let out a resigned sigh.

"Hello," James said.

"Boys," Samuel said, indicating this was a three-way conversation. "Eric's calling Ben. I'm patching it through."

Not now, James thought as his eyes met Mak's.

"Ben, what's the update? Has Mak moved in with him?"

"Yes, she moved in last weekend," Ben said, sticking to the plan.

James strained to listen for any background noise, but as always, Eric's phone calls gave away nothing of his location. It was eerily silent, but James didn't think he would be in the Amman house.

"It won't work out…she doesn't love him," Eric said, and James turned it over in his mind. It was an odd thing to say. Did Eric honestly believe Mak still loved him, if she ever had?

James' eyes met Mak's again. Eyes that were narrowing with each passing second. Eyes that would be slits by the time this conversation ended, he knew.

"I don't know," Ben said. *"She says she does love him… There's something you need to know, Eric. Mak's preparing to file the papers in court—she's asking for you to be declared deceased."*

Silence.

"What?" Eric's voice was as cold as ice, and James imagined Ben in his cell, cringing.

"We're assuming it's inspired by this new guy. Kayla asked her if she wants to get married again and she said she's thinking about it, although it's not the reason she's filing the papers. She wants closure and now that she has your body, or thinks that she does, she says she's ready to move on," Ben said.

James kept his face neutral as he waited for Eric's response.

"She's not getting married again. I won't let it happen. She's my wife."

Eric's obsession with Mak hadn't ceased after all these years, even though he'd appeared to remarry and even had a child. James didn't know why he was surprised by the conviction in Eric's words, though —he had even named his daughter Makaela.

"Maybe it won't come to that," Ben said, attempting to pacify him.

"You're fucking right it won't happen. I'm going to send you a package for Kayla. I'll include the instructions of how to set up the cameras, and I want her to put them in Mak's apartment when she goes for dinner. I want to know everything about this guy. I want to know every dirty secret of his. I want to know where his skeletons are buried, because I'm going to dig them up. He can't have my wife—I won't allow it. I'm going to destroy them. I'm going to rip them apart."

A defensive, protective urge rippled through James.

No you won't, Eric—because I won't let you.

6

MAK ASHWOOD

He held the phone to his ear but he hadn't spoken a single word.

Who are you talking to, James Thomas?

Mak tilted her head to the side, continuing to observe him. When he hung up and put the phone in his pocket, she waited to see what he would do next.

He took a step forward, closing the space between them. He wrapped one arm—the arm that wasn't injured—around her waist and drew her in.

"Please don't be angry, Mak," he said, tilting her chin up. "I promise, no more surprises like this in the future. I just want you to have a home again, and a home that's safe. That was my only intention."

She was momentarily stunned by his ability to continue their conversation with complete disregard for the strange phone call he'd just taken.

"Who were you speaking to?" she asked.

"I wasn't speaking to anyone. Samuel patched through a call from a client case, I was just listening to it," he said, tightening his arm around her waist so that their bodies were flushed.

"Don't try and seduce me, it won't work," Mak said.

James smirked and it took all her self-control not to smile.

"Are you sure? I can be very persuasive."

Mak pushed against his chest but James didn't let her go.

"Look, I promise I won't surprise you like this again. But, it's a great apartment, Mak, and I want you to live here. Take it," he said.

She bit her lip, still undecided, however tempting it was.

James shrugged his shoulders as a guilty grin spread across his face. "And, your stuff is already here."

"How convenient," she said, but her tone had little of the resistance she'd felt earlier, and she could see that James knew it.

"This is a good thing," he said.

"And you're going to stay here with me?" she asked.

"Yes, unless I'm away," James said as he lowered his lips. His tongue dove in, sweeping over hers. His hunger surprised her, but she liked it.

"What's gotten into you, James Thomas?" she asked, her voice breathy.

"You," he said, squeezing her ass. Her pelvis pressed against his erection and a moan slipped from her lips.

"You're cheating," Mak said.

"No, I'm playing by my rules, and I'll do anything to win," he said, biting her bottom lip. "Are you going to take the apartment or not?"

Mak sighed. "Yes, James. But no more surprises. I know that there are a lot of things that you can't tell me, and that you need to make certain decisions for me, but this wasn't one of them. This apartment is something we should've discussed together. Given what has happened in the past months, and what I've found out, I don't want to have any reason not to trust you. Nor do I want you to make every decision for me, even if your intentions are good. It is my life, and I don't want it controlled any more than it needs to be."

James looked deep into her eyes. "I'm sorry, I was wrong. I should've talked to you about this, rather than making the decision for you."

Mak nodded, accepting his apology and vowing to let go of the tension still humming in her chest. They spent so little time together and she didn't want to hold onto any feelings of bitterness. "What now?" Mak said, looking around them.

"I was thinking I'd leave you here for a few hours to unpack—with security, of course. I need to catch up on a few things at work, so I'll do that and then come back later and stay the night."

Suddenly Mak was excited now that she wasn't restraining herself —she had her own apartment again!

"Sounds like a plan, Thomas," she said, kissing his smiling lips. "Thank you for this amazing apartment," she added.

"I'll do anything for you," he said, and Mak didn't miss the under-tone of conviction.

Mak looked at the boxes towering around her and she felt a sense of déjà vu. She'd been in this situation not so long ago, but she'd been living a disillusioned life at that point. She'd thought the security threat a temporary thing, and that it would all be resolved within a few months. How wrong she'd been. How wrong she'd been about a lot of things—including James Thomas. She'd thought she'd never even see him again after their first meeting.

"Mak," Cami said, who'd arrived with an entourage shortly before James and Deacon left. "Let me know if you need a hand with anything. I'll be in here," she said, nodding toward the security control room.

"Sure, thanks," Mak said.

Cami disappeared into the room, but left the door open. Mak returned her attention to the boxes—she knew which ones she wanted to start with.

She pulled a box down from a stack and ran one edge of the scissor blade along the tape, opening it. The gray archive box was on top and Mak pulled it out. She lifted the lid, taking one last look at her wedding dress. Nothing welled within her except anger at how Eric had deceived her. She sighed, packing it back into the box. She pulled out her veil, her wedding shoes, and her wedding album. She sat down on the floor, crossing her legs and resting the album on her knees. She flicked through the pages, looking over each photograph. She wasn't doing it for old times' sake—she wanted to make sure that before she threw it out she wasn't missing something. Maybe a face she didn't recognize, or an image that hadn't looked strange to her before but might now, knowing what she did. She'd done the same thing when she'd gone through the boxes recently, but so much had happened even since then.

When she got to the photos of their reception she paid particular attention to the faces in the background. When she turned the last page, Mak pressed her lips together. Nothing. She looked down at the album for a moment longer and then put it back in the box along with everything else she'd pulled out. She got up and pushed it toward the door and then went back to the second box marked *Wedding*.

She opened it taking out a shoebox that contained all of the cards they'd been given.

She opened each one, reading who it was from. She struggled to match some of the names to faces of Eric's relatives but thought she had them right. She paused when she read the card from his parents. It had been a long time since she'd spoken to either of them. Initially, of course, they'd kept in contact. But, slowly, the contact had waned until it had ceased to exist. Mak had wondered if talking to her had been a painful reminder for them, or if it was just a natural progression. Thirteen years was a long time.

Mak felt a tightening of her chest at knowing she was withholding information about Eric—that he was alive—but there was no point telling them now because if all went to plan, and James delivered him to Biskup, Mak didn't think he'd live long anyway. At some point, though, she did want to be able to give them closure.

Mak sighed and put the card to the side, and then opened the next. She chewed on her lip as she looked at the name on the card she'd just picked up. She thought of the photographs she'd just looked over but couldn't match the name to a face.

She was about to brush it aside, but as she put the card down something inside her forced her to pick it up again. She stood up, moving toward the box she'd put by the door. She pulled out the wedding album again, and flicked through it once more, but she still couldn't place the name.

Who is Carl Junez?

"Cami?" Mak said, calling out her name as she walked toward the security control room.

"Yeah," she answered, swiveling in her chair to face Mak. "What's up?"

"I'm not sure…maybe nothing," Mak said. She passed Cami the card but didn't say anything—Mak wanted to test her.

Mak watched her, taking note of every minute change in her expression. When her eyes lingered on the name, Mak knew something about it had registered.

Cami looked up, her face blank. "What about it?"

Oh, you're good, Cami.

"The name… Does it mean anything to you?" Mak asked.

"Should it?" Cami said, and Mak wondered whether James had taught her that—to deflect the question with another question—or if her past had taught her that.

"I don't know," Mak said, but she thought it did in fact mean something. "I don't recognize the name, nor can I match it to a face. And I've been through the wedding album twice—including the background shots," Mak said. She shrugged her shoulders. "It could be nothing, but it seems strange to me."

Cami nodded, picking up her cell phone. "Samuel," she said, "I'm looking at a wedding card of Mak's, it's from a Carl Junez. Mak doesn't recognize the name. Can you please run a report? … Okay, thanks." Cami ended the call. "He'll look into it and get back to us."

"Why do you recognize the name?" Mak asked, putting one hand on her hip.

"I don't recognize the name," Cami said casually, passing the card back to her.

"Yes, you do. You're almost as good as James, but not quite. Then again, he's got a few years on you, so maybe the student will surpass the teacher."

Cami smiled. "I don't recognize the name, Mak."

"Okay, I'll rephrase. What about the name did you recognize?"

"Does this look like a witness stand to you?" Cami asked, looking around her.

Mak bared a smile. "It looks like *my* new apartment, and in *my* apartment I make the rules."

Cami laughed. "You're such a pain in the ass sometimes."

"You didn't answer my question."

"For the love of God, I don't recognize the name. I have no idea who Carl Junez is," Cami said.

"Okay," Mak said. "We'll see."

Mak returned to the boxes. Cami wasn't going to give her the answers—she never did—but someone else was going to. That card she had to play very carefully, though.

She pushed aside the two boxes containing her wedding items and then started on the living room boxes since they had all been deposited there. She pulled out items, one after the other, and placed them in their new home. She was lost in thought, both strategizing the unpacking and where everything was going to go, and still trying to place Carl Junez.

An arm wrapped around her waist, and Mak screamed.

"Always pay attention to your surroundings," James whispered from behind her.

Mak relaxed, melting into his embrace. She tilted her head back, kissing his cheek. "I was thinking," she said.

"I'm sure you were." He turned her around, cupping her chin and bringing their mouths together. "Are you hungry? I brought dinner."

Mak bit her lip. "I'm hungry for something else," she whispered, unsure of Cami's exact location.

James smirked. "What do you want, Mak?"

"You know what I want, James."

"I'm not sure I do," he said with an arrogant grin.

Mak pushed him away, giggling, but he grabbed her wrist and pulled her back in.

"Let's eat, and then I'll give you everything you want," he said.

Mak's cheeks flushed.

He pulled back, smirked, and then walked away.

Mak's legs felt like jelly so for a moment she just watched him, admiring his behind. Once she'd collected herself she met him in the kitchen, where she received another smoldering grin.

James began to plate up the food.

"Tell me about Carl Junez," Mak said, watching him like she had done with Cami.

He pushed a plate and cutlery set toward her, and then came to sit on the stool next to her. He angled his body so that his knees brushed against hers.

"Eric has had multiple aliases since he disappeared. One of them had the surname Junez, so, therefore, Carl Junez is of particular interest to us."

Mak didn't interrupt, but rather waited for James to continue.

"Samuel ran some reports this afternoon, and he got a match for a Carl Junez," James said, meeting her gaze. "Carl Junez, as it turns out, is also an alias Eric used."

Mak frowned. "He sent the card to himself?"

"Samuel has run a handwriting analysis and it doesn't appear to be Eric's, although that's not definitive. I'm thinking that someone else has also used the alias Carl Junez, someone that Eric was close to. A mentor, perhaps."

"A mentor for what?"

"A mentor for the underworld. Someone who showed him the ropes and gave him the resources and contacts he needed. Someone who helped him to disappear."

7

JAMES THOMAS

Someone with a link to the Escanta. Someone who saw the madness in him, and recruited him into the organization. Someone who fostered every single one of Eric's bad traits.

"Maybe he—Carl Junez—wasn't actually at the wedding," Mak said. "Maybe the card was posted to us, and that's why I don't remember his face."

James nodded. "It's possible. And it's possible that he was there, but you don't remember his face because he didn't want you to."

Incoming call: Samuel.

James answered the call with hesitation. He'd only just left, so what could be so important?

Samuel didn't even wait for James' greeting. "Big fucking problem... Eric sent Ben a message: I'll see you in an hour. Be home."

James' stomach clenched. That meant Eric was in Manhattan right now. James was growing tired of unwelcome visitors.

Samuel continued. "Deacon is setting up security teams, and then he'll go down to the cells to prep Ben and Kayla."

"I'm leaving now," James said, standing up. He hung up and slipped the phone into his pocket. Mak gave him a look that indicated she expected an explanation. He didn't give one to her.

"I'm going to have a look at something. Eat, continue unpacking, and I'll be back as soon as I can." Although he didn't have a minute to spare, he cupped her cheek and gave her a long, departing kiss.

As soon as he closed the door he ran for the elevator. Adrenaline threatened to rule his mind, but he refused to let it. Eric being in New York could be a good thing—it meant another potential opportunity to capture him. But James wouldn't risk it if it sacrificed Ben's cover. His contact with Eric was too important—without the telephone conversations, their leads on Eric might go so quiet James worried they'd never find him again if they failed.

When the elevator arrived in the basement car park James ran toward the car and turned on the ignition, lurching the car into reverse. He called his brother.

"Deacon, where are we at?"

"Security teams are en route to Ben's apartment. I'm waiting for you to get here and then we'll take him over. I'm thinking we'll drop him off several blocks away, and let him walk home. Eric could already be close by—watching. This could be a test."

"My thoughts exactly," James said, using the car mirrors to weave in and out of traffic. "Eric's injured," James continued, "so I can't understand what his motive would be. It would make sense for him to lie low and wait until he's healed—like I'm doing—but he's on the move. That either means he's got a lot of backup, or he's just crazy. Either is bad."

"Well, we know he's crazy," Deacon said, and James heard a door close in the background. "What's your ETA?"

"I'll be there in five minutes," James said, looking ahead. The traffic was thin, and Mak's apartment building had been chosen not only for its security features, but also because of its proximity to Thomas Security.

"We'll meet you in the car park. I've got your kit," Deacon said, and then added, "not that you should be doing anything."

His brother knew better than to argue with him on this one, though. James would try and stay out of the line of fire, but there was no way he was going to sit in Samuel's office with Eric on the streets of Manhattan.

James honked at the driver ahead and he moved out of the way, albeit with an unfriendly hand gesture, and James pressed down on the accelerator. It was a shame James had told Biskup to leave—it could've been a happy reunion for all involved.

He swiped his pass at the Thomas Security entrance and then drove into his designated parking bay. James jumped out of his car, jogging toward the assembled team. He looked at Ben, who was a shade whiter than usual.

"You're going to be fine," James said. "Play by our rules, and we'll make sure of it."

Ben swallowed, and then nodded.

James sat in the back next to Ben, and Tom sat on the other side. Deacon drove and James was surprised to see Lenny in the front passenger seat.

"What are you doing here?" James asked.

Lenny twisted in his seat. "Jayce is staying in so I came by to do some training. Good timing, I guess."

James agreed. He had his dream team—excluding Cami.

James turned to Ben. "What are your thoughts on why Eric is here?"

Ben shrugged his shoulders. "I have no idea at all. His visits have been less frequent than they used to be, but an unexpected visit like this isn't out of the ordinary. I would even go so far as to say we were lucky he sent that text message at all. I can't tell you the number of times I've turned up at home only to find Eric waiting there."

And that's what was worrying James. It could be a test, although Ben had done nothing to set off any warning bells for Eric—at least none that they could ascertain. But the same thought came back to James—someone else might be watching them. All of them.

Little could be done about that now, though, and they'd have to be prepared to deal with any potential consequence that arose from Eric's trip.

He looked at Ben again. "Does the name Carl Junez mean anything to you?"

Ben looked past James, his gaze less focused as he seemed to think it over, digging deep into the memories of his past—a past that James didn't envy. "No...I don't recall ever hearing that name."

James nodded, confident that was the truth. Eric had hid that part of his life from Ben, so why should the name ring a bell?

"Okay," Deacon said from the driver's seat. "We've got eyes on you, and micro-cameras in your apartment. We'll be watching and listening to everything you say and do. In the worst-case scenario, if there's a sign of trouble, we'll create a distraction and get you out of there."

Ben exhaled a wheezy sigh.

"Your loyalty is not to Eric," James said, taking a harsher tone than his brother. "Your loyalty is to Kayla, who is currently held with us." James didn't need to say anything more—he'd made the consequences known multiple times before.

"I'm aware of that, and I'm less excited about this impromptu visit than anyone, believe me," Ben said, running a hand through his hair.

"Okay, walk slowly to give us enough time to get into position," James said, opening the door to let Ben out. They nodded at each other, and then without another word, Ben began the walk to his apartment as James got back in the car.

Deacon met his gaze in the rearview mirror and James knew what he was thinking: this could get hairy.

James confirmed that all of his men were in position while Deacon parked the car, and James pulled out what he needed from his kit. He put on a bulletproof vest, and then slipped his sweater over it. James looked over his weapons, choosing two pistols, and a scalpel —he never went anywhere without one.

"We've got company, and a lot of it," Samuel's voice came through James' earwig. *"Four cars have pulled up out front. Security... They're getting out... Fifteen men... Damn, they're taking positions next to every entry and exit point... Bodyguards are ushering someone in now... It must*

be Eric... Okay, Eric's just entered Ben's apartment. Wow, he looks nothing like Nikolas Junez."

James loaded the surveillance footage onto his phone, taking a look for himself. His hair was cropped short and he wore a suit and black-framed glasses. His appearance was a far cry from his former alias, true, but there was one telltale sign—a bandaged hand. James turned his focus to the four, large, burly men standing beside Eric now. Nineteen men in total, James counted.

"Let's proceed toward that building very, very carefully," James said, exiting the car with his team. They split up, taking the routes Deacon had mapped out, each one weaving toward Ben's apartment.

"Stay deep in the shadows, we don't know if Eric has men outside watching," James said.

"He's got men watching," Samuel confirmed. *"I've just spotted three snipers set up on the rooftops of surrounding buildings. Keep very low."*

"What's Eric doing now?" James asked, covering his mouth like he was yawning.

"I don't know. He's carrying something—it looks like a box of some kind. He just put it in the refrigerator... He's sitting on the couch, looking at his phone. He looks relaxed, but that means nothing. Eric's capable of anything...and he has got extensive backup."

James looked over his shoulder, getting that familiar thrill of being in the field, amongst the action. The rush never failed to seduce him even in such a circumstance.

"In position," Deacon's voice came through first, followed shortly after by the rest of the team. James was the last to confirm, taking extra caution to stay out of the line of sight of Eric's snipers.

James drew his phone now that he was shielded by the building.

"Okay, here we go. Ben's walking in. I'm feeding the audio through but you'll hear my voice over it."

"Copy," the team said in unison.

"Ben, how are you, my friend?" James recognized Eric's voice immediately, even without looking at the footage.

Eric stood up and shook Ben's hand.

"I'm good. And you?" James halted his breath, listening carefully to

Ben's voice. It was steady, and that was a good sign he wouldn't buckle under the pressure. It was amazing what one could do when the stakes were raised.

"Good. I had some business to attend to nearby, so I thought I'd drop in," Eric said, walking toward the window. He stood in front of the glass panes, his head moving in an arc.

What business does he have nearby?

"It's been a while since you were here last," Ben commented casually as he seemed to do an assessment of Eric's friends.

"It has been, hasn't it?" Eric said, and there was a tone to his words that James didn't like. "A lot has happened since my last visit..."

Eric stared at Ben, but Ben's resolve didn't falter. *You can do this,* James thought.

It was an unusual conversation, but James couldn't say if their previous conversations—when Eric visited—were as halting and testing as this one. James thought they probably had been.

"How is Kayla?" Eric asked.

"Fine. Working...the usual. Can I get you a drink or anything?" Ben asked Eric but he looked at all of the men in turn.

"No, we're not staying long," Eric said. "I'm leaving tonight, but I've got a job for you."

"Sure."

"There's a box in the fridge. Go and get it," Eric said, and Ben did. He came back with the box, holding it out for Eric.

Eric shook his head. "It's for Mak. Open it. Tell me if you think she'll like it."

James wasn't sure if it was the tone of Eric's voice, or the twinkle in his eye, but it made James' skin crawl. And judging by the way Ben opened the lid, he must've had the same reaction.

"Jesus!" Ben said, slamming the lid back down, almost dropping the box.

Eric's laugh boomed.

"Careful, if you drop them I'll cut your fingers off and put them in there instead," he said, his maniacal laugh unnerving.

"Whose fingers are these?" Ben looked around like he was looking for somewhere to vomit.

"Mine, unfortunately," Eric said, holding up his bandaged hand. James knew what was coming next. "Someone—someone I can't wait to meet again—shot my hand, almost blowing it to smithereens. A few fingers had to be amputated, so I thought...what a perfect gift to send to my beautiful wife, who wants to declare me deceased."

"How is she going to know they're your fingers?" Ben asked.

Good question, James thought.

"Because you're going to give her this, too," Eric said, sticking his left hand into his pocket and pulling out a ring.

Ben frowned. "Your wedding band? Didn't I put that in her parent's house"

"This is a different ring, another I used to wear. Mak will recognize it—or at least the inscription will prompt her memory. That'll make her think twice about filing those papers. And it'll make her question her boyfriend. I just wish I could be there to see it. The sooner Kayla gets those cameras in, the better."

Ben nodded. "How should I deliver this? She's not exactly easy to get to at the moment."

"I'll send you further details soon. Just keep the package safe until then," Eric said, his attention returned to the window. "Put the box back in the fridge."

Ben moved fast, seemingly relieved by the prospect of not having to hold Eric's fingers any longer.

Eric flicked his wrist. "I need to get going," he said. "I'll be in touch soon." Eric's team of bodyguards moved in, providing full protection, and without even a nod goodbye, Eric exited. James watched them walk toward the elevators—thankful they'd installed cameras through the entire building—but he couldn't even see Eric above the towering men with shoulders the size of football players. They exited out onto the street and ushered Eric into the car.

James swore under his breath. Eric was so close, but so well protected. The only attack they could launch would be to chase them through the streets of Manhattan, but James didn't like the odds of it being a successful attack.

"Let them go," James said, defying every urge in his body to chase Eric down. "Samuel, track them for as long as you can.

"Copy."

James dialed Ben's number.

"Hello," he answered.

"Hey. You did well, very well. What is the inscription on Eric's ring?" James asked.

"In the Gods We Trust."

8

JAMES THOMAS

"Do you think Eric was crazy even as a child?" Deacon asked as they walked toward their car, having left the shadows only once Samuel confirmed the snipers had departed.

"I think he was probably an unusual child...a little malicious even...and I think someone saw that in him and has fostered it over the years," James said, his eyes roving over the faces that passed them. None of them were familiar, and nor did James feel like they were being watched, but he could be wrong.

"I think, particularly in the years he's been gone, he's transitioned into a madman. There is no way that neither Mak—even being distracted—nor Ben wouldn't have seen through the image he portrayed. I think the more power he's gained, the more insane he's become. Thirteen years is a long time."

"But why Mak?" Deacon asked. "I mean, aside from the obvious— she's beautiful and intelligent—but why the obsession even back then?"

"I don't know," James said, wishing he did.

"Do you think Carl Junez is the one who has conditioned him, so to speak?" Deacon asked.

"It's possible. If we knew who Carl Junez was, that would be very helpful." James thought it very likely Samuel would be able to find out who Carl Junez was, but James wasn't sure how long that would take. And even with a very likely alliance with Biskup, James still felt his clock ticking.

"What about the man we haven't yet identified from Sarquis' drawings? There were four portraits of that same man, so I'm thinking it was someone that worked closely with Eric. A mentor—as such—or a distant family relative wouldn't be unlikely."

"Mm," James mumbled as he recalled memories of those portraits. "I know we ran reports on all of Eric's family members, but I'm thinking we should widen that search. In particular, we should be looking for anyone listed as deceased. When I saw Marie in Paris, she told me he would have to have had a connection, or some contact, to get into such an organization. And we think now Eric was being groomed from a young age, so it surely had to be someone the family knew." James' speaking pace increased—it was another potential lead.

"I've lost them," Samuel's voice came through the earwig. *"The cars went several different directions and I couldn't keep track via the CCTV footage."*

"Okay. We'll see you soon," James said, opening the car door. He sat in the front passenger seat and when the doors were locked, and James was sure they didn't have a tail, he drew his phone and loaded up the security footage of Mak's apartment. He could see her in her bedroom, leaning over a box, still unpacking. He closed the app down and returned his thoughts to Carl Junez.

"The weather is turning," Deacon said.

The season was changing, and James thought its timing mirrored everything in his life. A sense of impending change bristled his nerves. Something big was going to happen soon. James knew it—he just didn't know what it would be.

Deacon pulled up in the car park, and no sooner had they stepped into the elevator did Samuel's voice sound in their earwigs, causing the hairs to stand up on James' arm.

"There's activity at the cemetery—at Eric's second grave. Two men—

that I can see—with torchlights and...shovels. Damn, it looks like they're going to dig up the grave."

The brother's eyes locked and Deacon slammed his hand on the elevator panel, halting it, and then sending it back down to the car park.

"Is Eric there?" James asked as they sprinted back to the car.

"I don't think so, and it doesn't look like they've got security with them," Samuel said. *"I'm trying to enhance the footage from the cameras we installed, but there's not a lot of light."*

Deacon had the engine roaring as James jumped into the passenger seat. "Get Lenny and the boys on site. We'll meet them there."

"Copy."

James listened half-heartedly to the voices coming through his earwig as he checked and reloaded Deacon's weapons, and then his own. He struggled to keep his balance as the car swung around a corner, and James didn't need to look at the dashboard to know Deacon was doing double the speed limit and breaking every traffic law in the book.

"Samuel, what's happening?" James said, as he looked at the GPS, trying to calculate their time of arrival.

"They're digging. They're going hit the casket soon."

"And find it empty," Deacon said, not taking his eyes off of the road. "If they can get it open."

"So let's get there and silence them before they can talk," James said. He presumed these were Eric's men, because no one else would have an interest in the grave.

"Five minutes," Deacon said as he continued to drive at a speed that made the world around them blur.

"The crew are seven minutes behind you," Samuel said, and then added, *"Tom's driving."*

Good, James thought. Tom was almost as good a driver as Deacon, and James knew he wouldn't lose any speed. The team had been taking Ben back to his cell when Samuel had alerted them and, therefore, a seven-minute turnaround was a good result.

"Lenny," James said. "Park at the rear and move in on foot. Fast but silent."

"Copy."

James mind flashed back to the cemetery in London. "Lucky Haruto's not here," James said, grinning as he looked at his brother. "He'd be freaking out right now."

Deacon chuckled. "Even the bad boys get spooked."

James grinned, but as they drove into the cemetery gate his mood sobered. Deacon turned off his lights and the car drove like a phantom through the night.

"Block it off here," James said, and Deacon slowed down, angling the car across the road. They parked it and left it there, potentially stopping a hasty getaway by Eric's men; although, it would likely lead to another vehicle write-off if it came to that. James passed Deacon his weapon and then they pulled their masks over their faces and strapped on their night-vision goggles.

"Are you okay?" Deacon asked as they jogged, light on their feet.

"I'll be fine," James said. Despite being overdue for both antibiotics and pain relief, his adrenaline was doing a good job of keeping the latter problem at bay.

They neared the two men and without having to say a word, the brothers split up. The purchase of this lot had been a carefully thought-out decision. The neighboring tombstones were tall, and provided cover. And the surrounding embankments meant that they could crawl up on their intruders and still be protected. They had all the advantages.

James dropped to the ground and his clothes stuck to him as they absorbed the moisture of the dewy grass.

"Fuck it's heavy," one of the men swore and James couldn't help the grin that spread across his lips. Yes, it was heavy, and that's because they'd filled it with concrete blocks to the maximum weight the burial rigging system was allowed. They had wanted to make it as hard as possible for anyone to dig it up.

Given what they'd known about Eric even then, they'd all agreed that him visiting his grave, or excavating it, was highly possible. So, they'd prepared for the day they might find themselves in this exact situation.

"Who the hell did they bury in here?" another man said, and James picked up an accent immediately but it didn't sound Russian. Greek, maybe? The man puffed from exertion and James assumed they were trying to lift the casket out as they hadn't been able to break the seal and open the lid.

James crawled up the embankment, trying to ignore the pulsing pain of his injured arm. His clothes were soaked by the time he reached the top. He peered over the ledge.

"In position," he whispered, acutely aware of his proximity to Eric's men.

James slowed his breath, in turn slowing his heart rate. Of all the things he'd been taught in his training, that was often the most useful. A clear, focused mind could be the winning edge on the field.

A roaring grunt came from the man with the accent, and then he swore again. James couldn't see him except for his head, sticking out of the grave. James had the perfect shot, but he didn't want to kill him —at least not yet. He couldn't see the second man, but the noises coming from the grave indicated he was in there, too.

"In position," Deacon said.

"Parking. ETA four minutes," Lenny confirmed.

The sound of a ringing cell phone sliced through the air. Both men seemed to pause—the silence palpitating. "It's him. Give me a second, Mikhail."

James saw him nod his head, and then knew who was on the other end of the call.

"Yes... It's taking longer than we expected... It won't open and it's heavy, but we'll get it. I'll call you back if there are any problems we can't overcome, otherwise we'll await your call in the morning." The man sighed. "He's not impressed. Let's get the fucking thing open and get this body out of here."

"Let me try something else," Mikhail said before putting his hands on the soil and hauling his body up and out of the grave. Lenny and the backup team weren't there yet, but with one man in the grave, and the other fully exposed, James knew he wouldn't get a better opportunity to disable him without killing him. He held his hand steady, not a single tremor, and aimed his weapon at Mikhail's foot. James readied his body for what he would have to do next, and then pulled the trigger.

Mikhail's jarring cry was loud enough to wake the dead residents.

James jumped to his feet as Mikhail fell to the ground and sprinted toward him, his weapon aimed and ready. James saw another figure moving in—fast—and he knew it was Deacon.

"Mikhail?" the man yelled from the grave, his voice laden with panic.

James lunged for Mikhail as the man tried to stand again. Mikhail's hand moved to his waist, but his reaction time was too slow and James knocked him over, taking him to the ground again. Mikhail wasn't about to give up, though, and he fought back, hitting James in the shoulder, sending an excruciating bolt of pain down to his toes. It temporarily blinded him, and James fought the dizziness that followed it. He grunted through clenched teeth as he held off Mikhail, giving his body some time to recover. When his vision cleared, their eyes met, and it was all the motivation James needed to fight through the pain. This man would never touch Mak, he'd never get near her, and James would make sure of it.

"Mikhail?" another urgent shout came from the grave and James slammed his hand over Mikhail's mouth. Using every resource of energy in his body, he rolled the man over, pinning him to the wet grass.

Mikhail landed a blow on James' cheek as he fought back like a wild animal. James lost his hold as Mikhail's arms swung like helicopter blades, blocking James' attempts. But, James only needed to land one blow, and when his fist connected with Mikhail's temple, the man went limp. James slumped to the ground, too, his chest heaving with exhaustion.

Shots fired from the grave and Deacon jumped back, dropping to the ground. "Put your weapon down!" his brother yelled.

"Fuck you," the man responded.

"Very well," Deacon said, throwing a gas cylinder into the grave.

"What the—" An alarmed cry came from the hole, and then all went silent. Deacon counted down from five, and then James turned his head, watching his brother crawl forward. He pointed his weapon into the grave, holding his hand over his nose and mouth. "He's down," Deacon said, before looking to James. "Are you okay?"

James nodded, swaying as he sat back on his knees.

"Lenny, bring in the boys. Let's move, quick," Deacon said.

James patted down Mikhail's pockets, and when he didn't find what he was looking for, he searched the ground around them. He found it: Mikhail's cell phone.

He turned the phone off and removed the battery, so that it couldn't be traced, and then slipped it into his jeans pocket. James stood up on his shaky legs and although he couldn't see it underneath his sweater, he felt a warm liquid trickling down his arm. James wondered how many stitches he'd busted.

Lenny and the boys came running in with battle gear on and weapons raised.

"One in the grave, and one here," Deacon said, nudging Mikhail with his foot. "Give them a shot of sedation each, and then put them in the van. We'll go and pick up our car and meet you at the rear. We'll tail you home. "

"Got it," Lenny said, kneeling beside Mikhail. He pulled a syringe from his kit, and slammed it into the jugular without hesitation. That's what James loved about the man.

Deacon took another look at James. "You wait here, too. I'll get the car."

James didn't object as Deacon ran off. He watched on as Lenny and Tom retrieved the man from the grave. When they pulled him up, James asked Lenny to shine a flashlight on his face. James didn't recognize him. He waved a hand for them to continue on. Headlights appeared behind them.

"Lenny, meet me in the cells. I might need a hand with this one," James said with his eyes on Mikhail. But, when he raised them to meet Lenny's, he saw a glint that wasn't the reflection of moonlight. Lenny had one of the most senior roles in his company, and protected one of their most important clients—Jayce Tohmatsu—and that meant he often missed out on the action. But not tonight.

Lenny was about to see something he'd never seen before.

9

JAMES THOMAS

James squeezed his eyes shut, clenching his teeth together as the local anesthetic stung like a swarm of wasps.

"You tore all of your stitches," Deacon said, his voice void of compassion.

"It was worth it," James said, his body slumping as the sting began to wither.

"You're not going to heal very fast if you don't rest this arm...and I don't just mean on the field." Deacon raised an eyebrow.

"He was right in front of me. It was a prime opportunity."

Deacon pulled his lips to the side but didn't respond. He began threading the needle through James' skin, knotting it, cutting the thread, and then repeating it over again.

James used the time to refuel and get some sugar into his body. He ate two energy bars and drank a liter of fluid. By the time Deacon was done, James felt like a new man.

"All right," James said, standing up, this time onto solid legs. "Let's have some fun."

Deacon gave a choking laugh as he packed up the medical kit, leaving it on his kitchen table.

James wondered how Samuel was getting on with Mikhail's

phone, but he knew Samuel would call the moment he had something useful. So, instead, James focused on the task at hand: extracting information in the cruelest way possible.

When the brothers arrived in the cells Lenny was waiting in the control room and immediately stood up.

"Did you get everything I asked for?" James said.

The corner of Lenny's lips turned up. "Everything. And he's just woken up."

James' lips mirrored Lenny's. "Let's do this."

Lenny picked up the bag at his feet and James led the way to the cell. He unlocked it, his eyes meeting Mikhail's once again, but this time James' face wasn't masked.

Mikhail's eyes tripled in size and his pupils dilated. James could barely see his irises.

"Liam Smith," he said with a hoarse voice.

"Surprise." James grinned and pulled up a chair, sitting in front of the bound man. He stretched out his legs, and crossed his arms over his chest, relaxing into the chair. James' aim was to throw Mikhail off as much as possible—the more uneasy he was, the quicker he would talk—and blunder.

"We've got all night," James said, widening his grin. "And I've got some friends."

Mikhail's eyes flickered to Deacon and Lenny behind him.

"I can't believe it," he said, and James didn't doubt him.

"It's a remarkable story how this all came to be, but that's not a story for your ears. In fact, I'd rather hear your story. How did you come to be in New York tonight, digging up a grave?"

Mikhail sat, tightlipped, so James gave him a nudge of encouragement: he drew his scalpel. Mikhail didn't look down, but the tensing of his jaw told James he'd seen it.

"I'm sure you know how this game works. I ask the questions, you answer. If you don't...you'll be made to. It's late, it's been a hell of a few weeks, and I'm not in a mood to be played with. Who are you working for?"

Silence.

"Lenny," he said, and the man came forward. He passed James a box. Mikhail's eyes flickered to it.

"I don't think I'll use this after all," James said, passing his scalpel to Lenny. "I think I'll use these instead..." Slowly, James removed the lid, revealing dozens of metals rods.

Mikhail swallowed.

"Who do you work for?" James repeated the question.

Mikhail's chest began to heave.

James looked to Lenny, and the man smiled. Lenny should've been his prodigy.

Lenny pulled out a set of gloves from his pocket and passed them to James. He put them on, and then Lenny pulled out a lighter, holding it up in front of Mikhail's eyes. *Nice touch,* James thought.

James took one of the metal rods from the box and then passed the box back to Lenny. He took the lighter, rolling his thumb over the flint wheel. He held the flame to the rod, locking eyes with Mikhail.

"Last chance," James said, not expecting him to answer. He wasn't ready to talk, but he would be soon.

Mikhail took a deep breath, as if to prepare his body for the ensuing pain. When the spiked tip of the needle glowed red, James wrapped his hand around the top of the needle and—locking eyes with Mikhail—jammed it into the man's thigh.

His piercing cry hurt James' ears and Mikhail writhed in the chair, only causing himself more pain. The man's breaths were violent, and his teeth clenched together as spit sprayed from his mouth.

"I have an entire box of these," James said calmly, relaxing back into the chair. He did have a full box, but James knew he couldn't use them all because Mikhail would pass out before then. He had to balance the pain with the response of Mikhail's body, otherwise the man wouldn't be able to say a word.

"Who are you working for?"

When Mikhail didn't answer, James gave him a few seconds of leniency in case it was the pain prohibiting him from talking. But a few seconds was all he got. Lenny passed him another rod.

James brought the lighter to the tip. "This could be so much easier for you," he said. "If you know me, you should also know that I always get my victims to talk—and you'll be no different. You'll break, and when you do, you'll just wish you'd given up earlier. This doesn't have to be painful."

"At least when I die I'll be with the Gods. You'll be in hell," Mikhail spat out.

James gave him a cocky grin. "Your Gods are liars. If I'm going to hell, I'll be meeting you there. Now, who do you work for?" James asked, and when he didn't receive an answer, he slammed the rod into Mikhail's other thigh. Mikhail let out a ferocious roar.

"No one can hear you," James said. "The quality of soundproofing materials these days is exceptional."

"He's going to find you," Mikhail growled. "You can hide from them but not forever. And when they do find you"—he wheezed in a breath—"you'll wish you never started this."

The man had touched on James' greatest fear, but he refused to show it. Instead, he decided to punish him for it instead.

"Put on some gloves," James said to Lenny.

Without muttering a word, or changing his facial expression, Lenny's excitement was nonetheless evident by the rate at which he moved. He pulled another set from his back pocket, slipped them on, and when James nodded Lenny took a rod from the box and began to heat it with a second lighter from his pocket. James lit the rod in his hand and Mikhail's eyes darted between them. He tried to sit back, but there was nowhere for the bound man to go. When both rods were alight, James counted down from three, and they jammed a rod into each thigh. Mikhail inhaled sharply, his voice like a rattle, and then his head dropped down. He was out cold.

"I'll get it," Deacon said from behind him and James heard the door open and close.

James looked to Lenny. "Four rods down. Want to place a bet on how long this is going to take?"

"I give him two more rods at least," Lenny said.

James nodded. "His loyalty to his Gods is greater than his fear of me. Or even his fear of pain or death."

"Can you crack him?" Lenny asked.

James didn't know. He never failed to get a man to talk, but then he'd never dealt with a member of a religious cult before.

The door opened and Deacon stepped forward with a bucket of icy water. He dumped it over Mikhail's head. The man jolted awake.

"Wakey, wakey," James said, kicking him in the shin. "Ready to talk yet?"

"You know who I work for," Mikhail said, his voice slow, almost slurred.

"I want to hear it from you," James said.

Mikhail shook his head from side to side, and James noticed he was beginning to shiver. Water dripped from his clothes, and onto the floor, amalgamating into the puddle that surrounded him.

"You know, as these rods get closer to your groin, the pain is going to increase," James said, as he held out his hand for another. Lenny passed it to him and James lit it up, holding it directly in front of Mikhail's eyes.

He closed his eyes. James wondered if he was mentally trying to remove himself from the situation, and therefore the pain, or if he just didn't want to see it coming. Either way, the action was futile, and James' patience was running out. He took the metal rod, and slammed it into the man's right thigh, an inch from his groin.

James sat back quickly to avoid the spray of spit that came from the man's mouth. Mikhail looked down, his eyes bulging as wailing noises sounded from his mouth. He eventually calmed down but continued to whimper and when his head began to sway, James brought his hand to his cheek, giving him a cracking slap.

"If you pass out again, you'll wake up missing a limb, and I won't be giving you any anesthetic. Stay awake," James growled, his voice deep and threatening. It was a voice he'd refrained from using until this point.

Mikhail shuddered and mumbled incoherently. James wasn't even sure it was in English.

"Repeat that," James said.

"Cerah zalû, cerah zalû."

James looked to Deacon but he shook his head.

"I'm running it though a language test," Samuel said through the earwig. *"No matches yet."*

Mikhail's head bobbled around like it might fall off, and James knew if he administered another rod the man might not be capable of talking. The extreme pain might also cause him to lose control and urinate on himself, which was something James definitely wasn't in the mood to deal with.

So James changed tactics. Mikhail might not consciously volunteer the information, but with a fraction more pain he might slip into a state of delirium and inadvertently crack. James took hold of one of the rods in Mikhail's thigh and turned it. The man hissed in a breath and his head fell to the side before righting itself.

"Did Christos ask you to dig up the grave tonight?" James asked.

"Yes..." The response was almost inaudible, but he had responded.

James turned the rod again. "Whose grave were you digging up?"

"Dunno," Mikhail said, his voice sleepy.

The strategy was working. Not how James had intended, and not how he wanted, but he was finally getting some information.

"How did Christos give you the job details?"

"Phone. Telephone." Mikhail's voice was fading.

"What were you supposed to do with the body?" James asked.

"Wait...wait for a call."

"How long have you worked for Christos?"

When Mikhail didn't respond, James turned the rod in a full circle and repeated the question.

The man screamed, his breath laborious. "From the beginning...years..."

That explains his loyalty, James thought. "What is your role in Saratani?"

"The girls..." Mikhail said, his head slumping forward again.

James kicked his shin and Mikhail partially opened his eyes.

"Spotter... I find the girls."

James didn't feel an iota of guilt for what he'd done to Mikhail tonight, but if he had, it would've been obliterated with that answer. He didn't even look at his brother, who had a special hate for men who trafficked women.

"Oh, you're definitely going to hell," James muttered. "How do I find Christos?"

Christos' name seemed to empower the man and in one last act of defiance, Mikhail shook his head.

James turned the rod nearest to Mikhail's groin, watching his pain response, timing his questions carefully.

"Where is Christos?"

"Sect..." Mikhail mumbled.

"Sect, what?

"...Sect meeting..."

"Where is the meeting held?"

"...Romania."

"When is the meeting?" James asked, feeling hopeful for the first time since Mikhail started talking.

"Tomorrow..."

"Where in Romania?" James pressed.

"Don't know..."

James turned the rod again. "Where is the meeting held?"

"I don't know," Mikhail muttered between labored breaths.

Sect meetings... James wondered what they entailed.

"Will Christos be there?"

"Sect meeting," Mikhail repeated, his words barely coherent, clearly unaware that he wasn't answering the question.

James didn't think Mikhail was going to tell him anything more— if he knew anything more in the first place.

"What is the address for the sect meeting?" James asked again.

"Dunno..."

Tension ate at James' stomach like a termite. He couldn't crack Mikhail the way he'd always been able to crack other men. Mikhail wouldn't betray his Gods, and he wouldn't betray his leader, not consciously, and he couldn't get as much out of a man in this state. It was becoming evident that Eric had created a zealous, religious cult with members who would die to protect it. The threat was even bigger than James had realized.

James turned another rod, adjusting Mikhail's pain levels once more. James repeated questions he'd asked earlier—Mikhail's responses were the same. James asked again where he could find Christos, and where the sect meetings were, but he got the same three words over and over: "I don't know."

Mindful of the time and that Eric's call could come at any point, James admitted defeat.

"Final chance," James said, pressing his scalpel into Mikhail's forehead. He swore weakly.

"Where can I find Christos?"

His wheezy voice again muttered the three words James didn't want to hear.

He sliced an arc from Mikhail's forehead to his ear and Mikhail began to chant words unfamiliar to James. Perhaps they were his final prayers to his Gods. James thought Mikhail was going to be very disappointed when he shortly discovered his Gods were nothing but a lie.

James looked into the man's eyes and then in one swift move, he slashed Mikhail's neck. He gurgled, wheezing in his final breaths. His body slumped in the chair, and the cell was silent.

"We'll use his body. We're going to send him, without a face and with charred skin to mask the decomposition of his body, to the funeral home. Samuel, get forensics ready," James said.

"Copy."

"I want Eric to have to figure out who the body is, and I want to scare him—I want him to fear us. I want him to see what we're capable of, how violent we can be, and for him to realize that if he threatens Mak, we will respond." James looked to Lenny. "Do you want to watch?"

He flashed a teeth-baring grin. "Sure do."

James nodded. "It's best to slice around the face," he said, demonstrating with the scalpel, "and then peel it back. It's the easiest method."

And James should know—he'd tested several.

10

JAMES THOMAS

The man was as white as a freshly painted wall when the brothers walked in.

"Enjoy the show?" James said, looking to the screen one of his team had placed in front of the bound man. The man had just witnessed everything that had gone on in the cell next door.

Blue eyes locked with James'. "I want an easy death. One clean bullet."

"All you need to do is talk then," James said, pleased their tactic had worked. They didn't know how long they had until Eric called, and so they'd wanted to make this process as efficient as possible.

"I know who you are, Liam Smith."

"And who are you?" James said, sitting down in front of him.

"Liev," he said. "I joined Escanta about the same time Christos did. He, however, was much more ambitious than I was—something I only realized later on. He's very deceiving—as you're aware—and it's hard to know what he's really up to. They say no one has ever risen through the ranks so quickly...some even say he's the son of a God." Liev rolled his eyes.

James knew immediately then that Liev had never truly bought into the fanatical religious cult, and that gave James a flicker of hope there were more like him, and that they weren't all like Mikhail.

"How long have you been in Manhattan?" James asked.

"I flew in earlier today. When I landed, Christos called with the job's details."

James nodded. "Why is Christos hunting me? What does he want?"

"I don't think he personally wants anything, but the elders do, and Christos is very ambitious, and very eager to please. He's become obsessed with you—I've never seen anything quite like it." Liev cleared his throat. "The rumor has it that your father betrayed the elders. He crossed them, and they do not take well to that. He made a mockery of them—a mockery that has not been forgotten to this day. In our world, in this group, if you betray the elders, your family must also pay for your sins. There is no leniency, no reasoning. And, given that you are your father's only child, there is even more incentive to find you."

James kept his face neutral, but his mind was reeling. "What did my father do?"

"I don't know. No one knows, at least not in Escanta or Saratani. We've all asked the question a million times: why have so many of our resources been committed to finding Liam Smith? If you want the answer to that question, I suggest you find Christos. I'm sure he knows."

"Does Christos have a family?" James asked.

"Yes. A wife, Marianne, and a daughter, Makaela."

"What about Eric's old life, did he ever mentioned that to you?"

Liev stalled, as if choosing his words carefully. "Yes, he has a wife here in Manhattan."

"So, he has two wives?" James asked.

Liev shrugged his shoulders. "We have some unusual practices. Or, those with power do, at least."

"Meaning?"

"The elders have several wives. But the lower men—men in Escanta and Saratani—are not allowed multiple wives. But, I think you'd struggle to find a monogamous relationship amongst them. Having a wife and multiple girlfriends is accepted."

"Eric's wife, his first wife, thought he was dead. That was Eric's grave you were digging up tonight. Did you know that?"

His forehead creased. "No, I had no idea. I was given the coordinates, and Mikhail's contact details, and told to carry out a job." He looked to the ceiling, and then back at James. "How do you know this?"

"Because I orchestrated his funeral," James said, his eyes never leaving Liev's. The man's face transformed.

"You?" His mouth dropped open and he leaned forward against the restraints. "You're Makaela's boyfriend."

James nodded.

The man looked at him in wonder. "What are the chances?" he muttered. "Oh, wow, Christos is going to fucking lose it when he finds out."

"He's not going to," James said.

"He will," Liev said. "You have no idea who that man is."

"I'm getting a good idea. How often do you see Christos?" James asked, curious as to how he led such a large number of men without seeming to have a base for his business dealings.

"No one sees him except at the sect meetings and at worship ceremonies." Liev began wriggling his arms. "Can you do undo these? My hands are aching."

"No," James said, keeping his face neutral. "What are sect meetings?"

"Local division meetings for the different sectors of Saratani," Liev said. "The Romania meeting Mikhail mentioned—the address wouldn't have been released yet. And if Christos asked him to come here, he won't be expected at the meeting and he won't receive the address. But, if there's a sect meeting scheduled, Christos will be there."

"Why wouldn't the address be released yet?"

"The addresses for the sect meetings are only released twelve hours before. The notice is always short. I'm not sure why."

James wondered if it was a security measure. "What are worship ceremonies?"

"They're our version of church. They are held about once per month, on a Saturday night. A series of rituals are performed, chanting..."

"Is Eric always at these ceremonies?"

"Always. He leads them. He's like the priest."

James almost choked on his breath. Eric was a special kind of priest, all right.

"When was the last one?" James asked, feeling hopeful.

Mikhail looked thoughtful. "Three weeks ago."

"When will you receive the address for the worship ceremony?"

"The notice will be short, but the address is always the same. They are held in a building in London. They say it's sacred, and it's been owned by the elders for centuries."

"Can you give me the address?" James asked.

Liev nodded and then spoke the address, which he said he had committed to memory. James untied the man's wrists.

"What language was Mikhail speaking?"

Liev scoffed. "The old language. It's used for portions of the ceremonies. Christos says the words of the language have the power of the Gods."

James sighed. "Is it a recognized language?"

"No, not that I'm aware of."

The two men looked at each other.

"Just get it over with," Liev said.

James shook his head. "I'm going to need you to do something first."

James squinted against the morning sun as he pulled out of the Thomas Security car park. He lowered the visor, giving his eyes some relief while he retrieved his aviators from the glove box. As he drove toward Mak's apartment, he reflected on the night's events. All-in-all it had been a good night, but now they had to wait for the call from Eric with further instructions. It could come at any moment, and given Eric's aptitude for calling at inconvenient times, James didn't think he'd be lucky with the timing. Nonetheless, he was hoping for a few hours of sleep, with Mak tucked up in his arms. There was nothing he wanted more. He didn't even want sex. He just wanted to hold her and close his eyes. *Just a few hours, that's all I'm asking for,* James thought.

He checked rearview and side mirrors, but there were few cars on the road, and none of them were tailing him.

James had made the right call not to pursue Eric once he'd exited Ben's building—even though it had been as anguishing as cutting off a limb. If Eric had gotten a whiff that they were that close, last night would've been called off, and James wouldn't have the information they had—and another chance to get close to him. Not to mention, a car chase through the city was never a good idea—the death tally could multiply exponentially and so could the media attention. Right now, more than ever, James needed to keep a low profile in Manhattan.

James had to check himself before making decisions now. He couldn't rush the hunt to find Eric, and nor could he make emotional decisions—not when there was so much at stake. The desire to resolve Mak's case before something happened to him gnawed at him every minute of the day. It hung there, like a cobweb in his mind, one he couldn't brush away. That did not, however, give him an excuse to make decisions he wouldn't other-wise make.

He parked and turned off the ignition, and then popped out four capsules from the boxes in his lap. He took a large swig of water and swallowed them before grabbing his bag and getting out of the car. He swiped his pass across the elevator control panel, bypassing every floor on the way up to Mak's.

He unlocked her door, walking into a warm but silent home. To his surprise, all of the boxes were gone. If she wasn't fully unpacked, she nearly was, which meant she'd been up all night. James went straight to the control room, checking in with Jack, who had replaced Cami for the evening shift.

"Morning," James said. "How is everything?"

Jack shrugged his shoulders. "Good. Nothing to report."

"What time did she go to bed?"

"About an hour ago," Jack said.

James nodded. "Okay. I'm going to sleep for a few hours," he said before walking toward Mak's bedroom. James slowly turned the doorknob, pushing it open and closing it without a sound. He put his bag down beside the bed. The duvet was pushed down to Mak's waist, and the strap of her silk slip had fallen off her shoulder. Her hair was splayed across her pillow and her lips turned up in a small smile. He wondered what she was dreaming about.

James put his phone and pistol on the bedside table, and then carefully, so as not to bust his stitches again, he removed his sweater and T-shirt, dropping them to the floor. He stripped off his jeans, adding them to the pile, and then crawled in beside Mak.

His hopes of not waking her were quickly dashed. She opened her eyes.

"Hey," James whispered, using his left arm to scoop her in, flush against his body. She slipped one leg between his and James felt his entire body relax.

He kissed her but reminded himself he needed to sleep right now, and not spend an hour making love to her, because that call could come at any moment and he needed to be prepared.

She cupped his chin and parted her lips. James deepened the kiss, moaning as her tongue brushed over his.

He pulled back before he couldn't. He rested his forehead on hers, noting her quick breathing. He ignored the throb that ignited in his crotch.

"You're just getting in?" she asked, lifting her head to look at the alarm clock.

"Mm," James said. "Late night in the office."

Her eyes penetrated his. "What's happening, James?"

"Work is happening, but right now, I have a few hours—maybe— and all I want is to do is hold you and close my eyes."

Her lips puckered, and James's groin pulsed. "Don't do that, you're turning me on."

"Don't try and distract me," Mak said.

"I'm not, I was being honest." He grazed his teeth over her bottom lip. "Seriously, though, I really need to sleep."

A few seconds passed before she spoke. "Okay, but when we get up I want to talk about my case."

"Okay," James said with a nod. *In a few hours I might not be here, and we won't have to have that discussion.*

Mak softened, and she finally gave him a smile. She tightened her arm around him and buried her head into his chest. James closed his eyes.

This is it, he thought, *this is all I want.*

And I won't let you take it from me, Eric.

Never.

James' eyes sprung open as his phone rang beside him. His hand darted for it, but when he answered the call he didn't speak—he listened. He rolled onto his back, ignoring a set of eyes he knew were watching him.

"Hello." It was Eric.

Deacon would be in the cell with Liev, and they'd rehearsed this call, but James still felt a pang of apprehension.

"Do you have the body?"

"We do. One problem, though, there's no face. I don't know if that's an issue for you, or not," Liev said.

"Does he have fingers?"

"Yes. All ten of them."

"Then it's not a problem," Eric said. *"I'm going to text you an address. It's a funeral home—take the body there at noon. They'll be expecting you;*

no questions will be asked. Just drop it off, and then get on a plane and head home."

"Sure."

"Well done, Liev. I appreciate your help."

"It's an honor. I'll get the body to the home at noon."

"Good."

The line went silent and James' eyes flickered to the clock. It was eight in the morning.

"Call complete," Samuel said.

Deacon spoke. "I'll deploy security teams to begin surveillance on the funeral home as soon as we get the address. There seems to be no rush in delivering this body, though, so I think we should get a few hours of shut-eye and then prep Liev."

"Okay," James said. "Get some sleep and I'll see you soon."

James hung up, and set an alarm on his phone before putting it down on the bedside table once more.

James closed his eyes, ignoring Mak's inquisitive gaze, and drew her in. Her breasts pressed against his chest and he sighed softly.

Two hours.

11

ERIC

The hands of the clock moved rhythmically and Eric couldn't draw his eyes away.

"Can I get you anything else, sir?"

The man's wrinkled fingers trembled as he pushed his glasses up the ridge of his nose. Dead people didn't give him the jitters, but an intruder who calmly sipped on tea, with a pistol in his lap, apparently did.

Eric shook his head. "No, thank you. I'm fine for the moment."

The undertaker cleared his throat. "Very well." The man—Ian—returned his attention to the papers on the desk. Eric studied him, concluding that he wasn't actually working but using them as a distraction.

They'll be here soon, Eric thought, his eyes dropping to his wrist once more. It was almost noon. This was a test for his old friend—one which, if he passed, would cause him to be promoted. Eric had another job for Liev—a job he could only give to someone who had proved themselves.

An alert, which resembled a doorbell, sounded and Eric's eyes honed in on the undertaker. He pressed a button on the intercom.

"Can I help you?" Ian said.

"Yes. I have a delivery you are expecting."

Eric nodded, and Ian responded. "Of course," he said, pressing another button. "Please come in and park at the left-side entrance. I will meet you there."

"Thank you," Liev said.

Eric loaded the surveillance footage from the cameras he'd installed yesterday. The wrought-iron gates opened, and a charcoal-gray sedan entered. Eric took a screenshot of the registration plate and sent it to Luke to run a check. The car pulled to a stop at the entrance and Eric tilted his head toward the door.

"Remember, I'm not here, and if you do something stupid—like tell him I am —I'll blow your fucking brains out." Eric lifted the gun and made a clicking noise with his tongue—twice. One for each bullet.

Ian paled—unaware Eric couldn't actually shoot with his left hand—and then left without another word. Keeping the surveillance footage in view, Eric crept behind him, following the old man. He stopped at the juncture of the hallway that led to the side entrance.

Ian opened the door and Eric peered around the corner. He saw Liev, but he seemed to be alone. *Where the fuck is Mikhail?*

Eric bit his lip, observing Liev as the car window receded. He smiled at the old man.

"Hi. He's in the trunk."

"Oh dear," Ian said under his breath.

Ian rolled out a gurney to the car and Liev got out, offering a helping hand.

Liev looked relaxed, striding casually around to the trunk. It popped open, and Ian paused for a moment before he seemed to collect himself.

"I'll help you, he's a bit heavy," Liev said.

Eric watched as the two men lifted the body—wrapped in white plastic sheeting—onto the gurney. A grin spread across Eric's lips.

Who did you bury?

I want to know, because one day soon I'm going to tell Makaela all about this.

When the body was strapped onto the gurney, Ian pushed it toward the door.

"I can help you get him inside, if you'd like?" Liev said.

Eric frowned. Was that suspicious, or was he just doing an exemplary job? The old undertaker did look fragile.

Ian responded exactly how Eric had told him to. "No, thank you. I'll take it from here. Good day."

Liev shrugged his shoulders. "Good day to you, too. Can I exit around this way?" he asked, pointing at the rear.

"Yes, it loops around to the front. I'll open the gates for you," Ian said.

Liev got back into the car, turned on the ignition, and drove off.

Ian opened the door and Eric pulled the gurney toward him, instructing Ian to wait. On his phone he watched Liev exit, and then he made a phone call.

"Did he have a tail? Was anyone watching him?" Eric asked.

"No. He looked to be alone."

"Good," Eric said, hanging up and drawing a knife from his pocket. The old man stepped back. "Relax, it's not for you," Eric said, laughing. He jammed the knife through the plastic sheeting and tore it open. A slightly charred but skinless face stared back at him.

What the fuck happened to you? Eric thought with a sadistic grin.

"Good," he said, looking at Ian. "I want samples prepared for analysis—I'll wait for them—and then you can cremate him. If this is ever spoken about, I'll be back, and you'll look just like this man."

Ian shrank back under Eric's glare but managed to find his voice. "I'll get started."

Eric busied himself while Ian prepared the samples. He looked around, observing the other bodies. He found death fascinating. He brushed his thumb over another body Ian had been preparing. It was like wax.

Fools, Eric thought. *If only they knew. If only they realized they could live forever.*

It took Ian several hours to prepare the samples, and when they were ready Eric made another call.

Ian opened the gates once more and a hearse drove in, pulling up at the same side entrance. Two men—Eric's bodyguards—dressed in suits, entered the funeral home.

Eric looked at the coffin and chuckled. "This is a first," he said, stepping into the box. Holes had been cut to allow for oxygen supply, but they wouldn't be visible to anyone watching.

Eric lay down, wriggling his body in and placing his hands by his side. Frankie—his primary bodyguard—closed the lid and Eric yelled out, "Don't make me come back, Ian!" His laugh boomed as he thumped his fist on the top of the casket.

Manhattan looked like a Lego city as Eric peered through the window of the jet. In the past, every time he'd been back to the concrete jungle he'd made sure he'd seen his wife—from a distance—but this trip had been different. He couldn't get near her, thanks to her boyfriend. Eric's gut clenched, twisting into knots. *Who is he? And how the hell is he so good, and so seemingly well-resourced?* Eric's teeth ground back and forth. If Kayla didn't find out soon, he was going to put a bullet in her head to punish her for being such a useless bitch. Eric wanted to know everything about Makaela's boyfriend, because something wasn't right about him. *James Thomas.* That's all he knew, and even that was a lie. His name wasn't James Thomas, but he did have a name, and Eric was going to find out what it was.

Eric inhaled, expanding his chest, and then exhaled. He didn't need this distraction right now; what he needed to do was focus on finding Liam Smith. Makaela's boyfriend should've been the last thing on his mind, but when he'd had to make the trip to Boston, he couldn't resist going to Romania via New York.

Since his disappearance, Makaela hadn't had a boyfriend—not a serious one. Nor had she declared him deceased. That had pleased Eric. Admittedly, she hadn't been the best wife. She'd been young, and distracted—focused on her studies—but he liked her ambitious nature. So he forgave her for her sins, because he understood ambition. Ambition was the reason he'd walked away from their marriage —for the short-term. It had all been for her—for them. And it wouldn't be long until he could share the fruits of his sacrifice with her, but first he had to find Liam Smith. If Eric could hand him over to the elders, his status would rise. He would have more power— more than he could've ever dreamed of. And then he could have Makaela back.

Eric often wondered how Makaela would adjust to life in Saratani. Marianne hadn't needed to adjust, she'd been born into their world. Eric knew Makaela would struggle at first. She'd come around, though—he'd make her. He'd have to, because once she was inducted into Saratani, there was no choice. No one left, not volun- tarily—not since Eric had become its leader.

Eric took another long, calming breath as the jet floated through the sky. He checked the time, wondering when he was going to have the dead man's identification. *It shouldn't be long now*, Eric thought.

The man could be a homeless nobody that Makaela's boyfriend had found dead on the street. Or, he could be someone that could potentially be a link to the true identity of her boyfriend. It was a long shot, but with little information coming through from Kayla, Eric had thought it worth the risk.

He'd desperately wanted to visit the grave himself; to see where his darling wife had buried him. But a complication in Boston had kept him on the phone, held up in his hotel room, so he hadn't been able to make the trip. That same complication had forced him to reschedule the sect meeting. He should've been in Romania now, but instead he was on his way back to Boston.

Next time, Eric thought, *I'll visit my grave.*

When his phone rang in his lap, his eyes lingered on it, counting the number of rings before he picked it up. It was a superstition he couldn't shake.

"Hello," Eric answered.

"I've got the lab results... The identification of the deceased is Mikhail Sined."

Eric's blood ran cold, then hot, then cold again. When he finally found his voice, it cut the air like a razor. "Are you certain?"

"Yes. The body has been identified via several sources."

"Thank you," Eric said, ending the call. Slowly, he put his phone back in his lap.

Small bumps broke out over his skin like a rash. He'd been deceived, and Mak's boyfriend had done that to Mikhail. What was the man capable of?

Eric paced the length of the jet, ignoring the inquisitive eyes of his security men, but it did nothing to calm him.

Liev.

He darted back to his chair and picked up his phone. He dialed Liev's number.

It rang twice.

"Hello, Eric."

Eric stopped breathing. He didn't recognize the voice, but it wasn't Liev's.

"Who are you?" Eric asked.

"I'm your wife's boyfriend. And I'm the man who is going to kill you."

"You're overly confident, that's what you are. What have you done with Liev?"

"He's been disposed of. As has Mikhail. But then, you already know that, don't you?"

"I do. I like what you did with his face...quite a masterpiece. You're obviously well-practiced," Eric said, buying himself some time to get his mind straight.

"When I find you, I'll show you how good I am. You'll be able to admire my artwork up close and personal."

"You'll never find me," Eric said, but as he spoke the words he found himself doubting them.

"I will," the man said, and Eric steeled at the confidence in his words.

I can't let that happen, Eric thought. *I've worked too hard, and sacrificed too much.*

"Tell me," Eric said, trying to regain some sense of control in the conversation, "does Makaela know who you are? A man of your skills? A man of your resources? A man like that doesn't come with a clean past... What would she think of you if she really knew who you were?"

"It can't be any worse than what she already thinks of you," he replied. "You have something Biskup wants, Eric, and I suggest you give it to him. If you don't, I'll make you wish you'd given him the code."

A sharp pain pierced his ear and Eric stretched open his jaw. "I will never give Biskup the code. And, believe me, you wouldn't want me to. He'll destroy the world with it, and we'll all be dead."

"I don't know what you've done, but I'm going to find out. You should fear me; you should lie awake in bed at night worried about what the next day will bring. Because when I find you—and I will find you—your life will become a hell that you can't even imagine yet. I'll be seeing you soon, Eric."

The line went dead and Eric's eyes lingered on his phone. His breaths were short and tight and the vein in his forehead pulsed.

No, no, no, Eric thought. *No one threatens me and gets away with it.*

I'll find out who you are.

And then I'll take my wife away from you.

12

MAK ASHWOOD

She didn't hear him, but when a strong, lean arm wrapped around her waist and she inhaled the masculine tone of his cologne, she knew it was him.

"Good evening," she said, giggling as he picked her up, holding her against his chest and letting her feet dangle. His hot lips seared her cheek.

"Evening," James said, carrying her toward her bedroom.

"I can walk, you know," she said, wriggling against him. "You should put me down, you'll hurt your arm."

"This is my good arm," he said before throwing her on the bed.

She shrieked as she went flying through the air, bouncing a few times on the plush mattress. She looked up at him, laughing at his huge grin.

"Why are you in such a good mood?" Mak asked.

He kneeled on the edge of the mattress, curling his index finger toward him. She sat up, their faces just inches apart.

"Because I have the night off—I think—and I get to spend it with you," James said. His mouth came down on hers—hard, and greedy.

"Not so fast, Thomas. We're overdue for that talk we should've had this morning," Mak said.

His smile faded and he sighed in resignation. "Move over," he said.

Mak crawled into the middle of the bed and he lay down beside her, propping his back up with cushions.

He took her hand, guiding her onto his lap so she was straddling him.

"What do you want to know?" he asked in that casual tone he used so well.

"I want to know about my case and where it's at," Mak said. It was to James' disadvantage that he'd left her alone all day, because it had given her lots of time to think, and to orchestrate a series of questions that just might trip him up.

His gaze diverted behind her.

Mak looked over her shoulder. "What?"

James chuckled. "Nothing. Just noting the fireplace is on. Remind me to turn that off before I remove your clothes."

Mak bit her lip, returning her gaze to him. "Do I make you hot?"

He bucked his hips. "You know you do."

"Stop distracting me," Mak said. "First question... When did Ben speak to Eric last?"

He raised one eyebrow, perhaps at the pinpointing nature of her question. "Yesterday."

"Was that one of the calls you were listening to?" Mak asked.

"Yes," James said.

"Are Ben and Kayla still living in the cells?" Mak asked. Although she was interested in the answer, the question was mostly important because it would determine her next one.

"No. We've moved them to another apartment building," James said.

Interesting. "You told me you moved me here because Biskup has agreed to cooperate. But that has nothing to do with Eric. What has changed that leads you to believe they're safe outside the walls of Thomas Security?"

"We believe Eric is busy in Europe. We think he's got his hands full there for the moment, so the immediate risk to them is low. At any point—as with you—if we need to move them back to Thomas Security then we will. Kayla and Ben are cooperating, so moving them is a reward."

"What makes you think Eric is busy in Europe?"

"He said as much on the phone. And other intelligence seems to back that up," James replied.

"Such as," Mak said.

"Such as I'm not divulging for security purposes. The less you know the better—that hasn't changed. Let me deal with Eric, and you focus on your work and living your life—as best you can at the moment."

"Have you worked out what the code is for?"

James sighed. "No, but I'm thinking our first assumption, that it relates to nuclear weapons, is correct."

"When will you make contact with Biskup again?"

"I'm not sure yet, but likely within the next few days."

"Isn't there a chance that Biskup might betray you?"

James squeezed her hand. "Yes, but it's a necessary risk."

"Why? Why not keep trying to find Eric and force him to give you the code? Or hand over Eric to Biskup? Why do you need Biskup's help?"

"For two reasons. One, forming that relationship keeps Biskup's guys away from you. Second, it's become apparent that Eric has a huge support network...a resource pool much greater than we have, in terms of men at least. An army of five against an army of hundreds doesn't stand a good chance, does it? With Biskup's men, we equal the playing field."

"As long as Biskup doesn't renege on his part of the deal. If he were to eliminate Thomas Security, then he would eliminate my security field, and then he gets what he wants. Either way, he wins."

"Come here," James said, gently tugging on her hand.

Mak leaned forward, resting her elbows on the pillows behind him.

"If he kills me, and gets you, and still can't get the code, he's back to square one. If he works with me to get Eric, he gets the code. His chances are much better to work with me, and Biskup is no fool. This is our best chance, Mak."

He wrapped one hand around her neck and guided her mouth to his. His lips were soft as they pressed against hers, lingering there. "I'm going to fix this, Mak. I'm going to find Eric, and give him to Biskup, and then we won't have to live like this anymore. We'll have the life we want, the kind of life I dream about."

"You sound so confident," Mak said, resting her forehead against his.

"I am. An alliance with Biskup is a good thing. I trust my gut instincts, I always have, and I feel like this is what we need—that this will work."

"I'm scared. I'm scared for you," Mak whispered, thinking of the white patch hidden underneath his sweater.

"You don't need to be," James said, and although she didn't see any doubt in his eyes, she wasn't sure if he believed that or not.

His hand slipped underneath her top and his finger left a trail of heat on her skin. He undid her bra, and then brushed his thumb over one nipple as he pressed his lips against hers once more.

"I'm not finished yet," she said between kisses.

"I am." James pinched her nipple and she moaned. "I want you. I need you. No more questions, please."

"Can they hear us?" Mak asked, thinking of the security staff in the control room.

"No. He's outside in the foyer office now."

That was all Mak needed to hear. She closed her eyes, parted her lips, and let James Thomas explore her mouth as she rubbed her pelvis against his.

James seemed to enjoy the teasing, evident by the throaty groans that slipped through his lips. Mak pushed up onto her knees and undid his jeans without breaking the kiss. His lips were too enticing, too seductive, and she'd missed the way he kissed her. And the way her body reacted to him.

She slipped her hand underneath his briefs, her fingers encircling his hard shaft. He groaned louder as she stroked him up and down, twisting her hand over the head of his penis. She repeated it over and over, taking joy when he pulsed in her hand.

"Mak," he said, pushing her back and pulling her top over her head. He tossed her bra onto the bed and brought one nipple to his mouth. Mak tilted her head back as he sucked and nibbled. Her breasts grew heavier, and her pelvis ached, throbbing with desire. She watched him now, and when he looked up through hooded eyes, locking with her gaze, a warm sensation pooled deep in her hips.

James stopped, and let out a groan. "Please tell me you've unpacked the condoms," he said as he gripped her waist, digging his fingers in.

Mak flinched, but she liked it when he was rough like that. The short burst of pain caused a rush of pleasure.

"Top drawer," she said quickly, leaning over him. Her breast basically fell back into his mouth, and he took full advantage.

Her concentration lapsed and Mak temporarily forgot what she was doing. She shook her head, clearing the lust enough to grab one of the little packets. Sitting back on his hips, she tore the plastic between her teeth, and then rolled it onto his cock. His eyes never left her.

Mak lifted her hips, and then lowered herself down, moaning as he stretched her. Mak felt everything shift. James' eyes were mesmerizing. Hypnotic. They were darker than she'd ever seen them, and unguarded. Mak slowly, teasingly, rolled her hips, grinding against his. His lips parted and his chest rose. As she lifted up and down, he groaned and his eyes rolled back into his head, breaking the static connection.

"Come here," he commanded, and Mak leaned forward, continuing to ride him.

He threaded one hand through her hair, grasping it at the base of her skull and guiding her mouth toward his. "There are so many things I want to do with you. As soon as this arm is healed...you better get ready." He drew her bottom lip between his teeth.

"Get ready? Whatever do you mean, James Thomas?" Mak asked.

He gave her that arrogant, sexy smirk she so loved.

"You know exactly what I mean." He pinched her ass and Mak gasped.

"Tell me more," Mak said, aware of the change in her breath. She was panting. James Thomas did that to her—every time.

"In one week I'll show you. You can wait until then," he said, kissing her neck.

Mak tilted her head to the side, and she shivered as his teeth grazed over her collarbone.

"In one week?" That seemed too fast. Even with a mind clouded by lust, Mak didn't think his arm would be healed.

"It will be good enough for what I want to do."

His fingers trailed the groove between her butt cheeks and Mak moaned. She slowed down, but James wrapped his arm around her waist, guiding her, keeping up the rhythm.

"Tell me," she begged, sucking on his earlobe.

He groaned. "No. It's always better to have the element of surprise. And you will be surprised."

"Please," she begged again, trying to ignore the coiling in her hips. She wasn't ready to orgasm, she didn't want this to end.

"Don't slow down," James said.

"I'm going to—"

"I know," he said.

Mak squeezed her eyes shut. "Not yet."

James smirked again, cupping her chin. "You're going to come multiple times. I promise."

James had never made her a promise he hadn't kept, so she submitted. She flattened her palms against the headboard, rubbing her clit against his pelvis. Their mouths crashed together and Mak's body felt so light it was as if she were floating. Her head spun as her orgasm consumed her body and a rush of heat preceded the burst of ecstasy that shot to her toes. She screamed into his mouth, as he wrapped one arm around her waist, holding her as she found her release.

Mak slumped onto his chest, fighting to breathe.

James ran his fingers through her hair, soothing her, and he kissed the crown of her head.

"That's one," he said.

"How many more?" Mak said, lifting her head to look into his sparkling eyes.

He ran his tongue across his teeth, his gaze heated and penetrating. His abdomen rippled as he suddenly sat upright. "I don't know, but we've got all night."

Mak curled her knees to her chest, tucking the sheet over her breasts and under her arms. She strained to listen, hoping to catch even one word, but she didn't hear a sound. She assumed James was in the security control room. Mak knew it served an official purpose, and that her team needed a base to work from in her apartment, but it also seemed to be a convenient office for James, too.

When he opened the bedroom door and strolled toward her he had the classic, calm, James Thomas face on.

"Good morning," he said as he climbed into bed next to her.

"Did you sleep at all?" Mak asked, wondering at what time exactly he'd snuck out of her room.

"Six hours," he said, grinning. "Sleep and sex... It's a good combination."

Mak shook her head but she couldn't suppress the laugh at James' expression.

"I do need to go into the office this morning, though," he said. "So, I was thinking I'll cook breakfast—we'll cook breakfast," he said, correcting himself. "And then I'll go to work."

"I need to practice at the range," Mak said. "I have to win this bet." She would not be handing over one hundred dollars to Cami. Never.

James smirked. "So come with me this morning. I'll go to my office, and you can go to the range."

Mak paused, realizing something. "I've never seen your office. I suppose I assumed you had one, but Samuel's office seems to be the headquarters."

"Of course I have an office. I do co-run the company. I'll show it to you before you go and practice."

"Okay," Mak said, smiling as she sat up. She was eager to see his office, even though she imagined it was much like his apartment—a blank canvas.

"Oh, and one more thing," Mak said, letting the sheet drop to her waist.

His eyes followed it. "Are you trying to distract me before you ask me this question?" He smirked again. "I like it when you play dirty."

"I need to go shopping before the Tohmatsu wedding. I need a new dress, and we need to get them a present."

"Easy. We'll arrange for someone to come to your apartment with a selection and you can choose what you want," James said.

"Like a personal shopper?"

"Exactly. We arrange it all the time for our clients—men and women. All you need to do is tell them what you like, or look at their online store and pick out a selection, and they'll bring it over so you can try everything on," he said. "Going shopping in an actual store is a risk I'm not prepared to take right now."

Mak thought it through. As long as she could choose the items she wanted to look at—in her price range—then she was more than okay with that. "Deal, Thomas."

"Good. Now, let's have breakfast before I eat you. Again," he said, his eyes glimmering devilishly.

13

JAMES THOMAS

"Where are we at?" James said as he walked into Samuel's office.

Deacon pulled out a chair for him as he simultaneously took a bite of a sandwich.

Samuel spoke first. "I've got the photographs ready to send to Biskup. Kayla and Ben are secured in their apartments. And we're still waiting on contact from Eric in regards to those fingers being picked up and delivered to Mak."

"Tsk." James was disgusted by Eric's *finger* present, but what worried him most was that although Mak's husband continued to have an obsession with her, he was not above playing cruel games.

James' eyes passed over the assorted food on the table. He'd already eaten breakfast with Mak, but he wasn't about to pass up a second serving. He took a ham-and-salad roll.

"Okay," James said. "Let's send those photographs now because I want to secure this alliance with Biskup. I want to be in London on Saturday in case a worship ceremony takes place, and I want his men as backup."

"I would try and talk you out of going—given that arm—but I know it's pointless," Deacon said. "But, I'm going with you. You cannot walk into a situation with Biskup's men without someone to watch your back." Deacon's hard gaze told James there would be no negotiating.

"Okay," James said.

He took a bite of the sandwich—it was delicious—and then washed it down with a large mouthful of water. While he couldn't train properly, he needed to make sure his nutrition was spot-on so that he stayed fit, but he'd more than earned the calories last night.

"Let's do it," James said, looking at Samuel.

Samuel wiggled in his chair, grinning, and the brothers chuckled.

He hit one button with his index finger, and then looked at them. "Done."

There was a lingering pause in the room and James knew they were all thinking the same thing. How long would they have to wait?

The door opened and Cami strolled in. James looked over his shoulder. "How is she doing?" he asked.

Cami sighed, shaking her head. "She hit four targets in succession today. I think I'm going to lose the bet."

Deacon laughed.

The news pleased James, but he wanted her to be better than good. He wanted her to be able to protect herself if he wasn't there to do it for her.

"She's determined when she wants to be, that's for sure," Deacon said.

The sound of a magic wand came from Samuel's computer and all heads turned in his direction.

He projected his laptop screen onto the wall, and as James read the message he felt a surge of relief.

I'm interested. But when we find him, I get him. If you kill him, I'll kill you. And then I'll kill Makaela Ashwood. Understood?

"Let's hope Eric doesn't get killed in a standoff," Deacon muttered under his breath.

James looked to Samuel. "Type this message: *If your men kill him—even on accident—I'll kill all of them. And then kill I'll you. Understood?*"

Another magic wand chimed.

Perfectly. One more thing... I'd like to meet you in person to make this deal. There are some questions that need to be asked, and answered.

James had known that was coming, and they'd already prepared for it. James nodded at Samuel, and James watched the letters appear on the screen as Samuel typed the response. They gave Biskup the location and time for the meet, both of which had been chosen for specific reasons.

I'll see you there.

"Book the jet," James said to Samuel.

James was thinking of Mak, and what she was doing, as he looked into the black darkness that surrounded them. The jet hummed along, a journey so far free of turbulence, although the pilot had already warned it was going to get bumpy as they neared their destination. *It's a good thing Mak's not on this flight,* James thought.

"How did she take it?" Deacon asked, crossing one ankle over his knee.

"Good," James said. "Maya is between trips so she's going to stay with Mak for a few days. That'll hopefully keep her mind off things."

James knew that even though he hadn't told Mak why he was leaving, she'd likely come to the assumption that this trip was to meet with Biskup. And by the way that she'd kissed James goodbye, almost as if not believing he was coming back, he was certain his thoughts were correct. The words had been left unsaid, but the silence told a greater truth.

Deacon nodded. "Good."

"I'm a little concerned about this new case she's working on. She passes one up, only to take on another different but still high-risk case," James said. He'd made it a protocol for Samuel to look into every case she received. Mak had progressed from prosecuting the mob to potentially prosecuting one of Manhattan's prominent gang leaders. James sighed.

"At least we've got time with this case," Deacon said, looking out of the window before returning his gaze to James. "It won't go to trial for a while, if it even does. This is her career, and the more cases she wins, the bigger the target she will put on her head."

Mak was racking up an impressive list of enemies. *Deal with it as it happens*, James was telling himself when his phone began to vibrate.

James answered, putting it on speaker.

"Samuel," he said.

"I've got movement at the location. Biskup's guys are scouting it."

James and Deacon looked to each other.

"How long have they been there?" Deacon asked.

"Ten minutes. There are six men that I can see."

"Have they found the escape route?" James said.

"No, not yet."

"Okay," James said, looking at his wrist. "We'll be landing in a few hours. But let us know if they find it."

"Will do."

James hung up just as the plane lurched in the sky. He grabbed the armrest, but Deacon laughed. His brother loved to fly, and James supposed that came from his time as a ranger. He'd been dropped behind enemy lines time and time again.

"I packed the chutes. We're all good," Deacon said, beaming a grin.

James cleaned and then reloaded his weapon. It was time to meet with Alexandr Biskup. He sat down on the stool, taking a quiet moment to reflect. This was it. If the alliance didn't pan out, if he couldn't get the backup he needed, James didn't know how he could possibly beat Christos and the Russians. An imaginary clock dangled above his head. One might say it was hanging from heaven, but James didn't believe in heaven or hell. Even if he did, though, he doubted he'd be going to heaven. He was okay with the things he'd done, but he doubted a god would be.

It's not over until it's over.

While he was still breathing, he would fight—because he had so much to fight for. Mak's eyes flashed in his mind. Eyes he'd searched a thousand times. Eyes he could barely draw his away from. Eyes he wanted to look into for the next fifty years—if age served him well.

Christos had chosen the wrong man to go after, because James never gave up.

Never.

Not even when things seemed impossible.

"Ready?" Deacon said, and James looked over his shoulder.

"Ready." He tucked his pistol into the holster, checked his earwig, and took a long, calming breath.

There was a chance Biskup could kill them today; he had enough men secured around the location to do that—easily. But James knew how a man like Biskup thought—because James thought the same way. He wanted blood—Eric's blood—and James intended to give it to him. And while they continued to deliver, James believed their lives were safe—from Biskup, at least.

They'd chosen a building in London, one that James knew well because he owned it. Or, rather, Patrick McCormack owned it via one of his many corporations. While James Thomas didn't have a dollar to his name, Patrick had hundreds of millions thanks to several lucrative businesses and Samuel's creative accounting.

"Are we sticking to the same plan?" Deacon asked as he veered the car into the lanes of traffic.

"Same plan," James said. "It doesn't matter that they've cased the building—we knew they would. So long as we have something to offer, I don't think they'll kill us."

Deacon nodded. His arms were stretched, cupping the steering wheel, but they weren't tense, and while he looked thoughtful, James couldn't see any tightness in his brother's jaw. Deacon believed they would be okay, too. For tonight.

Biskup had sent men in hours ago, and they were still there, hidden in the building. James didn't blame him—he wouldn't put himself in that position without supports, either. James hadn't chosen London just because he owned property there, though, he'd chosen it because the worship could potentially take place in just a few days, and if James was going to work with Biskup's men, he needed time to train them. He needed Eric alive, or there was going to be major consequences.

"We'll pull up at the front, use the building entrance and walk straight in. I want him to know we're not playing games. We have one chance to make this work—to gain his trust—so if things get heated, let's keep our weapons down until we're forced otherwise."

Deacon nodded once more, and James knew his brother would keep to the plan. Deacon was able to keep his cool even when a situation exploded like the lid off of a pressure cooker. It was one of the reasons Deacon had been so successful in the army, and it was one of the reasons that James had requested to have him by his side on the final mission he'd done with the agency.

James remembered the events leading up to that night as clear as the day they'd happened. And he supposed that should be no surprise—he'd replayed them a million times over, looking for any signs he'd missed—any covert looks, any shaking hands, any flickering of the eyes. Anything that conveyed that someone knew the slaughter they were being sent into. A CIA team and a ranger team. A total of thirty-two men. And only two walked out alive.

When James had initially been given the mission, and told he could request from a selection of profiles, he'd scrutinized every single team member. He hadn't worked with any of the rangers before, which was never ideal, but James knew how to lead a team. Deacon's profile—or rather, Nathan Wyatt's profile—had been the fifth that he'd looked over, and James had selected him immediately. The decision had been based on so much more than experience—it was based on his loyalty to his team. Deacon had been rewarded multiple times, even in that stage of his career, for things he'd done for his men. He never left an injured man behind, and he'd risked his life for his men multiple times. Both were qualities James admired and had made him the perfect candidate to be by his side. James had known even then, without knowing Deacon, that the Rangers would obey his every command. They respected him, they believed in him, and they would die for him. And they had. It was a story that didn't have a happy ending, except that James knew those soldiers would smile if they knew Deacon had walked out alive. It was just a shame that they would never know.

"Okay, brother. Game time," Deacon said as he pulled to a stop outside the entrance.

They looked to each other, nodded, and then got out of the car. They walked side by side up the stairs that led to the wide, wrought-iron security gate. James pushed it, taking the first step inside.

A step that would alter his future forever.

James heard his heart beating in his ears as he surveyed the environment. Deacon was a step behind him.

"Evening!" James shouted, announcing their arrival despite being one-hundred-percent sure Biskup was already aware. His greeting echoed through the multi-story building. James moved toward the winding staircase, his foot creaking on the first step. When they'd bought this place, James and Deacon had painstakingly set about rigging the staircase. Certain steps creaked, others didn't—if you knew where to step. Tonight, though, James wanted their attendance known. With Deacon by his side, they walked toward the living room where Samuel had advised their guests had made themselves comfortable.

James took a steadying breath, praying he hadn't been wrong on his assumptions about Biskup. They were vulnerable, two men against many, walking into a potential bloodbath.

From the doorway James could see two figures sitting on the couch, their silhouettes illuminated only by the streetlight glowing through the window.

James flicked on the light, taking a step to the side. Deacon came to stand beside him.

Alexandr Biskup sat with a pistol on his lap, one arm stretched out across the back of the couch. Maksym sat beside him.

"And so we meet," Biskup said.

"You can tell your men to relax," James said. "We have no intention of killing any of them. Unless they raise their weapons, of course."

Biskup paused, and then laughed. "Take a seat," he said.

The reality that one of the world's most violent and corrupt men had just told him to take a seat—in his own house—almost made James want to laugh himself. His life was a series of twist and turns, and this would be no different.

"Well, thank you," James said, grinning as he sat down on the couch opposite. He leaned forward and put his weapon on the coffee table. It was a risk—even though he did have other weapons—but it was a peace offering. Biskup looked to Deacon, who did the same. And then Biskup and Maksym followed suit. It was a very nice collection of pistols.

"Do you know what intrigues me most?" Biskup said, playing with his day-old stubble.

"Pray tell," James said.

"You...the two of you, actually." Biskup tilted his head to the side, seeming to study them. "I can't quite work out who you are, or how you seem to have the resources that you do. Nor can I work out how Makaela Ashwood came to secure your services."

"We're two brothers that, via a range of life experiences, came to acquire some very unique skillsets," James said, shrugging his shoulders. "Makaela Ashwood was introduced to us via a contact. We agreed to protect her—though if we'd known the circumstances we were getting ourselves into we might've made a different choice." James raised one eyebrow, and Maksym grinned.

Deacon spoke. "Your timing was well played. Targeting her during a press-covered trial against the mob was a good strategy—even we were initially fooled. But, as all things eventually do, the reality of her situation has become very clear."

Movement behind James distracted him. "If your man takes one more step, it will be the last one he ever takes." James' eyes were hard, nailing the man across from him.

Biskup waved his hand and James heard the footsteps retreat.

"How do you know that she doesn't have the code?" Maksym asked.

"She knew nothing about Eric's business dealings," James said. "She didn't even know about his software company. She thought he was a real-estate developer. Believe us when we say it came as a total shock to her to learn the things she has. We've been around the block a few times, and we have a good idea when people are lying to us. She isn't. She has absolutely no idea what the code is, nor what it is for."

Deacon continued. "But Eric does. And he's alive and well, as you've seen. He played you...which I can't imagine you'll forgive."

James saw it—the betrayal burn like a fire in Biskup's eyes—and James knew they had him. And that they would all walk out alive tonight.

Neither Biskup nor Maksym responded.

James cut to the chase. "I have information that a ceremony is potentially taking place in two evenings time, and if it does, Eric will be attending. I fully intend to be there and if I have your men, what I intend to do will be a lot fucking easier."

Biskup's lips parted and his eyes narrowed. "Hm... How exactly do you know this?"

"I extracted it from two men we captured a few nights ago. They'd been sent to dig up a grave—a grave Eric had been led to believe was his. He believes Makaela thinks he is dead, and he decided to find out who was buried instead of him."

Biskup was silent, but his eyes were busy darting between the two brothers. "Who *did* you bury?" he finally asked, and James thought it was a question asked out of interest more than anything else. Amusement, even, perhaps.

"When the casket was lowered into the ground, it was empty. But when one of our captives advised Eric—via telephone—that there had been a body inside, Eric instructed them to deliver it to an undertaker. We arranged that, sending one of the captives to the undertaker...minus his face."

Biskup's lips turned up. "Nice touch. What happened then?"

"Eric wasn't very impressed."

That brought a smile to Biskup's lips, and James thought anything that pissed off Eric was likely to make the man happy. The expression didn't last long, though.

"I'm concerned about his relationship with the Russians," Biskup said. "How far does it extend?"

"Eric is in bed with the Russians. Pavel Sokolov, to be exact."

"And now I see your problem. Sokolov is a very well-resourced man."

"As I said, had we known the full extent of Makaela's situation, we might've walked away. But, here we are. We can beat Eric, even if he's playing with the Russians, but only if we have backup."

Biskup tapped his fingers on his knee. "And if I say no?"

If you say no, then I'm fucked, James thought. "Then, you can continue your efforts to get to Makaela, which are pointless in every way you look at it. You won't get past us, and even if you did, she doesn't have the code. Alternatively, you can go up against Eric and Sokolov on your own, without our intelligence resources. Again, not good odds for you.

"Look," James said, steepling his fingers, "I get that you're not keen to start a war with the Russians. That said, they're siding with someone who fucked you. Maybe they don't realize what he's done, or maybe they do. Either way, it doesn't look good." James had shot an arrow into the man's pride.

"Tell me," Biskup said, "why is Eric connected with the Russians? What do they have to gain?"

Biskup had asked the one question James didn't want him to.

"We don't know as yet," James said, lying through his teeth. "But we will find out—of that I'm certain."

James held Biskup's hard stare, his resolve unwavering. Nine painstaking seconds passed—James silently counted them—until Biskup's expression softened.

"We both have a lot to gain from this relationship...and we both have a lot to lose if it goes sour," Biskup said.

James nodded. "I'm fully aware of that. Our playbook of rules is a very thin one, but when we give our word, it's set in stone. We mean you no harm, and have no intention of hurting you or your loved ones, nor do we have any interest in your business dealings. We come with one intention only: of gaining your support to capture Eric. Once that's done, we walk away...an amicable divorce, as such," James said, throwing in a light joke that earned him a small smile from Maksym.

"Okay," Biskup finally said, leaning forward. "We have a deal. You'll have the support of my men, but there's one condition...you have six weeks to find Eric and deliver him to me."

"Six weeks?" James said, his stomach curdling. If the worship ceremony didn't take place in the next few weeks, they had no idea where to find him. And even though the address of the building from Liev was a powerful lead, it wasn't enough. James needed six months, not six weeks.

Deacon leaned forward, mirroring Biskup's stance. "How long did you hunt Eric for before concluding that he was dead?"

"The deal is six weeks," Biskup repeated. "As they say, there's nothing quite like a deadline to motivate people." The sly grin that formed on his lips made James want to pick up his pistol and blow Biskup's brains out. If they failed to meet the deadline, Eric and the Russians might not be their biggest worry.

"And if that deadline isn't reached, what then?" James said, needing to clarify the terms of the contract. And this was a contract—a contract in the underworld. This was exactly how they were formed, and they were binding. Always.

"Then it won't be a very amicable divorce." The words came from Maksym, and James looked to him. If they failed, this was the man they would face.

As tempting as it was to try and negotiate, James knew it was pointless. Regardless, six weeks with Biskup's men were better odds than six weeks on his own. He could be dead by then anyway.

He turned to Deacon and, without speaking a word, he knew his brother didn't like the deal, but he also agreed with James.

James turned back to Biskup. "Six weeks, provided your men do exactly as we say. If they break the rules, if they disobey, we will kill them and this deal will be terminated, or renegotiated. Is that clear?"

Biskup held out his hand. "Crystal."

James shook it, and made a deal with the devil. *God help us all,* James thought.

Biskup shook Deacon's hand and then relaxed back into the couch. Maksym didn't move.

A silly, almost boy-like grin shone on Biskup's face. "You know what, I think this is going to be a lot of fun," he said with a slight chuckle.

"I'm glad you think that..." James said. "I want your men tonight. I want to start training them in preparation for the ceremony. And I want your best, including you." He nodded toward Maksym.

He wanted the man Biskup's men feared, the one who was in charge. The one James knew without a shred of doubt was an animal capable of inflicting horrors that made people scream in the night.

A man not unlike Liam Smith.

14

JAMES THOMAS

Four hours. That's all they had to prepare until Biskup's men arrived. Samuel had secured a warehouse in a rural village south of London. It would give them enough privacy, and space, to train.

James' eyes roamed over the stacked brick walls where sections had been previously painted but had now begun to peel away. Black boxes sat in the middle—boxes loaded with weaponry and ammunition.

"Remind you of anything?" Deacon asked as he came to stand beside James.

"Yes...unfortunately," James said. They'd trained countless men for Thomas Security over the past few years, but they were men they'd hired. Men they'd done background checks on. And the training had been done in a secure facility.

The last time James had been in a situation like this was the last one he'd done with the CIA. The one he'd led Deacon and his men into. The one that had been a setup to eliminate them all. A bloodbath.

Deacon crossed his arms over his chest as he looked at the black boxes. "I think we over-packed," he said, looking to James.

"You think?" James said with a chuckle. "Come on, let's get this equipment sorted before our guests arrive with more boxes."

Biskup was sending thirty men for this initial mission. It was a good number—enough to give serious ammunition power, but a small enough group to control.

James walked toward the boxes but halted when his phone rang. *Incoming call: Mak.*

"Hey," James said as he swiveled on his feet, walking toward a corner of the warehouse.

"Hi. Is this a bad time?"

"Good timing, actually. We've just checked into our accommodation." He looked over the warehouse again. He'd been in worse digs. "Are you okay?" James asked.

"Yeah, I'm fine. Maya left this morning—she told me about her travel companions," she said.

"I know Maya wasn't thrilled about having a security team accompany her, but it's a risk I'm not willing to take right now," James said. Given the amount of travel Maya did for her job—and the places she went to—she was a sitting duck for anyone wanting to use her to get to Mak. James had enough problems and didn't need to add that to his list.

"How serious is the threat to her?" Mak asked.

"There is no threat to her, as such—it's a preventative measure," James said.

"Okay..." Mak said. "How is your arm?"

"It's good." His arm was feeling better, although it was a long way from healed.

"So, have you met with Biskup yet?" Mak asked.

James was stalled by her question, but he shouldn't have been. He'd known she'd come to that conclusion.

"Yes," James said. "He's agreed to work with us, which is a very good thing."

"Is it?" Mak asked.

"It is," James said, leaning back against the wall.

"But how can you trust him?"

James heard the worry in her voice, and although he didn't want her to feel that way, it was still selfishly nice to hear it.

"Because it's a mutually beneficial relationship," James said. "When two parties have a common goal, there's really no reason to defy each other."

"Does he need a reason? He doesn't sound like a man of upstanding character," Mak said, and James smiled at her choice of words.

"No, but he's desperate to find Eric, not only for the code, but also to teach him and his friends a lesson. For men like Biskup, Mak, that's more powerful than anything you can imagine. He'll play the game for as long as it serves him."

Mak sighed. "I try and block it out, to not think about you and what you're doing, but I can't."

"I'm coming home to you, Mak," James said.

"But you can't promise that... And this is my fault. You're in this situation because of me—well, Eric. I—"

James cut her off. "Don't do that," he said. "You're forgetting who we are and what we do. We've been in situations like this before—worse situations, actually—and we've risked our lives time and time again for our clients. It's our job, and the choice is ours. The risks we take are always calculated, Mak. We stack the odds in our favor."

James wanted to tell her the truth, to let her know that the stars of the universe had so aligned that this situation wasn't her fault. James would've met her husband at some point, even if he'd never met her. His path with Eric had been fated the moment James' father had betrayed the elders. Maybe even before then. Maybe this had been his destiny from the moment he was conceived.

"I just want you to come home...alive," she said.

He heard the tightness in her voice, and he wished he was there. He wished he could hold her and promise her everything was going to be okay. But the reality was that he couldn't. And given his past, he knew that was a promise he was never going to be able to make.

"Don't worry about me, Mak. I'm a survivor, I always have been, always will be," James said. His eyes flickered to his brother, who was setting up the equipment. James needed to go and help him, but he didn't want to say goodbye.

As if she could read his mind, Mak said, "I should let you go. Take care, James. I love you."

James closed his eyes and took a deep breath. Hearing that would never get old. "I love you, too. Don't worry about me, Mak. I'm going to be okay." He couldn't promise her, but his chances had greatly improved in the last five hours.

He hung up, slipped his phone into his pocket and walked toward Deacon. It was time to focus. For the next few days he had to be Liam Smith—a man much more dangerous than James Thomas.

The roller door shrieked as it opened and headlights beamed in from the dark night. James motioned the vehicles forward with his hand. Six hummers entered in an organized procession, and James was relieved that this time they weren't hunting them—they were collaborating with them.

Biskup's main man stepped out first, striding toward the brothers. This time he did extend his hand. "Maksym."

James shook it. "James. Are your men ready?"

Maksym's eyes gleamed. "They're busting at the seams. I've never seen a more excited entourage."

James looked to Deacon, who smiled back. That was exactly what they wanted. Men eager for blood, men who were ready to get their hands dirty.

"Good to hear," James said, letting his own excitement show. "Now, time is crucial so I don't want to waste a minute. Let's get your boys unpacked, blanks loaded, and then grouped there," James said, pointing to the two whiteboards.

Samuel had secured a floor map of the building Liev had disclosed. It was an old blueprint, and they couldn't be sure renovations hadn't been undertaken in recent years, but it was a start. James had the floor plans tacked to one whiteboard, and two markers ready.

They were going to outline the strategy and practice the codes until Biskup's men were dead on their feet. And then they would repeat it relentlessly over the next few days. There was no room for error—not when they had a deadline of six weeks.

James snapped the cap onto the whiteboard marker and looked over his companions. Faces marred with various degrees of scarring and stubble stared back at him.

"Any questions?" James asked.

"Yeah," one man called out. "When are we going to practice?"

James grinned. "In a minute. Any other questions?"

The men shook their head. In theory, on a diagram drawn on a whiteboard, it looked simple. Easy even. Once they started practicing the drills, though, James knew questions would come up.

"One last thing," James said. "You're all experienced enough to know that this plan may change at any point. Communication is everything on a mission, and you are to obey all orders. Those orders, however, are only to come from one of us," James said, motioning his hand between him and Deacon. "If you hear a command from anyone else, you are to disobey it—regardless of who it comes from," James said, his eyes making his stance very clear.

Maksym stood, and James resisted the urge to look to his brother.

What are you doing, Maksym?

The man paused for a moment, and then crossed his arms over his chest. He looked to his men. "That is also an order from me. These two," he nodded toward the brothers, "are calling the shots. I will be following them, just like you will be. If you disobey a single command, I'll kill you myself." His thick accent added a touch of violence to his threat, and James liked it. Maksym sat down as calmly as he'd stood.

This is going to be very interesting, James thought.

"Get your weapons, it's time to train," Deacon said.

~

The first few drills were rough but the men improved fast. James stood back, assessing each one. Some were lighter on their feet, some were a better shot. One-by-one he assigned them roles as he identified their talents, inserting them into the strategy until each man had his position. It was a lengthy process and when James looked at his watch, he called time and ordered the men to eat and then catch a few hours of sleep.

The black sheeting they'd placed over the cracked warehouse windows gave them additional privacy during the night, but it would also shield the sunlight so the men could now sleep. Whether it was day or night would make no difference to these men. They had three objectives: and those were to train, eat, and sleep.

"You're very hard to read. Both of you are," Maksym said from behind James and Deacon.

James turned to face him. "We don't want to be read."

Maksym laughed. "No, given your evident operative skills, I'm sure you don't."

James didn't respond. Neither did Deacon.

"What are your first impressions?" Maksym asked, his eyes cast over the group.

"Some are much better than others, but that's always the case. They'll perform, though...and that's the most important thing," James said, looking at the men now rolling out bedding and joking amongst themselves. Biskup's men had the camaraderie of an army.

"They'll perform," Maksym confirmed, and James didn't hear a sliver of doubt in his voice. "What do you believe is going to happen at this ceremony?"

"Various rituals, injecting of alchemized blood, and a surplus of naked women. Beyond that, I honestly don't know," James said, noting his expression.

"Fuck, maybe we should just join in," Maksym said with a thunderous laugh.

"Just make sure they can concentrate. They need to think with their heads, not their dicks," Deacon said, raising one eyebrow.

Maksym winked. "They'll be fine. They've seen plenty of pussy," he said over his shoulder as he moved toward a spread of food assembled on a folding table.

"Someone help us," Deacon muttered under his breath.

James shook his head. "Let's eat and then I'll take the first shift. We've got to keep one eye on these boys," James said.

He wasn't letting his brother close his eyes without someone to watch his back. Not a fucking chance.

The men were silent as the vans drove through the streets. Silent and focused. Practice was over—it was game time.

The men had been pushed to their limits over the past few days, but James had given them a break for the last twelve hours. They had needed to sleep and eat, because the men needed to be at their best.

Maksym sat beside James now and, provided all went to plan, they'd stay by each other's side for the entire mission. Deacon would lead the team entering through the rear. Ideally, James would've had Deacon beside him, rather than Maksym, but James didn't know him well enough yet. He didn't trust the man not to veer off course, but he did trust him to perform. James knew his first assumptions had been correct: Maksym trained Biskup's men to be the brutal, hostile faces the underground world had come to fear. From what James had been able to gather over the past forty-eight hours, Biskup barely got his hands dirty anymore. Not unless he wanted to—if it was just for fun. *And just to keep his men on his toes,* James thought.

James noted the time on his watch, calculating how long until they would arrive at the ceremony's location. He wondered what they would find there. For all James knew, Liev's intel could've been incorrect. Or it wasn't a night of worship. There could be nothing at their location.

Six weeks.

James had six weeks to get Eric. If he didn't, James knew the renegotiations would be ugly. And bloody.

James saw Maksym look at his watch, and he guessed he too was calculating the time to their arrival, and mentally preparing himself for the next few hours.

Nothing else mattered, nothing except getting Eric. The thought that Mak's saga could end tonight was almost too good to be true, and James wondered if it was.

Don't think about, he told himself. *Focus on the mission. One thing at a time.*

James looked over the men in their van, huddled down in black protective gear. They were the team that was going to scale the building and come in from the top floor windows. He scanned for men that were fidgeting, or compulsively checking their weapons. He gave those men a reassuring look. He had to calm their nerves as best as he could, it was part of his job as their leader.

The car came to a stop and James angled his body so that he could see through the front windscreen. They had arrived. They were two blocks from the building, and they would weave through the shadows until they reached the adjoining building.

A rush of adrenaline kicked his body into gear and he stood up, motioning for the man closest to the door to open it.

"Remember," James said, altering the tone of his voice to convey his message, "do not deviate from the plan unless either Deacon or I issue the command. If you do, you're putting the lives of every single one of your comrades at risk."

They nodded in unison.

James grinned in spite of himself—no matter what was on the line, he lived for nights like this. "Let's go."

James moved toward the door, stepping out first with Maksym right behind him. His body pulsed with the beat of his heart as he moved toward the closest building, pressing his shoulders against it. He heard the door close, and knew all of his men were out. He took light steps, keeping his body agile, ready to react.

James held his pistol in his left hand, eternally grateful he'd trained himself so long ago to shoot with both hands. If he hadn't, he wouldn't be on this mission tonight. Even during all of their training drills, no one had questioned his left-hand ability. He'd hidden his injury well, although he didn't think it had escaped Maksym. James doubted much escaped him.

"Hold," James whispered, the hairs on his skin standing up. He pressed his back against the wall. He could hear voices in the passageway near them, but he couldn't hear what they were saying. "Stay in position," James said, giving the command via their earwigs, but he motioned for Maksym to follow him. James crept up to the corner, his lips pressed together as the voices became more audible. He still couldn't understand what they were saying, but James soon realized it was because their words were slurred.

"Drunks," James said, and Maksym nodded. James debated their options. They could move past the two men, hoping they wouldn't be seen. But the men could see them, and later alert someone to their arrival.

"We need to silence them. Put them out, don't kill them," James instructed.

Sorry, guys, James thought as he turned the corner, ducking as he paced toward the two men. He heard Maksym's footsteps behind him. James moved faster once they neared the men and could no longer hide their presence.

The reactions of the two men were slow—not surprising given their slurred speech. James lunged to the left, Maksym to the right, and they wrapped their arms around the men's necks. James ignored the shot of pain in his injured arm as the man fought back—luckily it wasn't much of a fight. As soon as the man slipped into unconsciousness, James let his limp body drop to the floor. He pulled out multiple bills from the stash in his pocket—a stash he always carried on a mission in the event things didn't go to plan and they couldn't get back to a safe house—and tucked it into the man's pocket. Maksym raised an eyebrow, but said nothing as they ran back to the building and James motioned for their men to continue.

"In position," Deacon's voice came through the earwig.

"Copy. Hold." James said, looking up at the buildings that loomed around them. The air was still, frozen in the tension of the night. If James hadn't learned to control his mind all those years ago, his body would probably be in a similar state.

One building to go, James thought as he remained alert, refusing to rush to their location. People made mistakes when they rushed forward without a clear head, and James would not allow himself to do that. Not tonight. Not ever.

James cast his eyes forward, assessing the building the worship was to take place in. From the street, it looked like no one was home. No lights. No movement. James wondered if that was because it was boarded up, or if it was because the ceremony was to take place in an underground level. Given the church he'd searched, and the warehouse in London, James knew Saratani liked underground locations. The floor plan Samuel obtained didn't show a basement, but that didn't mean there wasn't one.

James paused at the fire escape, looking over his shoulder, doing a quick count of the men. They hadn't lost anyone—yet.

"Let's go," James said as he began to take the steps two at a time. His ears strained to hear everything; to hear the footsteps of his men behind him, to hear Maksym's breathing holding calm and steady, to hear a rattle or movement indicating they weren't alone. His eyes darted constantly, like balls in a pinball machine. His body tingled with energy, with excitement, with adrenaline.

They reached the rooftop and James' breathing was heavier than it should've been. His fitness had dropped dramatically in the past few weeks and as soon as he could, he had to make rectifying that a priority. Unfortunately, sex alone wasn't going to be enough. He shook his head, shaking out all thoughts of sex—that was a dangerous tangent for his mind to go off on.

He kneeled down, keeping his body shielded by the brick wall that encased the rooftop, as they waited for the rest of the group to arrive and get their breath back. James gave them a few moments before they crawled toward the edge of the building. He surveyed it carefully, but he couldn't hear any movement, and his night-vision goggles didn't reveal anyone. James didn't know if that meant no one was in the building tonight, or if Saratani were secure enough inside that they didn't need exterior security. Both were unfavorable.

It was a small jump to the next building, and James stood, taking one step back and then a few quick steps as he propelled his body across the narrow passageway. He landed lightly on his feet. He kneeled down again, waiting for his men. They looked like ninjas flying through the night, one after the other.

When they were assembled, James ran toward the door that led to the stairwell into the building. It was an electronic lock, much like the one he'd seen at the abandoned church—one that was too new and too shiny for its surroundings. *Even if they're not here tonight,* James thought, *this is definitely a Saratani building.*

He pulled out a device from his pocket, one Samuel had given him. He used it to work the lock. It took longer than he'd have liked, but eventually the door clicked open.

His blood whooshed through his ears as he took the first step inside.

The stairwell was as dark as a cave and without his night-vision goggles James wouldn't have been able to see his own hands.

"In position. Move in, Deacon," James commanded as he began his descent.

"Copy."

James' eyes looked up, searching for security cameras—he couldn't see any.

"First check," James said, coming to a stop at the platform.

He pushed on the door handle but it didn't budge. James pulled out a scalpel and jimmied it until he felt it move. Using his fingertips, he opened the door wide enough for one eye to peer through. It seemed as lifeless as the rest of the building. He widened the gap, giving him a full view of the room. He moved forward, his weapon raised as he fought to keep his breath steady. His men split up, as they'd practiced in their drills, and scouted the entire floor. James listened for a confirmation—of anything—but his earwig was silent.

When his men regrouped, he led them back to the stairwell. The floor was a bust, but they still had three floors to go.

James descended the stairs, faster this time, but still not rushing. His body and mind had found their groove—they were in rhythm, focused, alert.

Liam Smith had entered the building.

They repeated the drill at the next floor down, once more coming up empty-handed. James refused to let it worry him for the very fact that it could be a good thing. He wanted Saratani, and whoever else was here, to be assembled in one location. An image of the cross monument he'd seen in the dilapidated church flashed in his mind, and he imagined a large group of people assembled around it. There was never a better scenario to set upon a big group.

"Holy fuck," one of Deacon's men said. *"You've gotta see this."*

"Keep to the plan," Deacon reprimanded.

James wanted to sprint down the stairs to see what Deacon's team was seeing, but they hadn't finished casing the building. He couldn't leave the upper levels unsecured. He had to know all risks had been eliminated before he met Deacon on the ground level.

"Stay in the shadows," James warned as they stopped at the next floor. James paused at the landing, knowing that all of his men had heard Deacon's man, and were likely to be experiencing the same temptation James was. James just didn't trust them to be as disciplined.

"Focus," James instructed. "Scout every corner of this floor and do not come back until it's done."

"Copy," the group said in unison.

James jimmied the lock, assuming he'd have to do this at every level. Carefully, he opened the door and moved his team in. James searched the first room, which was empty save for one plastic tub. James opened the lid, but it held nothing. James wondered what it had stored earlier, but didn't have time to ponder on it.

He stood up, meeting Maksym by the stairwell door. The team assembled together, moving into the stairwell once more.

One more floor.

They descended the stairs, stopping on the platform. James heard, or rather felt, the vibrations of the music before he'd even opened the door. James tentatively pushed on the door handle—it was unlocked. *Strange,* James thought. With even more caution, he opened the door. The smell of dinner greeted him. Someone had eaten here recently, and James' gut told him they'd only just missed each other.

James made a silent hand gesture, signaling the men in.

Unlike the other levels, which were vacant, this one was filled with navy-blue velvet couches, woven floor rugs and tall lamps which cast a soft, yellow glow across the room. The music seemed to echo, bouncing off the walls in the vast space. There were fewer partitions on this level, and fewer rooms to search, but James felt the tension hanging from his skin. He felt uneasy, but he couldn't pinpoint why. He took one small step forward. And then another. His finger was steady on the trigger of his pistol as he moved into the center of the room. James motioned the men in when he didn't see a flicker of movement.

"This is weird," Maksym said under his breath.

"Pre-ritual room?" James whispered, voicing aloud his thoughts.

"It looks like someone should be here. Or they're coming back," Maksym said.

James moved toward a table, spotting empty takeout containers. He wrapped his hand around one—it was still warm.

"Proceed with caution," James instructed.

Maksym picked up a book on the table, flipping the pages. He looked to James, holding it up. It was bound in red leather and had a gold-embossed circle with an *X* crossing through it. It looked like a bible of some sort, but if it was, James had a feeling it was a different version of the best-selling book of all time.

Maksym passed him the book and James slipped it into his pocket and went to check the windows.

James' eyes surveyed their surroundings constantly, silently counting the seconds that passed until all of his men returned.

They all shook their heads.

James turned to move toward the stairwell but he stopped, looking over his shoulder. It was a move born out of instinct. He didn't know why he did it, and he thought to go back and check the floor once more, but he was conscious of the time. Gauging by Deacon's team's comments, James thought the ritual was already underway—and who knew how long it would go for.

He moved back into the stairwell and descended the last flight of stairs.

"Deacon. Confirm location," James said.

"Alcoves of the main room."

"Hold position," James said, and then turned to his men. "Two at a time, on my command."

James opened the door, immediately noting the music. It was the same music that had been playing upstairs. James stepped into the room, pressing his back up against the wall. Maksym was only a second behind him. They looked to each other, nodded, and then followed the sound of the music, keeping the floor plan in mind. Light streamed in from the hallway to their left and James turned, taking a cautious step toward it. He took a steadying breath with each footstep, his eyes pinned to the light.

Movement at the end caught James', attention and he pressed up against the wall, mentally reminding himself to breathe. A silhouette passed by, and James recognized the stance—security.

The man stopped, seeming to lean up against the wall, his shoulder exposed in the hallway. James looked at Maksym and gave him a hand gesture: *Neutralize him.* Maksym passed James his weapon as he lunged toward the man, wrapping one hand over his mouth and twisting his neck with the other before he dragged him back into the shadows of the hallway. James passed Maksym's weapon back to him and they inched forward, taking positions on either side of the hallway. James peered around the corner.

His breathing halted as his eyes rapidly surveyed the building. This was not on the floor plan. Once James was sure their path was safe, he motioned Maksym forward. They dropped to the floor, crawling toward the glowing source of light in the center of the room.

The floor had been cut out, revealing the basement below. From their position, it gave them a bird's-eye view of the horror scene below.

James exhaled a shaky breath as he looked at the mass of people below—three hundred, maybe more—circled around a giant cross. Hypnotic music boomed from the sound system but it wasn't the naked women holding silver trays of glasses, each filled with red liquid, that made James' heart stop. It was the supine naked bodies tied to the marble crosses. There were six of them—three males and three females. And standing in front of each one was a man. A man holding a knife. A man carving into the flesh of their abdomens while they whimpered in pain.

"This is my kind of party," Maksym whispered.

James ignored the comment and forced himself to draw his eyes away. He didn't know if they were volunteers, or if they were being subjected to this by way of punishment, but right now he couldn't afford to care. He was there for one man. And one man only.

His heart found its beat again, sending a rush of adrenaline through his body. James' eyes bounced from face to face, searching for a familiar pair of eyes. With each second that passed, the lump in his throat grew. James worked from the inside of the circle out, clockwise.

James closed his eyes, pressing his lips together as an invisible rope wrapped around his chest, tightening.

Eric's not here.

Where is he?

15

ERIC

The tip of the needle pressed into his skin and a sharp sting followed before it disappeared under the flesh, piercing through his vein. Eric moaned, feeling a rush of power as she pushed the plunger in, injecting the blood. Petra had good, steady hands...hands that were skilled in more ways than one. Eric closed his eyes, letting his head rest against the oversized couch cushion. The world came alive. He felt his blood pulsating through his veins, tingling. His body was still, but he felt like he was dancing to the music.

Petra pulled out the needle and then climbed onto his lap. "Are you okay?"

He opened his eyes, smirking. She was a devil of thing. He wrapped one arm around her waist and his mouth came crashing down on hers. "I think you know exactly how I am. You know how this makes me..." He bit her lip and she squealed. A squeal he quickly silenced.

"Now?" she asked, looking around the room, her eyes passing over their companions.

"Later," Eric said. Later, he would have her every way he wanted. And there were many.

Eric, mindful of the time, looked around the room, catching the eye of one of his bodyguards. Frankie nodded.

"Meet me here after the worship," Eric said, giving her a nudge to stand.

She drew a line down the center of his chest with her finger. "I'll be waiting." She bit her lip before turning her back to him. Eric watched her ass sway as she walked out.

"They're waiting for you," Frankie said.

"I'm ready," Eric replied. Worship had made for some of his favorite nights, and over the years he'd made them more frequent. They were a heady rush of power, and he always wanted more. He always had.

Eric followed Frankie toward the door, watching as he swung the large painting to the side, revealing the door. Eric stepped through the cutout in the wall, and then straightened the frame, making sure it hung even before he left. He hated when things weren't properly aligned.

Eric's body hummed to the music, and now that he was moving and increasing the oxygen to his blood, the magic of the alchemy kicked in. He felt weightless. He felt like a God.

Eric's eyes looked over the table, and then to Frankie. "Where is it?"

Frankie frowned. "Where is what?"

"My Korsa. I left it right here next to the containers," Eric said, not hiding his agitation.

"The red, leather-bound one, right?"

"Yes!"

"I don't know. Maybe one of the boys took it down for you," Frankie said, seeming to grasp for some logical excuse. "Here is mine, use this." He pulled out a green Korsa.

Eric snatched it from his hands. "I always use the same one for worship. Find out who took it—and kill them."

"Yes, Christos," Frankie said. "I'll make sure it's done."

"Where is my wife?" Eric said, slipping the Korsa into his back pocket. He followed Frankie toward the door, his steps now fueled with anger.

Who dared to take my Korsa?

"She's waiting for you in the axial chapel."

"Good," Eric said, almost running into Frankie as he came to a sudden stop. He paused.

"What?" Eric said.

"The door... It's unlocked..."

Eric swore. "Fucking hell! Find out who left it unlocked, and bring them to me." Eric clenched his teeth together. This night was not off to a good start. Something didn't feel right, but Eric put it down to the Korsa. He was superstitious even at the best of times, he knew.

Eric took a calming breath, calling on the powers of the blood—the powers of the Gods. "We need to go," Eric said, more calmly now.

They took the elevator down to the basement and walked through the hallways to the chapel. Eric's eyes landed on his beautiful wife as he opened the door. Unlike the other women at the ceremony, she was dressed, but she was far more seductive. She wore a white—almost sheer—draped gown that showed her cleavage beautifully. The fabric collected at her hip, held in place by an emerald-diamond brooch. The fabric then fell away, revealing her lean, toned leg that shimmered from whatever lotion she'd used. It was hard to draw his eyes away from her legs, but the dazzling, jeweled headpiece with three large teardrop diamonds made her look truly exotic.

"You look like a goddess," Eric said.

Marianne gave him a beautiful, beaming smile that reminded him of how she'd looked at him when they'd first met. Over the last few years, he'd rarely seen that smile. But in recent weeks, he'd seen it time and time again. She'd said that she had thought they were going to die in the house in Amman, and that she was grateful for another chance to fall in love all over again. At first he hadn't believed her, his thoughts bordering on suspicious, but with each day that had passed since, she'd been the wife he'd always wanted. Sweet, caring, attentive. Even when he'd been traveling, she'd made sure he'd known she was thinking about him. He supposed he had one thing to thank Liam Smith for.

Eric let Frankie attach his microphone, test it, and then Eric held out his arm and Marianne linked hers through.

The music changed as they stood waiting at the entrance to the chancel. Eric closed his eyes, taking a moment to savor the feeling that overwhelmed him. The chanting began, growing louder and louder. Chanting for him—their leader. Eric called upon the power of the Gods to guide him through the worship and then he opened his eyes, nodding to Frankie.

Frankie reached up, pressing a button, and the velvet drapes parted, revealing the couple. The chanting intensified as the men and women kneeled on the ground as they made their entrance. Eric looked over the gallery; he had never seen it so full. The sound of their voices were unified to create a gospel that one day the world would hear. Never had a leader of Saratani been so successful, and so admired.

This is just the beginning, Eric thought.

He looked to his wife, who beamed a smile down on the crowd, waving to them. She was perfect for the role she had to play. But his life was not yet complete—he still needed the missing part.

He still needed his first wife.

Eric took the first step, leading Marianne toward the crowd, which opened up to welcome them. Hands reached for him, desperate to touch the leader that would give them everything they desired.

"Cerah zalû, cerah zalû," the crowd began to chant. Even though the worship was conducted in English, they still used the old language for the chanting. It was one of the changes Eric had made. The old language gave the words power. It created unity. *Praise the Gods,* they chanted.

When the hands reaching for him became more needy, clinging to him, Frankie stepped in, but Eric told him to move back. This was his time with the people, and Eric loved it. They worshipped him, they would die for him. They were his people. They had started as a group, but now they were something much bigger. They had a sense of purpose in life, and they knew secrets that society had failed to discover. They could prolong life, they could live a life of abundance and pleasure that was beyond comprehension. The groups were a progression to the Gods, and Eric was so close to the next level. So close to the elders. Just one man stood in his way.

When a young woman clutched at his leg, wrapping her arms around it, Eric came to a stop. Her breasts parted around the fabric of his pants, and she sang, "Cerah zalû, cerah zalû," over and over again. Eric kneeled down, keeping a hold of his wife's hand.

"Cerah zalû," Eric said, kissing the woman's forehead and gently removing her from his limb.

"I love you," she whispered and Eric smiled. They all loved him.

"Practice," Eric told her. "Learn the scriptures. Devote yourself to the Gods. If you do, you can have anything you want in life."

She nodded, a tear dripping from the corner of her eye. He swept a lock of hair off of her wet chin, nodding as he stood. He began to walk again, moving toward the front of the galley where tonight's sacrifices were being prepared.

He stopped at the first of eleven steps that lead up to the stage, and then turned to his wife. He cupped her cheek, and then kissed her, sending the crowd into a roaring cheer. Eric pulled back, winking at her as they took the first steps up to the platform. In the few seconds that had passed, Frankie had positioned two intricate silver chairs on the platform. Thrones.

Eric's chest expanded, doubling in size as he breathed in the energy of the crowd. *I was made for this,* Eric thought. He led Marianne to her chair and she sat down, crossing one leg over the other. The fabric of her gown fell away, further exposing her leg. Eric knew every man in the room wanted her, but she was his. His, and only his. She was allowed to "play" with women, but only when he permitted. And only when he was watching.

He drew the Korsa from his pocket, resting it on his lap as he sat down on the throne next to his wife. But as he looked down, bile bubbled in his stomach.

It's wrong. The Korsa is wrong. It should be red. It is always red.

Eric pushed the thoughts aside. He didn't even need the Korsa anymore; it was really just for show. He knew the verses by heart, he could recite paragraphs without hesitation. *I don't need it, but I want it,* Eric thought. And he always got what he wanted. *I'll find that Korsa, and I'll rip the intestines out of the person who took it.*

"To honor the Gods!" Eric shouted, beginning the service. "We must show them our faith. We must do everything that they ask of us. And we give thanks to those who so willingly give themselves for the greater good of us all."

Eric's eyes went from sacrifice to sacrifice. Their white, naked bodies were already painted with ribbons of red and their eyes turned to him now.

"Let us begin with the devotion," Eric said, opening the Korsa on his lap. He flipped to the applicable page, but he didn't look at the words as he began to chant. "Merăhpărare suda leii." *Redemption of our eternal souls.*

The group chimed in, joining him. As Eric continued, the chorus charged his soul, and he knew the Gods were looking down upon him.

As he said the last words, "Namem cei bănicevu"—*We are the blessed ones*—he closed the Korsa and handed it to his wife as he stood. He walked down to the lower platform, stopping in front of the first sacrifice.

"Are you ready to be received?" Eric asked her.

She nodded. It was a common response—fear was a great silencer.

Eric took the knife that had been given to her, the knife that had already prepared her for the sacrifice. The number six—the number of Gods they worshipped—had been carved into her abdomen. And now Eric would make the next cut. It was an honor to be cut by the leader, for he had the power of the Gods.

As he raised the knife, she squeezed her eyes shut.

"Look at me," Eric commanded.

Her eyes sprung open, wide with fear.

He brought it to the soft skin of her neck, making sure it didn't cross paths with her jugular. He didn't want to kill her, not yet, not before the worship was concluded.

With practiced precision, he pressed the blade of the knife into her flesh and the crowd roared with cheer. She whimpered, but her lips remained sealed. He sliced over her collarbone, stopping at the midpoint of her breastbone. He twisted the knife, and this time she let out a cry.

"You look so beautiful," Eric told her. "Where are you from?"

She hesitated, and he nodded, encouraging her to speak.

"Manchester," she said, and Eric smiled.

"For every life to follow, you will blessed. You are a gift to the Gods," Eric said. With one swift move, he sliced up to the other side of her neck, creating a bloody V.

Her body began to tremble and he put a hand flat on her chest, pressing it against the traumatized skin. "Cerah zalû," Eric whispered in her ear, her breath hot on his neck.

Eric closed his eyes, taking in the power that now leaked from her body, and from her soul.

"Please, don't do this," she whispered.

Eric opened his eyes. "You volunteered for this. You are a sacrifice," he said.

"No, no I didn't," she said in a rushed, hushed voice. "Please, please don't hurt me anymore."

Eric grinned. "You did volunteer, and if a word otherwise slips from your lips, I will make your sacrifice so unbearable that you will regret ever saying that aloud again. No one is coming to save you, princess. I control your fate, and I don't want to hear another word like that," Eric growled, and then took a deep breath. "Understood?" he asked, this time his voice more gentle, more charming.

"Yes," she whimpered, closing her eyes.

"Good," he said, running the blade of his knife up to her chin. "You truly are beautiful." He flicked the blade off of her skin, noting her trembling body, and returned to the stage.

The crowd began to sway and chant and Eric stood before them, his hands held up in prayer. *My people,* he thought.

Eric's eyes flickered to Frankie, in order to give their unspoken signal that the sacrifice might be trouble—but he saw something else instead. Confusion. Or was it fear? Frankie's eyes were diverted, roaming the floor above them. What was he looking for?

Eric, not wanting to distract from the ceremony, began to recite the next verse, but the bile that had been bubbling in his stomach returned, inching toward his chest.

Even with a distracted mind, he got through the entire passage without using the Korsa, but when he looked to Frankie again, his lips were moving.

He's talking to someone, Eric thought. Who? What was happening? Was one of their worshippers drunk and out of control? It wouldn't have been the first time such a thing had happened.

Eric followed Frankie's eyes again and he soon realized it wasn't what he could see that was worrying Frankie—it was what he *couldn't.* Where was security? They should've been in every alcove above, but Eric couldn't see a single man up there.

The chanting continued as the crowd sung their praises, and Eric let it go on longer than normal while he tried to get a grasp on the situation. Eric turned his attention to security on the basement floor, but with the large crowd in attendance, it was difficult to see them. He looked to Frankie, wanting to get his attention, but the moment Eric's eyes landed on him blood sprayed from Frankie's forehead.

The crowd stilled, and then screamed. They began to scatter, causing a stampede. Pandemonium followed as Eric looked around wildly.

No! No! Out of instinct, Eric looked back to the spot where Frankie always stood, but the man was already on the ground, being trodden on.

Eric grabbed Marianne's hand and ran toward the edge of the stage.

"What's happening?" she screamed, her voice barely audible above the scene, which sounded like a massacre.

As they neared the edge of the stage, he lifted his eyes, seeing men in full SWAT gear abseiling down from the floor above, landing amongst the crowd.

"Come on," Eric said, fleeing down the stairs, keeping low.

Eric could feel the fear in the room, but this was one form of energy he wasn't going to feed off of. He had to survive. He had to think.

More rounds of gunfire followed and Eric kept his head down as they plunged into the crowd. A thought struck him, but it didn't comfort him.

He'd been sitting on the stage, in full view, without protection. Whoever was here, they were coming for him. They wanted him— alive. Who wanted him alive?

Liam Smith.

Eric was pushed from behind and with it went his train of thought. He gripped Marianne's hand, holding it tight.

"Christos! Christos!"

Eric heard his name being called but he couldn't identify who was calling it, or where the voice was coming from.

"Christos!" He heard it again, but he didn't dare raise his head above the sea of bodies, risking a fate matching Frankie's. Even if their intruder wasn't intending to kill him, there were so many bullets flying that Eric couldn't be sure one wouldn't land in his skull.

A strong hand grabbed his forearm, pulling him through the crowd. It was Frankie's brother, Stephen. A burst of confidence— confidence that they might get out of this alive—fuelled Eric's feet. Stephen used his booming voice to command the wild crowd. The space began to clear around them, giving Eric enough room to breathe without his chest being crushed.

"This way!" Stephen yelled, and Eric knew he was leading them to the escape route.

A gun fired in close range and Eric ducked down instinctively, but Stephen didn't stop. When people didn't move, Stephen pushed them out of the way. And when a few of the smarter crowd began to realize Eric was among them, they started to follow them.

The only time Eric did raise his head was when they passed the sacrifices, still tied to their death crosses. His eyes met with the young woman's, and she gave him a defiant look. If he'd had a gun he would've put a bullet between her eyes.

Marianne tripped and Eric yanked her hand, keeping her upright. He couldn't let her die tonight either, not when she was the daughter of an elder. That was a sin for which he'd never be forgiven; for that he'd have his title stripped. She had to survive, along with him. "Don't let go!" Eric said.

Stephen came to an abrupt stop and Eric crashed into the back of him.

"Not so fast," a voice said.

Eric knew the voice. He recognized it instantly, even though he couldn't see the face masked by protective gear. It was not who he had been expecting.

A gun shot rang and Stephen buckled, stumbled, and then fell to the floor. Eric looked around him, searching for a weapon, for anything.

"Hello, again," Maksym said. "You're a smart fucker, but this time you're done."

Biskup's men? How the fuck—

A pistol pointed at Eric's head, and he looked through the barrel.

No! No! This is not the end! This is the beginning!

Marianne screamed behind him and Eric closed his eyes, calling upon the power of the Gods. With no weapon, prayer was his only option.

Protect us, almighty Gods—

Eric's prayer was cut short by another gunshot. Instinctively he looked over his body, expecting to see a patch of red seeping through his clothing, but then realized he didn't feel any pain.

It was Maksym who had been shot. He dropped to the floor, clutching at his neck.

Another set of arms propelled Eric, and subsequently Marianne, forward. Suddenly they were enveloped by security. *Finally,* Eric thought. *Where the fuck have my men been?*

Eric began to run now. *Five more steps,* he told himself. Five more steps and they'd be out of this alive.

They dashed for the door and Eric's body, fuelled by fury and fear, bounded across the floor. Security swung it open and ushered them in.

"Lock it," Eric said, gasping for air as he leaned forward, resting his hands on his knees. The metal door slammed behind them, and Eric's eyes didn't leave it until he saw every one of the four locks—manual and electronic, a security precaution he'd insisted on after Amman—had been activated.

They began to run again, their footsteps pounding on the concrete of the winding tunnel. Eric tried to piece together the puzzle.

Biskup's men had found him. But how? They'd searched for years and come up with nothing. Eric thought back over recent events. There were only two men—that he knew of—who had been captured in the past few weeks: Liev and Mikhail. But how had Biskup's men gotten the intel from them?

Eric could only come up with one conclusion.

Makaela's boyfriend.

Eric's blood turned as the realization hit him like a like a tidal wave.

His teeth sawed back and forth. If he'd created an alliance with Biskup, he was even more dangerous than Eric had predicted.

I don't know who you are, Eric thought.

But I know how to find you.

What I'm going to do next is your fault.

16

JAMES THOMAS

James held the device to the door once more. Again the green light came on and the device beeped, but the door wouldn't open.

His mind raced, his vision darting between the door and a bleeding out Maksym.

James had to make a decision. If they couldn't get through this door and ensure Eric's capture, then he couldn't go back to Biskup with Maksym's dead body.

Deacon appeared at his side.

"It's not opening!" James said, firing another round of shots at the lock, and Deacon then gave the door two thumping kicks. It still didn't budge.

James looked to Maksym again. Time was running out.

"It's metal," Deacon said, looking at the hole his feet had left in the wooden finish.

The brothers looked at each other, and James' heart sank down to his feet. They had explosives, but given the state of the building, James thought the force of the explosion would likely cause the escape tunnel to collapse—and subsequently kill Eric. They weren't getting through. James wanted to scream, he wanted to strangle Mak's husband until the last of his oxygen leaked from his body, but that moment would not come tonight. Twice—twice he'd slipped through their fingers.

With the decision made for him, James ran back to Maksym, leaning over his body. The man spluttered and red liquid sprayed from his lips.

Oh, damn, he thought.

"You're not dead yet," James said. "Hang in there! Don't you dare fucking die on me!"

Deacon kneeled beside him. "We've got to get him in the van," he said, his eyes on James' blood-covered hand as he applied pressure to the wound.

James' eyes swept over the gallery. The crowd was pushing each other, scrambling to get out. Whatever practices they honored, caring for one another amidst a crisis wasn't one of them. The advantage, though, to launching an intrusion on a worship ceremony was that most of them were naked, which meant they weren't armed.

The frenzied shouting made communication through their earwigs difficult, but that's why James had instructed some men to stay on the level above. They were the exit strategy team and their role was just as important as the men on the ground level—if not more important. Even if they had captured Eric, it would've been no use if they hadn't been able to get him out.

"Code 17, left exit!" James called. He pulled a bandana out of his pocket and wrapped it around Maksym's neck. It wasn't going to do much—the wound needed to be stitched—but while they were moving James wouldn't be able to keep pressure on the wound as easily.

Despite their limited training, Biskup's men appeared in front of James within seconds and took a protective stance. James knew he couldn't lift Maksym and move with the speed and agility he would need to get out of there, so he called in one of the men.

"Lift on the count of three," Deacon instructed the man and they hauled Maksym's body up, James pressing his hand over the neck wound as they began to transport him. They were exposed as a group, but James didn't know how many security guys were still standing. Some had escaped with Eric, and he was almost certain they'd taken out the majority of them before they'd scaled down into the arena. One by one they'd orchestrated the attack, silently eliminating Eric's defense—and it still hadn't been enough.

Focus, James. Get out of here. Keep Maksym alive. Restrategize. That's your best hope, he told himself.

Hands reached for James, the hands of a panicked woman. He pushed them off, refusing to slow down. Another set of hands tugged on him, hoping to join their entourage, and again James pushed them off. "Keep up the pace," James instructed. "Keep moving, don't stop for anyone."

"Copy."

His eyes darted up, to the side, down, to the side. Constantly roaming. Constantly surveying. He monitored Deacon and the man assisting him. Maksym was a big guy, and lugging an almost dead weight and moving through a panicked crowd wasn't an easy task. Their breathing was labored, but his body was still being held high.

They reached the center of the gallery. *Halfway,* James thought.

"Keep going, keep moving. We're almost out," James said. It was a lie, they were far from out, but once they got through the crowd James thought they'd be okay. He thought that, but he had no idea what waited for them. Had Eric called in recruits? Was Eric waiting outside ready to launch a counterattack?

James didn't know, and he couldn't prepare for any of it. The best thing he could do was to keep his men alert, light on their feet, and positive that they weren't going to die tonight. Morale was everything in a war.

"Help me! Please! Don't leave me here!"

The desperation of the woman's voice pierced through James' thoughts. He turned his head, noticing his men do the same thing. Some even faltered.

The plea came from one of the young women on the cross. One of the evening's sacrifices. Her plea tugged on his conscience, but he wasn't here to save her. He wasn't here to save anyone.

"Keep going," James instructed. A couple of the men hesitated, their bodies swaying, but their feet didn't move. "Keep going!"

"Please! Please! I didn't sign up for this. This wasn't my choice!" Her scratchy, strained voice had stopped his men again.

But his time his Deacon stalled too. James looked at him, and he knew where Deacon's mind had gone. Nicole.

"James," Deacon said. It wasn't a plea, it was a demand.

James looked around them, praying this wasn't going to get them all killed.

"You," James said as he pointed over his shoulder. "Cut her down. Bring her with us and don't let her go. Lose her, and I'll kill you."

If they risked a man, and the time to cut her loose, James was going to use that to their advantage. He wanted to know how she came to be their sacrifice, and what she knew about the organization.

James looked over his shoulder. The girl was with them, the front of her naked body covered in red, the crimson color fading to a lighter shade as it reached her legs.

"Keep moving," James said, and his men moved again. "Faster, let's pick up the pace." The men in front—clearing through the crowd and debris—became a touch more aggressive in their efforts. It worked, and they were making up for the lost time. However, when Maksym's eyes rolled back and he gave another splutter James didn't know if it would be enough.

"Keep your eyes open," he said, looking down at the wounded man. "We're nearly there, and soon I'm going to load you up with that many meds you'll have the best time of your life. You're going to make it."

Maksym's bleary eyes looked at him and James wasn't even sure that he'd heard him, but then Maksym nodded. James sighed in relief.

The relief was short-lived after he heard a gunshot echo through the hall.

"Keep moving!" James shouted. They weren't stopping for

anything or anyone. The crowd was thinning as they neared the exit of the arena, but they still had to get up one floor, out through the left exit, and into the van. Without the multiple hands tugging and pushing them, causing them to stumble, it would be a lot easier.

They reached the stairwell door and the men at the front opened it, allowing for a seamless entry. James looked over his shoulder one last time, looking at the destructive scene they had left in their wake. James didn't know how many had been hurt, or killed, in the process, but he knew at least some of the red puddles on the floor were wine and not blood. He couldn't be sure how many, though, and he didn't bother to count the lifeless bodies scattered about. Most of them had been trodden on, crushed under the weight of the moving crowd. It was a horrible way to go.

James noted Maksym's body dipping lower.

"Swap out," James said, looking at the man holding up Maksym's feet. James didn't want him to be dropped on the stairs. He instructed another man to take his place and then looked to Deacon.

Deacon's chest was heaving but his brother shook his head. "I'm fine, let's go."

"Let's go," James said. "Up one floor, exit the stairwell and take the left."

His men were already jogging up the stairs, the sound of their feet like a marching band that intensified as the men at their rear joined the ascent.

The door was unlocked—as they had left it.

The man at the front swung it open, surveyed the hallway, and then led them out.

"Faster," James said, moving the group into fast-paced jog. James was glad he'd swapped out the man helping Deacon. The hallway was deserted, and if not for the images in his mind, he would never believe the scene that lay a few feet below them.

They reached the exit door.

So close, James thought, but he didn't let his guard down. Hell only needed to be allowed a second to unleash itself.

The door opened, and a gust of frosty air blew in. James inhaled, filling his lungs. He heard the van door open.

"Clear."

"Let's go!" James said as they moved forward, striding toward the van.

Six steps.

James counted them in his head, hurdling into the van on the final step.

"Put him in the middle," James said, and when he heard the door shut behind him he knew that they were all in. "Pass me the boxes."

James dropped to his knees, swaying as the van veered away from the curb.

Deacon kneeled beside him and together they began pulling items out. It wasn't the best makeshift clinic, but it was the only one they had right now.

"Hold him steady," James instructed the men sitting next to Maksym as he snapped on a pair of gloves and then jabbed the tip of the needle into a vial and withdrew the plunger. He took a second—only one—to look across at the sacrifice. She trembled, and her eyes were bleary. "Put a blanket around her."

James jabbed the needle into Maksym's skin as Deacon inserted an IV catheter into each hand. James didn't wait for the anesthetic to take full effect, and he didn't need to—Maksym was barely conscious.

The bullet had gone straight through the neck, and James did a quick assessment of the entry and exit wounds. He couldn't believe the man was still alive. With steady hands, James prepared a needle. The wounds were messy, and if he'd had more time he would've changed the way he stitched them. But right now time was everything.

The van veered around a corner and James swayed. One of his men reached out a steadying hand, applying pressure right onto his injured shoulder. James winced as the pain knocked the wind from his chest.

He took a deep breath. "Hold my waist," James said. "Keep me steady."

He pushed the needle through and Maksym groaned, which was a good sign. If he had a pain response, he was feeling something at least.

Deacon hooked up the blood and fluids and was using one of their men as an IV stand. He connected a monitor, and then prepared another needle and they angled Maksym—much to his angst—so that they could stitch at the same time.

James' ears pricked, listening to the monitor as the time between the beeps grew more vast.

We're losing him, James thought, but he pushed the hopelessness back into the recesses of his mind. He loaded a syringe of adrenaline and gave him a boost.

"Come on," James muttered under his breath.

He went back to stitching, working faster than he ever had before, but Maksym began to flatline.

James kneeled over, grabbing the defibrillator pads. James could see all eyes on him, but he didn't look up. He didn't wonder what they were thinking. His only focus was to keep this man from dying. If Maksym didn't come out of this, the alliance could be over.

The unit charged and James held the pads down on Maksym's chest.

"Now!" James said to Deacon, and James jolted back as they zapped the unconscious man.

James looked to the monitor.

Flat line.

"Again!"

Flat line.

James refused to give up.

"Again!"

The third shock was delivered and James held his breath, his eyes laser focused on the monitor.

Flat line.

Flat line.

Beep.

Beep.

Beep.

James sat back on his heels, his chest slumping forward. He exhaled.

"Thank you," he quietly, without even knowing who he was thanking.

James picked up the needle again to finish the stitching.

Maksym wasn't out of the woods yet.

17

MAK ASHWOOD

Mak looked down the range, her eyes focused on the target.

I can do this, she thought, steadying her hands, her finger on the trigger.

In five minutes time, Mak or Cami would be one hundred dollars richer. Mak hoped it was her, and not because of the money. She just hated to lose.

"Perhaps I should've set a time limit, too," Cami said from behind her, but Mak ignored her jab. Cami was playing dirty, and that meant she thought she might actually lose. Her taunting only inspired Mak.

I've got this. She took a long, calming breath and then pulled the trigger until the magazine was empty. Mak lowered her pistol and without even seeing the target, she had a good feeling.

Cami came to stand behind her and pressed the button to bring the target forward.

"Damn!" Cami said as a superior grin spread across Mak's lips.

Mak held out her palm, nodding.

Cami shook her head and a choked sigh left her lips. She dug her hand into the pocket of her jeans, pulling out a note and passing it to Mak. Mak held it by each end, moving her hands in and out to create a snapping sound.

"You don't have to gloat, I'm already going to cop it from James. And Deacon, for that matter."

"Let that be a lesson in betting against me," Mak said.

Cami laughed. "Okay, smartass, clean your pistol and put it away, and then we'll get you home."

Mak began cleaning her weapon. She was meticulous about it, something James, Deacon, and Cami all insisted upon.

"Can I get my own weapon now?" Mak asked. She didn't really want her own weapon, but she was interested to see whether they thought she was capable of having one or not.

"That's something you need to talk to James about," she said, shrugging her shoulders.

James Thomas. It had been days since she'd heard anything from him, but judging by Cami's demeanor, he was still alive. It didn't get easier not to worry, and with each day that passed without hearing from him, it got harder. But Mak kept herself busy with work, and settling into her new apartment. She'd also bought a dress for Zahra and Jayce's wedding—thanks to the lovely personal shopper that had brought over a selection for her—but she wanted to speak to James before she bought their gift.

"I'll do that," Mak said, finally replying to Cami, but she wondered when she would have a chance. And as she only got a few minutes to speak to him, she didn't want to waste time talking about having her own gun.

Once more Mak wondered what he was doing—what he and Deacon were doing—and another thought occurred to Mak.

"Do you miss it?" Mak asked.

"Miss what?" Cami said.

"Not being with James and Deacon, doing whatever they're doing. I don't know what your life was like before joining Thomas Security, but I assume you saw a lot more action than you're seeing being my bodyguard," Mak said. Although they'd had a few terrifying moments, for the most part it hadn't been a very exciting past few months.

"I think part of me will always miss my old life," she said, shrugging. "But no, I don't miss being with them now. I don't wish I were there instead of here with you. Every role is important, Mak. I trained to be a bodyguard for James and Deacon, and I enjoy doing it."

Mak nodded. "Do you think James misses his old life?"

A small smile formed on her lips. "I know that a little part of him does. But I also know that he wouldn't trade the life he has now for anything in the world. I've never seen him this happy." She looked thoughtful. "I think, for people that do what we do, there's an underlying addiction to the adrenaline. An addiction that's not necessarily healthy, and one that could easily get you killed. The life we have now gives us enough to satiate that craving, but still removes us enough from the field that we can have a normal life. Or somewhat of a normal life."

Mak was glad she'd met James long after he'd made the decision to walk away from his previous career and start Thomas Security, because it meant that she never had to query whether he'd done it because he'd wanted to or because of their relationship. Mak would never ask a partner to give up their career, and that same reasoning was why she never even thought to complain when James' career dragged him away and kept him away for days, sometimes weeks at a time. If you know the circumstances going into a relationship, it's unfair to complain about them later on. *You made your bed, now lie in it,* as Mak's mother had so often said to them as children. It was age-old advice that was always applicable.

"Do you miss having a personal life, Cami?"

She looked at Mak, and for the first time shared a detail of her past. "I've never had one—not really. My parents had very unusual careers, and therefore we had a very unusual childhood...I used to resent them for that, but now I thank them."

There was a nostalgic tone to her words and her eyes drifted to the right.

"*We,*" Mak said. "So, you have siblings?"

Cami grinned, a sparkle gleaming in her eyes. "And it's time to get you home."

~

Mak pulled the sheets up to her chin, but tonight she didn't feel tired. Her mind was awake, and it had been busy all evening. She'd been thinking about Cami's past and what she could possibly mean by *unusual*. The possibilities were endless. She'd then thought about James, and what it must've felt like to feel so alone as a child. She was surprised he'd turned out as normal and successful as he was. And then she thought about Deacon. Mak wondered if she'd ever know his story. Whether or not she did, she already knew parts of it were very sad.

Knowing sleep wasn't coming any time soon, she reached over to her bedside table where a pile of case notes sat. One of the few positives from this security case was that she'd become extremely productive. With nothing else to do but focus on her career, she'd been working day and night, trying to keep her mind busy.

When Mak's phone rang, she looked to it in disbelief. It was getting late, and there was only one person who would be ringing at this hour.

"Hey," Mak said, grinning as she wiggled herself lower on the pillow.

"I hear congratulations are in order," James said, and Mak thought she could hear a smile on his lips.

"Thank you," Mak said. "That will teach all of you for betting against me."

"When did I bet against you? I never did. I knew you'd win, just to stick it to Cami." He chuckled, but Mak noticed the difference in his voice.

"You sound tired," she said, fishing for details.

"Mm... I am, it's been a long night."

"Are you okay?" Mak asked, knowing he probably wouldn't tell her if he wasn't. He hadn't mentioned the bullet wound until he'd come home and couldn't hide it.

"I'm fine. The arm is healing, which is good. I've got one more thing to do tonight and then I'll get some sleep, but I wanted to call you first."

Tonight. Where was he? Was he in America?

"I'm glad you called," Mak said, leaving it at that. She wished his calls were a little more frequent, if not just to ease her worry, but she didn't want to nag him either. Without knowing what he was doing, Mak knew he'd call if he could—if he wasn't in the middle of something. Mak didn't even want to think what that *something* was.

"So, I've organized a dress for the wedding, but I wanted to talk to you about the gift."

"About the wedding..." James said, stalling, and Mak knew what was coming next.

"You're not coming, are you?" Mak said, helping him out.

James sighed. "At this stage, it's looking very unlikely. I may not be home for a few weeks, Mak."

Mak pressed her lips together, but didn't voice her disappointment.

"I'm sorry, Mak. I want to be there but I can't be right now," James continued.

"I know, and it's okay," Mak said. Even though she'd been excited at the possibility of them going together, she didn't need him there. "I've been to plenty of weddings on my own, James, and I survived," Mak said, trying to lighten the mood.

"I have no doubt you'll be fine, but it would've been nice to go together. Anyway, what were you going to ask about the gift?"

"I was looking at the gift registry but I wasn't sure what to buy them, or how much to spend," Mak said.

"Buy them whatever you want, it doesn't matter about the price. You do need to let Samuel know, though, so that he can purchase it for us. I don't want the transaction on your credit card," James said.

"Who is looking at my credit card?" Mak asked.

"I don't know if anyone is, but I'd rather not find out the hard way," James said.

"My credit card didn't get charged for the dress, either, did it?" Mak said, recalling that the personal shopper had advised the purchase would be charged to the credit card on file. Mak had assumed Thomas Security had given her Mak's credit-card details, but now she thought otherwise.

"No," James said unapologetically. "Samuel took care of that, too. Money is not a problem, Mak. Your security is, and until that's resolved, everything is paid for via one of my accounts."

A thought entertained Mak's mind, but she wasn't actually sure how funny it was. "How many bank accounts do you have?"

James chuckled. "I don't even know, but more than I should, I'm sure. Samuel is my accountant, and investment banker..."

"Oh, God," Mak said, smiling despite herself. She could only imagine how Samuel conducted his accounting business.

"He can be yours, too, if you'd like?"

Mak knew he was smirking, and she wanted to kiss it off his lips. "No, thank you. I like my current accountant."

"I like him too, actually. He's squeaky clean," James said, laughing louder.

"James Thomas," Mak said, giggling at the sound of his laugh.

James' laughter slowly settled and he sighed. "I miss you. I cannot even believe how much I miss you."

Mak closed her eyes. She didn't doubt his words, not when they were laced with emotion.

"I wish you were here," Mak whispered, bring her knees to her chest, wondering when he would be home next. He hadn't been gone a week, but it felt much longer than that.

"Me too..."

Other than the few playful moments they'd had during the conversation, James sounded different tonight, but Mak couldn't put her finger on it. *Maybe he's just tired*, Mak thought, but immediately dismissed it when it didn't sit well in her mind.

"Any leads on Carl Junez?" Mak asked, still plagued by that wedding card.

"Nothing new, no. Samuel will find out, though, he always does. He just needs time."

Mak nodded. There didn't seem to be much Samuel couldn't do.

"James," Mak said, making an effort to block the hesitation from her voice. "Why did you tell me about your past? And about you and Deacon not being brothers? Why now? What's changed?"

"I told you because I want you to know who I am. Of the things that you can know, I want you to know all of them."

Mak wasn't sure if she believed him. "Okay. But one more question... Are Cami and Deacon siblings?"

James chuckled. "What? No. What made you think that?"

"I just wanted to check, seeing as no one had actually said otherwise. If I don't ask the questions, I rarely get the answers."

"I promise you, none of us are related. Samuel included," James said.

"Good to know," Mak said, and James yawned. "I should let you go. You sound exhausted."

"Yeah, I need to get going, I just wanted to hear your voice, and to say good night. I love you, Mak. I'll call you when I can."

"Good night, James. Be careful. I love you."

A second passed before the call ended, but it did, and Mak put the phone down on her bedside table.

Come home to me, James Thomas.

18

JAMES THOMAS

James looked at the phone, wishing he hadn't had to hang up. Wishing that Mak were in his arms now. But wishing wasn't going to get him anywhere.

James tilted his head back, resting it against the rough brick wall. Tiny sparkles lit up the black sky, and James looked for the constellations, finding some peace in the task he'd done so often in the past. He'd never known what it was about space, but it had always helped to calm him. Under the stars he'd always done his best thinking. Even as a child he'd spent countless hours, up long after the orphanage curfew, sitting in the windowsill of his room, finding the stars in the night sky. *Some things never change, and some things never stay the same.*

What a night, he thought. Maksym had flat-lined again just as they'd reached the warehouse, and then James and Deacon had had a standoff with one of his men over taking him to a hospital. James had shook his head. Going to a hospital wasn't an option, not when Eric would be searching for him. Eric might assume Maksym had died—it was a very possible conclusion—but until he had a body, Eric would keep looking.

Deacon was with him now, monitoring his vitals, and while James' cell phone was silent he took a few deep breaths. There was

one more thing he had to do tonight, and that was to speak to the girl
—the sacrifice. They desperately needed information and she might
just have something that could help. If she hadn't volunteered, then
James very much wanted to know her story and how she'd managed
to end up bound to the cross.

James looked at his watch. It was nearing four in the morning. He
pushed all thoughts of Mak aside, and stood up, brushing off the dirt
that had been transferred from the concrete steps to his jeans. He
went back into the warehouse. The lights were dim, many of the men
already in their makeshift beds. He walked over to where Deacon sat.
He was flipping through the red book they'd taken from the
building.

"Anything useful?" James asked.

"Nothing useful, but plenty of radical thoughts."

"Any change?" James said, looking at Maksym's pasty-white skin.

"No, but I suppose that's good," Deacon said.

"We need to talk to the woman, and clean her wounds," James
said, watching his brother's reaction carefully.

"You do it, I'll stay here," Deacon said without meeting his gaze.

Deacon might've wanted to rescue her, but James thought the
memories that had since surfaced were too unbearable to face
tonight.

"Okay," James said, patting his brother on the shoulder. "Call me
if anything changes."

James left him alone with his traumatic memories—memories
that unfortunately he couldn't erase or help his brother deal with.
James picked up a medic box and a bottle of juice on his way to the
room where the sacrifice was being held. He paused, turning on his
earwig.

"Samuel?"

"*Copy.*"

"I'm going in to talk with the girl."

"*Copy. I'll be listening.*"

James closed the door behind him and dragged the chair from the
corner of the room, setting it directly in front of her. It was the same

position he'd normally use for an interrogation, but tonight he hoped she'd offer up the information voluntarily.

Despite the blankets wrapped around her shoulders, her body trembled. She'd been through hell tonight. James handed her the juice.

"Drink this, it'll help," he said, undoing the cap for her. With her shaking hands he knew she wouldn't be able to do it herself, at least not without spilling half of it.

James waited until she'd taken a few mouthfuls.

"You're here because we think you might have information that is helpful to us," he said.

"Please don't hurt me," she said as more tears rolled down her cheek.

"All you need to do is answer my questions, and I won't touch you."

She nodded rapidly.

"What is your name?" James asked.

"Julia," she replied. "Julia Lewis."

James nodded. "Where are you from?"

"Manchester." Her voice was hoarse, but James thought it was emotion rather than strain. When Eric's men, and then Eric himself, had cut her, she'd barely made a noise. Although, she could've been clenching so hard she'd strained her vocal chords.

"Tell me how you ended up where you did tonight," James said.

Her lips turned down and she wiped her wet cheeks with the back of her hand.

"I... I started dating this guy. We met at a bar in Chelsea a few weeks ago. He seemed fine, normal... I could never have guessed." She inhaled shakily, and James gave her a moment to collect her thoughts.

She continued. "I think it was our fifth, maybe sixth date, and we were driving to dinner—he was driving—and he got a phone call. It connected through his car, through the sound system, but he answered it on his mobile. He didn't want me to overhear the conversation, I guessed.

"He didn't say anything for the entire phone call until the very end, when eventually he said, 'I'll be there in a few minutes.' And then he apologized to me and said we had to take a detour because he'd left something at work. It seemed odd, but I didn't question it. He pulled up out front of the building, and I could see the sign on the door. It was a legal firm, and he'd said he was a lawyer, so I thought then maybe I'd interpreted the conversation incorrectly... I hadn't," she said with a shudder.

"He told me to stay in the car and he'd be back in a minute. I watched him enter the building and then I started using my phone, responding to a few messages. I don't know how much time passed— a few minutes, I think—and then I heard screaming. Even from inside the car it was so loud, so I got out. I thought someone was in trouble in the passageway."

Julia began to sob now. "The screaming got louder and before I had thought it through I was running toward the screams. They were coming from a window in the basement, and I could see her palms banging against the windowpane. And then— " she swallowed "— and then red... The glass splattered red and I screamed. And then another set of eyes looked up at me through the window. It was him.

"I started running. I kicked off my heels and just ran. I don't know where I was going—I wish I'd had a better plan. I didn't get far before I heard footsteps behind me. I got caught, stuck in a dead end, and he found me. He told me I should've stayed in the car, and that this was my fault. And then he said he couldn't let me go, so I had two options..." Julia's eyes locked on James'. "He said he was giving me a choice—that I could choose my future. He would either sell me to the highest bidder, or I could die. I pleaded with him, begged him, but he told me they were my only two options. I broke down, sobbing. I fell onto the ground but he dragged me up by the hair and told me that I had ten seconds to make a decision or I was going to the basement with the other girls to be sold. I chose death. I suppose I should've asked him to clarify how my death would come."

James understood why she felt that way, although he thought it was usually best not to know.

"What then?" James asked.

She searched his face, and he wondered if she was trying to get a read on him.

She rubbed her eyes and then sighed. "He dragged me inside the building, but not into the basement. He took me up to the third floor and locked me in an empty room. He would come in a couple of times throughout the day with food, and to take me to the bathroom. I stayed there for six days—I knew this only because I could see a little of the sunlight creeping in behind the boarded windows and began to count the days. I didn't talk to anyone. I didn't hear anything else. And then earlier this evening he came in and told me it was time to die. He told me to remember that I chose this, to sacrifice my life, and that if I said anything to anyone he would sell me to a man that loves to burn young women alive."

James gave her a moment to collect herself. "How did you get to the building that the ceremony took place in?"

"He made me shower—to be clean for the *worship*. I had no idea what he meant by that. Once I'd finished in the shower, he gave me a robe, and then bound my hands and feet. He carried me downstairs, and laid me on the backseat of the car. A black Mercedes sedan. He drove me there on his own."

"Did you note the registration plate?" James had to ask the question, but he thought he already knew the answer.

"No... I didn't think about it. I was thinking about how to get my hands free."

"What did you say to the man—the leader—when he was cutting you? I saw you talking to him," James said.

Her eyes welled up once more. "I couldn't die like that, not without trying. I'd watched him walk in with his wife, and saw how affectionate he was to her, and how everyone bowed at his feet. I thought...stupidly...that maybe he was different. I pleaded with him. I told him I didn't volunteer for this and that I didn't want to be one of the sacrifices, or whatever they call them...I don't think I'll ever forget his voice. I don't know who he is, but there's something wrong with him. He's...crazy."

"What did he say to you?" James pressed.

"He told me that he controlled my fate, and that if I said another word like that he'd make my sacrifice unbearable—" Julia scoffed between sobs "—as if it wasn't already. He told me no one was coming to save me."

James wondered if they had saved her or just delayed her death. If she'd been held captive for a week prior to the worship, someone would've reported her missing, which meant she'd have trouble crossing any border. And she would need to cross a border and get far away from London, because Eric's men would be looking for her. The life she knew, the family she loved: she had to forget them. She couldn't go back to her life, or they'd find her—and she'd find herself in a worse hell than she'd experienced a few hours ago.

"You've got a bit of a problem, now," James said. "Someone would've seen you leave with us and they're going to look for you. They are a very far-reaching organization with eyes everywhere. I'm sorry, but you are no longer Julia Lewis. She died tonight. You're now someone else—anyone, you get to choose—but if you ever go home, or make contact with your family, they will find you."

She buried her face in her hands and began sobbing.

"Pick a name that is familiar to you, but that isn't a family member. Create details of your past based on a colleague or a high-school friend. The more familiar the details are, the easier it is to remember them—to live the lie."

James wasn't sure she'd heard him through the sobs, but her next question indicated she had.

"I don't have anything. He took my phone, my money... I can't do this, I don't know what to do...where to go." By the end of the sentence her voice was high-pitched and her words running into one another. James couldn't give her back her life, but he could help her create a new one.

"We can help you—a little. We'll get you false documents, give you some money and clothes, and get you out of London. But from there you'll be on your own," James said. He waited for her to look up, and then added, "We'll also give you some medical supplies so that you can look after your wounds."

Julia huddled the blanket, drawing her arms around her.

She looked into James' eyes. "You were going to leave me there, weren't you? Why help me now?"

"I was focused on getting my men out of there alive," James said. "Stopping for you was an additional risk, and my responsibility was to them."

She didn't respond but wiped a tear from her cheek.

"Can you tell me the address of the legal building?"

She nodded, and then gave the address.

"Got it," Samuel said. *"I'm linking in the CCTV footage. It is a legal firm. She's not lying. I'll let Deacon know to rally the boys."*

"Good," James said. "We're also going to prepare a series of images from the worship. I need you to identify the man who kidnapped you—the man you were dating."

"Okay," she said, her voice stronger. He thought she'd take some pleasure in that.

James continued. "Before we do anything, though, I need to look at your wounds."

She shook her head, tightening the blanket around her.

"I'm not going to hurt you, other than giving you some anesthetic. But if your wounds aren't treated, they will become infected very quickly and you'll never get out of London alive." James leaned over, opening the medic box.

He snapped on a pair of gloves, and then drew up a syringe of local anesthetic. He was primarily concerned about the gouging hole Eric had left on her breast bone. He'd really twisted that knife in deep.

"I'm a doctor," he said without looking at her. He was aiming to calm her enough to give him access to her wounds.

"Where did you train?"

"Stanford," James said. He laid out the packages he needed, tearing open an alcohol wipe. He was about done playing doctor tonight, but this patient was an important lead.

"You don't look like a doctor," she said, and then pressed her lips tight.

James ignored the comment. He was achingly tired and all he wanted to do was to crawl into bed beside his girlfriend. Instead, he had to stitch up a different girl that had been marked by many men, including his girlfriend's husband. James pushed the thoughts aside.

"Lie down," he said. "Keep the shirt on, just open the first few buttons."

Her fingers shook as she undid them, exposing a raw, bloody chest.

James nodded. "Hold the fabric there," he said. It was open just enough to give him access, but he didn't want to see any more of her than he needed to. She'd been exploited enough already, regardless.

He used several wipes to clean the smeared blood from her skin and she winced, curling her hands up into fists, digging her nails into her palms.

James assessed the V-shaped wound, and refrained from sighing. He could use a few butterfly stitches, but the rest had to be sutured. And he hadn't even looked at the carvings on her stomach.

He heard noise outside the room, and he knew the boys were preparing to go again.

He smiled grimly. *Your time is running out, Eric.*

19

ERIC

Eric stood before the Commission. Eighteen pairs of eyes stared back at him. Eyes of the men who had the power to control his fate.

"The damage that has been caused by the events of tonight will be more far-reaching than you can realize." It was Lucian who spoke first, his deep voice and ice-gray eyes reprimanding.

Eric resisted the urge to clear his throat. He could not show weakness—not now. Now was the time for strength. "I understand the consequences. I am their leader, and I will need to prove to them once again that I can protect them, and that I can deliver them their salvation."

Lucian gave a slow nod.

Lucian was the oldest of the elders. He was also his father-in-law and the master of the entire organization. Only one man had more power—Sorin: the Dumnezeu. *The lord.* Eric had never seen Sorin in person, but when he received the summons to appear before the Commission this evening, he'd wondered if the man would be here. The fact that he wasn't gave Eric a sliver of confidence, but Eric worried it was false hope.

The worship—a sacred event—had been turned into a blood-bath. Never in the history of the organization had such horror played out at a ceremony. That horror had come under Eric's leadership, and that was why he was now standing on trial for the events. He could be stripped of his leadership. He could be sacrificed for redemption.

No, Eric thought. *I've come this far. I've dedicated my life to this organization. I've made it wealthier than the Catholic Church. I've recruited more members than any leader before me. All of that can't be pushed aside because of one failed worship. It can't be.*

"What is being done to rectify the security breach?"

Eric met the gaze of the elder seated beside Lucian. A candle on the table in front of him flickered, enhancing the grueling glower of the man.

"Additional security personnel are being recruited as we speak. They'll undergo induction within the next few days, and we'll have a full security team—three times as extensive as what we had previously. Until the time when that is complete, all men have been advised to stay low and wait for further instructions," Eric said, feeling little beads of sweat form on his brow.

Eric continued. "One of the sacrifices was taken by the men. This was sighted by several recruits, and I've confirmed it via the surveillance footage. Subsequently, my men—those that aren't injured—are dismantling the Nicu House. Once it's cleaned out, it will be rigged with explosives. We have a team dedicated to finding the sacrifice."

Lucian spoke again. "How did this happen, Christos? This is *very* unfavorable for your advancement."

"I fully understand that," Eric said, bowing his head. He counted to three, as was customary, and then lifted his head. "I believe that one of our recruits—Liev—passed on the information. The men were Alexandr Biskup's men—of that I'm sure. The link between Liev and Biskup is not yet confirmed; however, I believe that Liev was captured —and interrogated by—Makaela's security team in New York. I believe they have formed an alliance with Biskup."

Lucian's eyes widened and the elders looked amongst themselves, eliciting a series of hushed whispers. Eric's heart raced.

"This security team is a real problem," another elder said.

"Yes, they are. We're currently creating a plan that will bring them to us. I don't foresee them being a future problem," Eric said.

"And what is that plan?" Lucian asked.

"We're going to take one of Makaela's family members," Eric said. "We're going to force them to come to us, and they won't be returning to New York."

Lucian raised an eyebrow as a small smile spread across his lips. "It's a punitive move. However, after tonight's events, I think it's just. Does that present a problem for Makaela? She may now be aware of things about you that we wish she did not know."

"I've considered that, too. Therefore, I'm asking for her indoctrination into Saratani to be moved forward—to be undertaken as soon as her security team has been eliminated."

Another round of hushed whispers circulated.

"We've discussed your future plans for Makaela before, but she cannot be taken as your wife at this stage. You do not have the status."

"I'm not asking to take her as my wife, but only to begin her indoctrination as a means to solve a problem. I believe her adjustment period will be lengthier than standard—given her strong spirit—and therefore I believe the additional time will serve her well."

Lucian looked over the Commission, and then back to Eric. "You may step outside."

Eric bowed once more, and then retreated from the room, never turning his back on the Commission. He closed the intricate paneled door behind him, but his demeanor didn't change. He stood with a straight back, his arms hanging, his fingers woven together. Eric knew the Commission could watch him from the chamber, and he had to remain strong. He had to show them he could handle the pressure.

Eric began to count the seconds, but then stopped himself. Instead he focused on his surroundings. He inhaled the scent of the jasmine incense that burned from the candelabras on each side of the door. He focused on the musky wood of the bench seat that he refused to sit on. He listened to the silent halls, halls that kept the secrets of generations of elders.

One day I will be an elder, too, Eric thought. He wouldn't let one night defeat him. He would show the Commission who he was and what he was capable of.

The door creaked as it was opened by the guard.

Eric prayed to the Gods for another chance, and then stepped back into the chamber. He walked toward the Commission, stopping on the star tile in the center of the floor—the exact location he'd stood before.

"We have come to a unanimous decision," Lucian said. "You have been given grace, only because your past record has been flawless. Never has such an incident occurred within our organization, and never again will it." Lucian's eyes were hard. "You have one chance, and one chance only to prove yourself. We suggest you begin by eliminating Makaela's security team so that they cannot cause any future incidents. But at the same time, you must find Liam Smith. As you know, time is running out. His mother is dying, but she must not die without seeing the fate of her son. That is her punishment, and that task was given to you because we believe in you. Prove you are capable. Prove yourself worthy of such a task, and the Gods will reward you. If you do not, we will find someone who can."

Eric bowed, exhaling the angst that had been eating his insides alive.

"I will," Eric said, raising his eyes from the floor. "I thank you for your forgiveness and leniency."

"Regarding Makaela...we have approved your request based on one condition," Lucian said, and Eric held his breath. "If you fail to find Liam Smith before his mother dies, Makaela will be given to one of the elders. She will never be yours to take as a wife. That will be part of your punishment for failing Sorin."

No! No! She is my wife!

Lucian continued. "It is a decision you should think very carefully about. We expect your answer in twenty-four hours. You may go now —you have work to do."

Eric retreated once more, his feet fueled by raw determination. Once out of the chamber, he breezed toward the next door, and then the next, until he was in the car park.

He climbed into the back seat and once the door was closed behind him he leaned forward, screaming. Over and over again. His hands pulled his hair as he rocked back and forth, releasing the anger and humiliation that the worship had caused. When his throat burned, he slumped his forearms onto his knees, resting his head on them.

He felt better—a cathartic release. He took two long, invigorating breaths, and then looked to the man in the front passenger seat.

"Get Pavel Sokolov on the phone," Eric said.

Cell phones were forbidden in the chamber, and it was one of the only times it ever left his side. Eric held out his hand, taking the phone, and when he brought it to his ear it was ringing.

"Zdravstvuyte," Pavel said in greeting.

"Hello to you, too," Eric said. "It's time."

"When?" Pavel asked.

"I need a week to organize a few things," Eric said. "So, I want your men ready—in all six locations—in ten days. Can you do that?"

"To wage war against Liam Smith? Of course I can. You tell me when you're ready, and I'll make sure we are, too. This is a day I never thought I'd see. It can't come soon enough."

"Just remember one thing: you get him for three days, and that's it. After that, I'll take him. He must still be alive, and be able to withstand further torture. If he's not, we're going to have a very, very big problem."

Sokolov chuckled. "He might be missing a few fingers and toes, but he'll still be suitable for you... You never did tell me what you were planning to do to him."

The corner of Eric's lip turned up. "Perhaps once it's done, I'll show you."

"Please do. That is one photo album I'm very keen to see."

"Have your men—and your resources—ready. I'll speak to you in a few days."

"Proshchay," Pavel said, hanging up.

Eric's chest swelled with confidence.

Time is up, Liam.

≈

"Daddy! Daddy!" Makaela squealed as she ran toward Eric.

He scooped her up with one arm and she giggled as her body flopped and bounced like a rag doll. Eric lifted her upright and she pressed her small, pudgy palms pressed against his cheeks.

"Hello, Daddy," she said with a beautiful grin that only a child could wear. The grin of innocence.

"Hello, my beautiful girl," Eric said, kissing her forehead. Movement over her shoulder caught his eye and he saw his wife walk toward them. She too wore a smile, but Marianne's wasn't one of innocence. She knew better—she knew where he'd been.

"Hello," she said, kissing his cheek. She rubbed his back and their eyes met.

Eric nodded and smiled.

"Good," she said. "Breakfast is ready. Let's eat."

Eric carried Makaela to the kitchen where a spread was laid out on the table. He put her down, and then slid her chair in and sat down beside her. He poured some juice into Makaela's plastic cup and listened to her chatter about the cartoons she'd been watching earlier. She didn't stop to take a breath and Eric wondered how it was possible she had any air left in her lungs. He raised his eyebrows and looked to Marianne, who shrugged her shoulders, laughing.

"Makaela, you can't eat if you're talking," Marianne said, giving her a look that said she meant business. Marianne was the disciplinarian, and more often than not had the role of a single mother but with the bonus of financial support. While they had help around the house, Marianne refused to have a nanny.

She's my daughter, and I will raise her.

Marianne's mother—Lucian's fourth wife—had died during childbirth, and Eric often wondered if that was why Marianne had been so adamant about her role as a mother. When they'd found out Marianne was pregnant, Eric had prayed every hour of the day for a girl. In their world, girls of elders were not shunned—they were honored. More so than men, even. Eric would become an elder, and Makaela would one day be given as a wife.

"Daddy?"

Her sweet voice pulled him from his rambling thoughts.

"Yes, Makaela," he said, glad he'd made the effort to come home for breakfast. He would be gone for the rest of the day, perhaps even for the rest of the week, so this time with his family was precious. He also wanted to make sure that Marianne was okay. It was the second close call they'd had in weeks, and he couldn't let his wife's respect for him wane. Not when she was Lucian's daughter.

"Mommy is sick. You have to give her a kiss to make her feel better." She pressed her lips together and her head bounced up and down.

Eric's skin prickled. What did she mean?

"I will give her a big kiss," Eric said, smiling at his daughter before turning his attention to his wife. Had she not mentioned it deliberately? Or was it that this morning's events hadn't given her the time?

"Are you unwell?" Eric asked, giving his wife a very different look than the one he'd just given his daughter.

She waved her hand. "I'm fine. I think it was something I ate last night...it put my stomach off," she said, meeting his gaze.

Eric narrowed his eyes. If she lied to him, there would be consequences—and she knew them. She did have a tendency to vomit when she was stressed, though.

"Are you feeling better now?" Eric asked.

She looked into his eyes. "Yes. Last night has passed, and with it the bad food. I'm feeling much better."

"See, you always make her feel better," Makaela said.

Eric chuckled. "That is right. I will always take care of Mommy."

He was monitoring his wife's reaction but when his phone rang, he excused himself.

"Yes," Eric said, walking toward his office.

"Calling with the update you requested. The building is being cleaned out, but it's a big job, so it's going to take some time. There's been no other activity at the site. Perhaps the girl didn't talk."

She'll talk, Eric thought. He knew Biskup's men. She'd tell them everything she knew and then they'd use her and abuse her until she was a bloody pulp.

She hadn't been saved—she'd just been handed from one wolf to another.

20

JAMES THOMAS

His brother's eyes were unrelenting. "Someone has to stay, and it's you," Deacon said. "God only knows if he's going to make it—" he pointed at Maksym "—and you can't leave the girl alone with these men."

"You can treat him, Deacon. You know what to do," James said, keeping his voice low. They'd kept up a unified appearance thus far, but James knew if Biskup's men saw any cracks, they'd use it to their full advantage.

"You're a better doctor than I am, and you're injured. You're staying, and I'm going."

His brother was not backing down, and James thought his only option to stop Deacon was to knock him out and tie him up. But, given James' injury and Deacon's superior fitness, that wasn't a fight James thought he'd win.

"Deacon, please. I can't let you do this. We have no idea what will be inside the building, or who will be inside." James knew his words were falling on deaf ears.

"You don't have to let me, I'm going regardless," Deacon said.

"So what happened to your rule about both of us agreeing or we find another solution?" James asked.

"You were going to break that rule the moment it suited you, so don't even try and play that card," Deacon said, his voice low but firm. "I'm going."

So he had seen through his lie after all. James sank into the chair beside Maksym. He didn't like this, not at all. James rubbed his palms over his face, listening to the conversations around him. Biskup's men had been teased last night, and now they were ready for the main course.

Speak of the devil, James thought as he looked at an incoming call.

"I hear we have a problem," Biskup said.

James wondered which of Biskup's men had reported back to him.

"Yeah, we have a problem," James said. "We have a problem because Maksym decided to gloat instead of pulling the trigger and delivering a disabling shot. A mistake like that has consequences."

"In less than seventy-two hours you've managed to get five of my men killed, wound a handful of others, and my main man is fighting for his life. I'm beginning to regret this alliance."

"In less than seventy-two hours we found Eric—which you hadn't managed to do in the many years you hunted him. And we would've captured him if Maksym had done his job. Instead, Eric ran straight over the top of him and into the safety of an exit tunnel. Don't blame me for the mistakes of your *main man*," James responded harshly.

"If any more of my men die in the next twenty-four hours, the deal is off," Biskup said.

"A deal is a deal. I have six weeks, and if you try and renege on the deal, your men will die because I'll slit their throats before they can step a foot outside this building." James' temple was pounding and this conversation wasn't helping.

There was a momentary pause, and then Biskup said, "Very well," in a tone much less ugly than it had been a minute ago. James knew it had only been a threat, and he didn't think Biskup truly cared about the men—excluding Maksym, because he was a valuable asset. Given how close they had gotten to Eric, James thought Biskup would let his entire army die before he'd renege on the deal, although he'd never admit it.

"How is Maksym doing?"

"Stable," James responded. "I'm getting a doctor here to help with his treatment, but it may be twenty-four hours before he arrives."

"Good. I hear the boys are preparing to go out again. You're not going with them?"

"No," James said. "I have a patient and a hostage to attend to."

James looked over the scene in front of him, wishing he were going.

"Tell me, where did you get your medical training from? My boys are most impressed."

"Stanford," James said.

A loud laugh came through the phone. "Well, then, doctor—your patient should make a full recovery. I hope for Makaela's sake he does."

"Are you threatening her?" James said with a voice of steel.

"No, not while we remain friends... All men have a weakness, and I know she's yours."

James had had enough of the man for one night. "Your threats and intimidation techniques won't work on me. And you're wasting my time. So, if there's nothing else, I'll get back to commanding your men and doing the one thing you haven't been able to do: find Eric."

Biskup chuckled and James shook his head.

"You do that. Call me if anything changes."

James hung up without saying goodbye and went to stand beside his brother. He listened as Deacon prepared the men for what they might find, but warned them to remain vigilant, because they were walking into uncharted territory.

As the men hollered and grabbed their packs, swinging them over their shoulders, James looked to Deacon. "Be careful, brother," James said.

"Always," Deacon said.

James watched them walk out, and heard the door close behind them. He looked at the remaining men, those Deacon hadn't selected for the mission, and told them all to get some more rest.

It was daylight, and taking a huge group in would've attracted attention. Deacon and his men needed to be stealthy. For such a mission, what they needed was a smaller team of highly skilled men.

James unlocked the door to Julia's room. She was supine, her eyes closed. James had given her a mild sleeping tablet—just enough to block the horrors from her mind so that she could rest and her body could heal. When she awoke, she'd still be in hell, he knew.

James went back to Maksym and took another round of vitals. Nothing had changed, but as long as he wasn't crashing, James supposed he should be thankful. He sat down once more and listened to the chatter through his earwig. It was all nonsense talk, but when they got closer, Deacon would shut it down.

Incoming call: Samuel.

"Hey," James said.

"Today is your lucky day!"

James looked around him—Samuel definitely wasn't seeing what he was. "It is?"

"Oh yes, it is. I think we were wrong about Carl Junez—I don't think he's the person that inducted Eric into the organization. I actually think Mak was right—that he wasn't at the wedding. The card was probably mailed in, or given to Eric at some point. I've got a visual for a Carl Junez. Nothing about the profile looks sinister, and I wouldn't have paid it much attention except for someone in the background. Take a look at your phone..."

James opened his messages. The man looked to be sixty, maybe seventy years of age. And he looked to be of European descent. The photo looked like it was taken in a shopping mall, perhaps. James held the phone closer to his eyes, scanning the background. His jaw dropped into his lap. "Eric's wife."

"Bingo!"

"Interesting," James said. "But how are they connected? Through Eric?" James scanned the image again, but Eric definitely wasn't in the background. "Where did you get this image from?"

"A database picked up a credit-card transaction for a Carl Junez. I looked at the time, and then hacked the footage from the mall. It was taken one week ago in London."

"Well done, Samuel. Well done," James said. "I want to know more about Carl Junez. His face wasn't in the set of portraits we found in Sarquis' house, so I'm thinking that maybe Carl is higher up. And if he is, then Marianne is also a link to the higher levels. She might be incredibly useful."

"I think she might be, too. I'll keep digging."

"How is everything at home? How are Ben and Kayla?" James asked.

"They are doing well. I might be concerned about the lack of phone calls between Eric and Ben, but I'm thinking it's only because you're creating multiple problems for Eric at the moment and he's preoccupied. The package of cameras arrived for Kayla this morning, though. I'm thinking we can stall on that for a few days by saying that Mak's waiting until you're settled in to have guests over. At some point, however, we're going to have to find a solution that doesn't blow Kayla's cover. And, lastly, still no word on the fingers...I don't know what to make about that."

"I wondered whether Liev or Mikhail were originally going pick up the fingers... Perhaps Eric is in the process of making alternate plans," James said, worried what those plans might be.

"Possibly. Otherwise, everything else is pretty quiet, which is just how I like it."

James smiled. "Unlike the crap coming through our earwigs."

Samuel scoffed. "There are multiple reasons why I'd like this situation over and done with, and those boys are one of them. I'm going to get back to digging on Carl. I'll talk to you soon."

"Find me some more gold, Samuel," James said and then laid his phone in his lap.

James continued to listen to the communication stream through his earwig, aware of his body's response as they neared their destination. James retrieved his laptop and then sat down beside Maksym once more as he waited for the feed from Deacon's camera to come through. Samuel would have it linked in any second now.

Please don't let him get hurt, James prayed silently.

The footage began to play and James leaned forward. The men were on the ground, inching toward the building. It was a risk to enter in daylight, but James didn't think the building would be occupied for long. The daylight did provide an advantage, though—it would be difficult to clear out a building of this size without someone seeing something they weren't supposed to, which meant it would take more time.

James listened to his brother's commands, and the men followed blindly. They were good in that sense—they never questioned. Never. James wondered what Biskup had done to instill that in them. Whatever it was, it couldn't have been kind.

When all eleven men were in location, Deacon moved in first— going in through the rooftop. He paused at the door that led to the top floor, pressing his ear against it. Deacon opened it and three men followed in behind him.

The rooms appeared to be offices, but they were lacking one important element: computers.

They've cleared it out, James thought. Or the computers had never been there in the first place. The building had been purchased three years ago from a legal firm, and therefore it was possible that they'd bought it furnished. From what Julia had told them, James doubted it had ever been used as an office in the traditional form.

"Give us something," James said to himself as his eyes remained glued to the live stream from Deacon's camera.

The men searched the level, office by office, opening drawers and cabinets. Nothing—nor did they encounter any of Eric's men. James didn't know if that was a good thing or not.

"Let's go down," Deacon said to his men, and then instructed the next three to move in from the rooftop. It was a good strategy, because if they were spread out, they couldn't all be taken out at the same time by a grenade. And having too many men on one floor—if they

ran into company—meant that they wouldn't be able to duck behind the shelter of a wall and use the element of surprise. Too many men meant congestion, and attention.

Deacon flew down the stairs to the next level, again pressing his ear to the wall before entering. He opened the door handle and then rapidly closed it again. If James had blinked he would've missed it.

"*Hold,*" his brother instructed, opening the door at an achingly slow pace, just enough to give him one eye's view.

James couldn't see what his brother was seeing, and the powerless feeling of watching him and not being able to cover his back was excruciating. James wondered if this was how Deacon felt when he watched him.

When his brother passed his weapon to the man beside him, James thought there must be someone on the floor. Someone close to the door, someone Deacon thought he could silence. When he moved into a crouch position, James knew his assumptions were correct.

Deacon swung the door open wide and James saw a flash of the man before the footage went black as Deacon lunged at him. James heard the telltale sign—the puff of breath—and he knew his brother had his arm around the man's neck. James counted the seconds, knowing how long it should take for the man to be rendered unconscious. When the man's body dropped to the floor, clearing the camera lens, James exhaled.

"*Move in,*" Deacon instructed, dragging the man under one of the desks.

This floor too looked like offices. And it looked just as empty as well, which made James wonder what the man had been doing.

James' eyes flickered to the monitor beside Maksym. Stable. James returned his attention to the footage.

Deacon was casing another office, but as he pulled open the drawers, they were empty. James noted the time again. Even if Eric had instructed the building to be cleared out the minute he'd escaped, they couldn't have cleared out a building of this size already. Thomas

Security was efficient at relocating client's homes and business premises, and James had overseen the production many times. It just couldn't be done, not in daylight, and not without clogging the streets with moving trucks—which they hadn't done.

James sighed. Something wasn't right, but he didn't know what it was.

"*Clear out, third level,*" Deacon said, and then once more issued a command to the next group to move in from the rooftop.

Nine men inside.

Julia had said she was in a vacant room, so James was interested to see if there were any vacant rooms on the level Deacon was about to enter. He'd told Deacon to check, because if there weren't, and they were all filled with office furniture like the floors above, it was possible she'd lied to them. James didn't think so, but he wasn't ready to rule it out.

Deacon was out of the stairwell and stalking the hallway when the first shot was fired. Deacon spun around—James saw one of their men on the ground, and he felt his heart lurch. James leaned forward, his foot tapping on the floor. It was a nightmare he couldn't look away from.

Deacon fired back as he dove toward the wall.

"*Move in! Move in!*" Deacon instructed the men on the floors above. The element of surprise had passed.

The third man with his brother was also firing, but as Deacon turned, James saw the man up against a glass wall. *Move, move,* James thought, shaking his head. His brother obviously had the exact same thought because he started screaming out the command James could only think to himself.

Deacon was too late. The glass walls shattered, falling in on the man.

A deafening thunder of gunfire ensued and James held his breath, exhaling only when he realized it was coming from Deacon's men.

Deacon darted across the hall, pulling the man up from underneath the glass as shards fell by the side.

"Don't brush it off! Just let it fall," James heard Deacon say above the gunfire.

The shots ceased, and that palpable silence that always follows a shootout hung in the air. The moment you barely dare to breathe in for fear it wasn't over.

Deacon took a moment to look over the bleeding man and James thought, all considering, he'd fared pretty well. James did know, though, that the man would be his next patient when they returned.

"Regroup," Deacon said, assembling the group and splitting them up. Time wasn't on their side—it never had been—but if there were men on the floors below, they'd now be coming for them.

James watched as Deacon issued new commands, responding to the situation. His voice was calm and firm.

"Move quick," Deacon instructed as some of the team went to case the floor and others stood by the entrances. Two by the elevators. Two by the stairwell. It severely limited the number of men available to search, but it was a necessary precaution.

Deacon breezed from one office to another, and James noted a ladder in the hallway. He'd seen one on the floor above, too, but hadn't thought anything of it. Why would they need ladders when the offices were vacant?

"Deacon, look up," James said, wanting to see the ceiling.

His brother did, simultaneously asking, *"What is it?"*

"That ladder. Why would they need a ladder?" James asked, as a manhole came into view. He didn't need to tell his brother what to do next.

Deacon dragged the ladder into the middle of the hallway, opened the legs and climbed the rungs. He lifted the cover up with his fingertips and pushed it aside. He waited a moment, and then hauled himself up.

James stopped breathing.

"Oh, fuck!" Deacon said and James heard the panic in his voice. The same panic that was whirling like a wild storm in James' chest.

"Get out, Deacon! Get out now!" James yelled, standing up. He couldn't sit still, he couldn't simply watch this.

Explosives. Bundles of them sitting neatly on the insulation. That's what the man had been doing.

"I can't see the wires. I can't see a detonator," Deacon said, ignoring James' command.

Maybe Eric's men hadn't had time to finish setting it up, but either way, James didn't want to find out. And just because the entire building wasn't rigged didn't mean that they couldn't set off the explosives via other means.

"Deacon, get *out!*" James yelled but his voice was drowned out in a fresh wave of gunfire.

James looked on, helpless. Powerless.

He saw six men walking toward Deacon, their weapons raised. They weren't Biskup's guys. Deacon fired back, retreating into the hallway.

Wrong way, Deacon. Get out of there. Move back toward the stairwell.

But his brother had no choice; there was no way forward with six men coming at you.

"Six, northwest!" Deacon shouted as James paced back and forth the length of Maksym's bed.

When two of Eric's men went down, James paused. Glass divisions were shattering, and blood was spraying from the men like they were aerosol cans as a small war played out in Eric's building.

Two more went down and James nodded as Deacon pushed forward again.

Come on, James urged silently, so as not to distract Deacon. His brother needed to focus, to pay attention to every movement and every sound if they were going to get out of this. James wasn't sure how many of Biskup's men were down, but he thought a few, at least.

James folded his arms over his chest, his body rigid. A bullet ripped through the arm of one of Eric's men, and a second bullet landed in his forehead before he fell to the floor.

That eerie, pulsating silence followed again.

James could hear Deacon's labored breathing, but his brother didn't stop. He ran toward a fallen man and hauled him up. *"Abort! Exit through the rooftop!"*

Come on, come on, James prayed. How many more of Eric's men were in the building? Was each ceiling level loaded with explosives?

Deacon held open the stairwell door, ushering his men through.

Nine, James counted as he watched them pass by Deacon.

We've lost two.

When the last man entered the stairwell, Deacon closed the door behind him. James wished his brother had gone up first but he knew Deacon and he knew he'd never do that. Deacon always made sure his men were out.

They climbed the stairs fast but they were only up one level when James heard the familiar echo.

"Keep going!" Deacon urged, turning to fire back. He pulled the trigger twice and James heard a scream.

Deacon climbed another few stairs and then fired again when the gunfire didn't cease.

The scene was nail biting and all James could think about were the explosives. Even with Eric's men in the building, James didn't trust Eric not to blow it up.

And now he thought he knew Eric's plan. He wanted Deacon and Biskup's men captured, but, if it looked like they were going to get out, he'd call it. James knew Eric was watching this, he knew that Eric was aware of exactly what was going on. And, like himself, James also thought Eric was sitting somewhere far removed from the building.

Move, move, move, James thought, but the higher his brother climbed, the more the hairs on his arms rose. As Deacon reached the top floor, James felt his stomach contract, knotting itself into a tight ball.

"Out!" the calls started coming through James' earwig. Biskup's men that were at the front were getting out. Deacon turned his back on the gunfire and ran—sprinting up the stairs. James saw the light of the door that opened up to the rooftop.

"Go, go!" James said. His shoulders were burning with tension.

Sunlight flooded the camera and the footage bounced in motion with Deacon's feet, but James heard it before he saw it play out on the camera.

Thunderous cracks followed one after the other like dominos, and Deacon's scream pierced James' ears.

James stopped breathing as he saw an image of the sky before everything went black.

"Deacon! Deacon!" James screamed.

21

JAMES THOMAS

"Deacon!" James' throat burned like hot coals.

No response.

"Deacon!"

No response.

James covered his mouth with a shaking hand. *No!*

"Hang on!" Samuel's frantic voice came through James' earwig. *"I've got his tracker. It's showing a pulse. It's weak, but it's there."*

James sat down, fell down, on the edge of Maksym's bed.

Deacon has a pulse, but for how long? And even if he survived, what injuries will he have?

"Deacon! Deacon, wake up!" James said over and over again. It was likely—almost certain—that his brother was unconscious, his body thrown from the blast.

"The building is falling, James. There's fire and smoke everywhere," Samuel said, pushing the congested words from his mouth.

James knew he'd be looking at CCTV footage, but James couldn't draw his eyes from the black screen.

"All communication is down," Samuel said. *"Come on, Deacon. Get up, get up."*

James looked at Maksym, but the decision was already made—

and it was any easy one. Family came first, and if Maksym arrested and died before he could get back, so be it. That was a problem James would deal with later.

"I'm going to get him," James said, jogging to his makeshift bed where his kit sat beside it. He couldn't leave Deacon there. Even if his brother didn't make it, he'd do everything he could to bring his body home.

"You, you, and you," James said, kicking the men awake. "Get up and get your kits. We're going to get the boys."

The men sprung up to their feet. While they were grabbing their kits, James ran to the door of Julia's room. He put a second lock on it.

"Let's go," James said, running toward the exit. James slammed the warehouse door behind him, locking it, and sprinted toward one of the vans. He wasn't as good a driver as his brother, but he could drive fast when he needed to.

He unlocked the vehicle and they piled in.

"What's going on?" one man asked from the backseat.

"Eric blew up the building. We'll go in and get everyone who survived and bring them back here," James said as he tore out onto the street.

"I've got him," Samuel said. *"His tracker location indicates that he should be in, or on, the building next to Eric's."*

He'll be on the rooftop, James thought. If Eric's building had already fallen, the blast would've been powerful enough to catapult him to the next building. But that's also where Eric's men might look for them. James had to get to him first.

James looked at the speedometer. He wasn't sure how much faster this car could go, but he didn't take his foot off the accelerator as he weaved in and out of traffic.

"He's moving. His tracker is moving," Samuel said.

It was hard to drive at the speed James was and have a conversation, at least for him. Deacon had always seemed to do it so effortlessly.

"His pulse is too weak, though," Samuel continued. *"I don't think he's moving on his own. I think someone's got him."*

James prayed it was one of Biskup's guys, and not Eric's.

"We need some communication, Samuel," James said, swerving the car into the left lane.

"It's down. All of their devices. Mobile and earwig. I've tried all of the men."

James marveled at how Samuel was able to do so many things so quickly, even in the highly stressed state his voice indicated.

"Where are they going?" James asked.

"I'm not sure...I'm trying to map it. I've got a feeling they're going down the fire exit, but I don't have a view via CCTV."

"How far away am I?" James asked.

"Fifteen minutes. Don't crash, James."

On any other day James would've smiled at Samuel's lack of confidence in his driving skills.

James looked to the road ahead. Cars littered the lanes, but they weren't gridlocked. James concentrated on the road, making split-second decisions as he veered between the traffic.

Several minutes passed before Samuel spoke again. *"Okay, I think they're on the ground. From what I can see it's chaos there, which should help them."*

"If it's one of Biskup's guys who has him," James said.

"I'm thinking positive here. It's all we've got," Samuel replied. *"His pulse is fading, James."*

The world seemed to move in slow motion. James couldn't push the car any faster and yet he felt like they were crawling—every other driver seemed to be out for a leisurely drive while his brother's life was slipping away.

"They're moving west but I can't see them on CCTV. There's so many people, and so many vehicles and obstructions. I can't get a good view."

And they probably wouldn't until James could get on the ground. James used the car horn, demanding a path through.

"Where are they, Samuel?" James asked as the sound of sirens penetrated the glass windows of his car.

"I'm updating your GPS. I'm going to divert you away a few blocks so

that you can move around to the west side and get the car as close as possible."

"Okay," James said. His speed was slow enough now that he could follow the navigation system and not total the van.

The diversion was frustrating, but James knew Samuel was right. If Deacon's pulse was fading, he'd need to get him in the car as soon as possible.

"They've stopped. I don't know if that's good or bad," Samuel said, and James agreed.

James turned the wheel as instructed by the GPS. He could see thick clouds of smoke and he knew it was coming from Eric's building. James pressed his foot down again.

"You're so close," Samuel said. *"Hold on, Deacon..."*

"Is he moving again?" James asked.

"No."

As James drove the last few blocks, he calmed his mind and focused on the task. He wasn't rescuing his brother—he wasn't emotional. He couldn't be, not if he wanted Deacon to survive.

Think like Liam, James told himself.

He parked the van and grabbed two pistols from his kit, tucking his cell phone into his pocket. He turned to the men. "We've got a location on Deacon, but we don't think he's alone. Hopefully it's one of our guys that's got him. We'll pick them up first, and then go from there. Follow everything I say and do."

They nodded.

"Direct us, Samuel," James said as they zipped across the street, heading on foot toward Eric's burning building.

"One full block, and then he's midway along the next one," Samuel said.

James moved fast until he reached the second block. He moved across the footpath, walking close to the building, and checked to make sure his men were behind him. James slowed to a cautious pace as he neared the midway point of the block.

"Can you see him?"

"No," James said, his eyes scanning the building. He could potentially be on any level. James looked to the ground.

"I've got a blood trail," James said, retracing his steps. There was a small space between the buildings, so narrow that James' shoulders brushed against the walls. A sparkle of light caught his eye and he ran toward the broken glass on the ground. A basement window.

"He's inside," James whispered.

James kneeled on the ground, pausing to listen.

Silence.

"Wait here until I call you in," James said to his men. "Keep your back up against this wall and your weapons ready."

Protecting his hands, James climbed in through the window, dropping silently to his feet. His heart was thundering in his chest but his hand was steady and his mind focused. He surveyed the basement, which looked like some sort of utility room. His eyes searched the floor, but he could no longer see the blood trail.

James pressed his back up against a wall division, and looked at the tracker screen on his phone. Deacon couldn't be more than ninety feet from him.

James stopped breathing, but only to listen for any movement.

Silence.

He drew a breath and began edging toward the dot on the screen.

His eyes were like rovers, never stopping. He raised his weapon as he turned the corner.

Where are you? James thought as he looked at the screen. The two dots—his tracker and Deacon's—were almost joining.

James paused, assessing his options, when he noticed a small red smear on the floor.

That's why there isn't a blood trail, James thought. Someone had cleaned it up, but they'd missed one mark.

James couldn't risk calling out his name, not when he wasn't sure if it was Biskup's men or one of Eric's that was with him. James didn't even know how many men were with his brother.

James' eyes focused on a tank that had a door on it. It was the place he'd hide if he were Deacon. He did a quick calculation, estimating how many men could fit in the tank. *At least twenty,* he thought.

James retreated, moving back a little so that he could open his kit without it being heard. He withdrew a flashlight, closed his bag and slung it across his body. He inched back toward the tank. With one palm on the handle, and the flashlight in the other, he yanked open the door, using it to shield his body. He shined the light straight into the tank, blinding its occupants.

"Deacon!" James said, rushing forward.

His brother had been laid on his side next to one of Biskup's men. His eyes were closed.

James looked at both men. Their faces were covered in dried blood and black ash was smeared across their skin. When James saw why his brother was lying on his side, his stomach churned violently. The back of his head was covered in blood.

"How did you get here?" James said.

Biskup's guy answered. "Danny. He's gone to get help, to try and contact you."

That explains the blood trail being cleaned up, James thought. He knelt beside Deacon, shining the flashlight on his wound. James parted Deacon's bloody hair, looking for pieces of fractured or broken bone. He couldn't see any, but there was a lot of blood.

James turned his attention to the other man who had a laceration on his forehead, and a deep gash on his shin.

"Did anyone else make it?" James asked.

"We don't think so. Another one was on the rooftop with us, but he had no pulse. And we saw two bodies crumpled on the ground, in the passageway. I think the blast blew them off the roof." The man raised his hand to his head wound but James shook his head.

"Don't touch it, it's starting to clot," James said as he did a mental count in his head.

He'd seen at least two men go down in the building. Plus the one on the rooftop, two in the passageway, and the two men with Deacon; that was eight accounted for. Eight out of eleven. James wasn't hopeful for the remainder. But he'd rather they be dead than injured and captured. Eric would get them to talk.

James drew his cell phone and called the men outside, instructing one of them to get the car and bring it out front.

"Can you walk?" James said.

The man nodded. "Just."

James heard a noise behind him and he spun around, raising his weapon.

"Fuck am I glad to see you guys," Danny said, out of breath. "I got a burner phone," he said, holding it up, "but I guess we don't need it. Let's get out of here!"

"How did you get out so unscathed?" James asked him.

He raised an eyebrow. "I was already on the next building when it went off."

James nodded, satisfied. "Good. Let's get these men out."

James called in the supports and supervised as they gently lifted Deacon's body, carrying him toward the window. Once James had confirmation the car was ready, the supports hauled the injured men through the window.

"We need to move fast," James said. "We don't know who is watching. I'll sit in the back and start treating these wounds. Who's the best driver?"

Danny put his hand up and when no one disagreed James nodded.

"Let's go," he said, leading the pack forward. The car doors were opened and for a group that had only been training together a few days, they did well.

The injured men were lifted in safely and they were driving through the traffic within seconds.

James recruited one of Biskup's men as an assistant. The man clearly had no medical training but he could open packages and hand them to James, and that was better than nothing.

James pulled on a pair of gloves and started working on Deacon first.

"Samuel," James said. "Have you got in contact with the doctor? We need him. Today."

"He's on a flight from Zimbabwe as we speak. How does Deacon look?"

"I'm not sure yet," James said as he looked at the head injury. James took a pair of scissors and began cutting the hair around the wound so that he could at least clean it and make a proper assessment. If—*when*—Deacon woke up, he was going to be pissed about his new haircut.

James lost track of time, his concentration laser focused on treating his brother, and his head snapped up in surprise as they pulled up at the warehouse. Deacon was still unconscious but James was more confident than he'd been half an hour ago that his brother would pull through. James hadn't found any broken bone, but he couldn't be sure there weren't any fractures or other injuries that he couldn't see visually. There was also the risk of brain-tissue swelling, which James was not equipped to treat.

James had sent the doctor images—via Samuel—of Deacon's wound and he was going to advise treatment as best he could. It was far from ideal, but it was better than nothing.

"Let's get inside," James said as the back doors opened. While Biskup's men carried the patients, James checked in with Samuel.

"Have you got another location?" James asked.

"I secured it a few minutes ago. I'll send you the address."

"Thanks," James said. "And documents for the girl?"

"They'll be ready by nightfall."

"Thanks, Samuel," James said as he walked into their warehouse.

He had three patients to move, a hostage, and an entire warehouse to pack up. James took a deep breath, staving off feeling overwhelmed. They had to start moving now. If any one of the unaccounted men had been captured by Eric, it was only a matter of time before the warehouse location was disclosed. James intended to be long gone by the time they came.

"Okay, come in," James said, commanding his men. "There are three men unaccounted for and we can't rule out the possibility that

Eric's men will find them—if they're alive. I've secured a new location. Start packing. We've got one hour to clear out."

There were many things about Biskup's men that James didn't like, but there was one thing that he loved: their ability to follow orders. The boys moved with unprecedented speed and, as James went back to his patients, he estimated they'd clear out before the hour was up.

It was a small win, but James hung onto it.

22

MAK ASHWOOD

They sat side-by-side, surrounded by enough products to start a cosmetic store. Mak glanced sideways at Cami. She wasn't James Thomas, but she was proving to be a good wedding date.

"When was the last time you had your hair and makeup done for an event that wasn't work related?" Mak asked.

Cami seemed to think it through. Mak assumed it had been a while.

"Prom," Cami finally said with a laugh. "It's not that I don't like having it done, it's just that I rarely have an event worth making the effort for."

"You went to prom?" Mak asked, not letting the opportunity pass for another glimpse inside Cami's past.

"Yes, Mak. I went to prom like most ordinary teenagers," she responded with a sneaky grin.

"I'd like to hear more about your prom."

Cami rolled her eyes. "I'm sure you would, but unfortunately we're running out of time." She looked to the woman curling her hair. "Are we almost done?"

"Just another few minutes," the woman said, as fluently as she was turning the straightening irons through Cami's hair.

Cami looked down at her watch. Mak's hair and makeup was done, so she went to her bedroom to get changed. She threw her robe onto the bed and slipped into a mint-colored, asymmetric gown. The color made her eyes pop and she was glad her makeup artist had been so insistent on the pink lip. She sat on the edge of the bed, strapped on her jeweled gold heels, and then did one last check in the mirror, smoothing her hair into place.

She'd never been a woman to dress for a man—she'd always dressed in whatever made her feel good, and feel confident. But, as she looked at the woman in the mirror, she wondered what James would think if he were looking back at her. She'd seen him in a suit, and it was a sight that had made her insides tighten. Unfortunately, she would never know what he thought because he wasn't coming. Mak hadn't even heard from him for three days.

He'd been gone for weeks now, and the nights she'd spent alone had given her a lot of time to think. She'd spent much of that time thinking about his lack of phone calls. At first she'd accepted his reasoning—that he was with Biskup and he had to be on his game, not on the phone and distracted by his girlfriend. But, even doing what Mak thought he did—and that was still an assumption—she didn't believe that he was flat-out busy every minute of every day. That he couldn't take one minute to call her before he closed his eyes for the evening.

Mak thought there was another explanation for his lack of communication when he was away. On the night they'd been chased by the Hummers she'd seen it in his eyes. She'd seen a man she didn't recognize. And when he was away, she wondered if he was the man she'd seen in the car. Adopting another personality was a mental strategy she used in the courtroom and it helped her to think in a certain way, to make decisions differently. When James Thomas was away, Mak didn't think he was James Thomas—she thought he was someone else entirely. The million-dollar question was: *Who was he?*

"Mak? Are you ready?" Cami said, opening the door.

"Ready," Mak said, picking up her clutch bag and putting her phone and lipstick inside before following Cami out. Mak had arranged the gift; or, rather, had told Samuel, and he'd arranged the gift. Mak couldn't stop thinking about James' comments regarding their accounting system, either. Mak was certain that wasn't one of the parts of Thomas Security that was run legally.

"You look very nice, Cami," Mak said, giving her a nod of approval. Cami pulled off a pantsuit better than anyone Mak knew, although Mak didn't think it was the only reason she'd worn it—it was also practical.

Cami grinned as she ushered Mak into the elevator and down into the car.

The practice of detouring was such a normal occurrence now that Mak no longer paid attention, nor did she try and predict the routes they would take. That had seemed like fun at first, but after daily commutes to and from work, the fun of it quickly wore thin.

Instead, Mak liked to watch the people on the street. Of all the things she missed most, it was just to walk the streets of New York and to be amongst the people, soaking up the energy of the city that was like no other. *One day,* Mak thought, but she didn't dare to add *soon*—especially given her new case.

When they arrived at the hotel where the ceremony and reception were to take place, Mak was ushered in through lines of security —security that for once was not related to her case. Mak was aware that it was likely that the only reason she could attend today, especially without James or Deacon, was that this was Jayce Tohmatsu's wedding. A family of gangsters, an assassinated brother, and a bank account with plenty of zeros meant that this wedding would be highly guarded. Mak didn't feel any unease, though. When she'd first hired Thomas Security, Mak didn't think she would ever get used to it. But she had—without even realizing it.

Cami and Tom flanked Mak as they walked into the hall where the ceremony would take place. She almost stumbled on her feet. She'd never seen anything like it. The walls were like vertical gardens and flowers hung from the ceiling. Mak couldn't see a speck of paint in the room—it was the floral equivalent of the Sistine Chapel.

"Oh, wow," Mak whispered, taking it all in. She turned to Cami.

"Had you seen this?"

"No. I had seen the plans, because we approved everything and all of the suppliers, but this is far beyond what I imagined," she said. But Cami's eyes weren't mesmerized like Mak's—they were alert and focused. Cami was on the job. "We're seated near the front with your family."

Mak followed Cami, looking for familiar faces. She smiled and waved at a few of Zahra's friends she'd met on various occasions. Her parents were already seated and she snuck up on her mother, wrapping her arms around her.

"Hello," Mak said, kissing her cheek.

"Mak!" her mother said, turning to embrace her. "Oh, you look so lovely. And so do you, Cami."

"As do you, Mrs. Ashwood," Cami said giving Mak's mother a sweet grin.

If only she really knew, Mak thought, grinning at her inside joke. Mak's mother knew Cami was her bodyguard, but Mak doubted she had any idea what Cami was capable of. Mak didn't either, truthfully, but she had a fair indication of her talents. Talents that would terrify Mak's mother.

"Hi, Dad," Mak said, giving him a big hug.

"We've missed you," he said in a low voice.

"I've missed you too. I've been okay, just hanging out with these two." Mak nodded toward Cami and then Tom.

Mak noticed the tissues in her mother's hand. "Oh, look at you! Don't tell me you're starting already?"

"I can't help it," she said with sparkling eyes. "I just get so emotional, it's so beautiful."

Mak saw Jayce walking toward them, wearing a beaming grin.

"She's going to be bawling through your ceremony," Mak said as she moved forward to greet him.

Jayce's head tilted back as he laughed. "Remind me not to look at you then," he joked to Mak's mother. He kissed Mak's cheek. "It's good to see you again."

"How are you feeling?" Mak asked. "Are you nervous?"

"No. I'm excited." Jayce's smile grew. "I spoke to James a few hours ago, he called to wish us well."

Mak raised one eyebrow. "He did?" she asked as a flame of irritation flickered. It had been days since she'd heard from him and yet he had no problems calling Jayce?

"When *are* we going to meet this man?" Mak's mother interjected.

"I don't know," Mak said, holding out her empty palms. "He's busy. He works hard."

"He's always *working*." Jayce gave Mak a knowing grin. "I need to keep moving, I'll leave you to it," Jayce said, waving at another guest who had just entered.

"He is so handsome," Mak's mother whispered and Mak shushed her. He'd only moved to the row behind them. Cami chuckled.

They had a few minutes until the ceremony was scheduled to start, so Mak said hello to the familiar faces she recognized, and also greeted Jayce's father.

Today—and maybe only because it was his son's wedding—he seemed like such a big softie. Mak couldn't imagine him as one of the Tokyo's most powerful gangsters, but there was a time when he had been. Mr. Tohmatsu's twin brother, Haruki, stood next to him. Mak introduced herself.

Unlike Jayce's father, Mak immediately sensed that this man was powerful. "I've been looking forward to meeting you," Haruki said.

Mak pressed her lips together. It wasn't the response she'd been expecting. "You have been?"

"Yes, I heard about your recent case. I hope I never end up on your witness stand," he said, laughing at his joke. Mak took it as a compliment. Haruki continued. "And... I also heard you're dating James Thomas. Now that must be a *very* interesting story."

"It's not, really," Mak said with a smile. He might be powerful, but she knew his game, and she wasn't playing it.

"It's a shame that James isn't here," Haruki Tohmatsu said. "I would've liked to have caught up with him again."

Mak nodded, not letting her expression falter. Mak wondered how well James knew Haruki. If James had known Kyoji Tohmatsu well, then she supposed he also knew Haruki well. And again she thought that relationship fell into the illegal section of Thomas Security's dealings.

"Busy working," Mak said, and the twins' eyes crinkled in unison. It was unfortunately a joke they all understood.

The music changed and Jayce's father touched her arm. "I think we need to take our seats. It was nice to meet you, Mak."

"And you both," Mak said, bowing her head.

She joined her parents and took her seat, scanning her eyes over the program.

When guests began to stand, Mak felt a rush of excitement. She did love weddings, even if she didn't have such fond memories of her own.

"Oh, look, there's Maya," Mak's mother said and Mak leaned around her, seeing her sister walking down the aisle. She looked beautiful in her silver gown that sashayed as she walked.

Maya gave them a big smile as she passed by and Mak saw her wink at Jayce as she took her place at the front.

Jemma followed closely behind and Mak almost had to look twice —it could've been Zahra.

When hushed whispers floated through the room, Mak knew Zahra had made her entrance—and Jayce's face confirmed it. His chest rose and his eyes welled. Mak wondered if he might need to borrow some of her mother's tissues.

Mak turned her attention back to the aisle as Zahra was approaching and Mak wondered if she'd ever seen a more beautiful bride. Her hair was pinned at the nape of her neck with a few loose curls framing her heart-shaped face. Her eyes dazzled like emeralds and her strapless gown enhanced her tall, lean figure. But Mak thought it was something else that made it impossible to draw her eyes away: it was the happiness radiating from her.

The congregation sat as the Buddhist priest began the service. The ceremony was an interesting mix of Buddhist and Christian traditions but despite that it didn't seem overly religious. Nor was it long. In fifteen minutes they were husband and wife.

Mr. and Mrs. Tohmatsu.

The guests cheered as the couple kissed for the first time and when Mak saw the look in their eyes, a previous comment of Jayce's came to mind. He'd said, "We've both made so many mistakes in the past, there was a day when I never thought we would make it."

Mak thought of James, and she too wondered if they would make it. If they would make it as a couple, and if they would make it out of this situation alive. The deal with Biskup had created a well of anxiety within her. James said it was a good thing, but Mak wondered if it was good because it was their only option—their last chance.

When Mak tasted blood she realized she'd been biting her lip. She dabbed a tissue, glad her pink lipstick would hide it. Cami gave her a sideways look but didn't comment.

Zahra and Jayce wore matching dazzling smiles as they began their exit.

Mak's mother sighed. "Oh, that was so lovely."

"It was a very nice ceremony," Mak agreed.

Maya quickly said hello as she passed by.

"Did I tell you that we've hired a cabin for the weekend of your father's birthday?" Mak's mother said.

"No, you didn't," Mak said, her gaze flickering to Cami.

"Oh, don't worry, it's all been approved by Thomas Security. It's instead of the Bahamas trip we had planned to take. We know traveling at the moment creates a security risk, so we'll go on that holiday once your case has settled down. James has arranged for two security teams to accompany us and it's only a few hours from the city, hidden in the mountains. It looks amazing," Mak's mother said.

"Good, I'm glad to hear that everything has been organized for you," Mak said, looking directly at Cami.

James seemed capable of organizing a lot of things lately, except a single phone call to let his girlfriend know he was alive and well. Mak forced herself to swallow her anger.

Cami cleared her throat. "If you're ready, we'll take you all downstairs. Drinks have been organized while the wedding party has their photos."

23

JAMES THOMAS

With one hand on the steering wheel, James' eyes darted to the clock on the dashboard. He then checked the rearview mirror. No tail. He was alert and more cautious than ever. His life had become an invisible juggling act, and every ball was in the air. All he needed was for one to drop and his fight would be over.

But it's not over yet.

And after the past few weeks, he had wanted to see Mak more than ever. He wanted to hold her. To feel her. To remember what he was fighting for. But he'd been so consumed with the situation that he didn't have the emotional space to even make a personal phone call. He couldn't afford a single distraction. He couldn't let himself want—dream—of being somewhere he couldn't be. He had to be focused, and the best way he knew how to do that was to be a man that Mak didn't know.

Even with Biskup's support, they hadn't yet been able to get the upper edge. They'd evened the playing field for sure, but with two equal forces, the only guarantee was that there would be blood.

Deacon had been moved to a makeshift hospital in their safe house, but he was recovering well. It had been a close call—too close.

Maksym was also there with him, as was the man with the leg wound. All were expected to make a fair recovery in time. But it was time James didn't have and Biskup wasn't relenting on the time frame. He had, however, dedicated more men to James. Men that were waiting for him in London. James hoped they were resting, because when he returned he was going to train them until they were too exhausted to stand.

11:30 p.m.

James pulled into the underground car park and into one of the parking bays his company had been dedicated for the evening. He took the stairs up to the lobby and collected a room key from one of his men. Unfortunately, James wasn't here for the wedding—he was here on business. After what had happened in the past few days, James had made a worst-case contingency plan. He couldn't predict what Eric was going to do next, but he knew it was going to be something big. Eric had to redeem himself, and a desperate man was a dangerous man.

James took the elevator to room 902, and then slid the room key across the electronic lock. When he opened the door he saw Haruki Tohmatsu sitting at the table by the window. He turned to look at him.

"James Thomas, your call was very unexpected," Haruki said, and James noted he'd poured himself a glass of whisky.

"Thank you for meeting me," James said, sitting down. "How was the wedding?"

"Interesting... I met your girlfriend."

"I assumed you would've," James said, wondering how that introduction had played out.

Haruki gave an odd grin. "I don't think she's intimidated by me."

The corner of James' lips turned up ever so slightly. "Don't be offended. She's not intimidated by me, either."

Haruki chuckled. "Make sure you add that part to my bedtime story. Now, tell me why we're meeting here when the wedding is upstairs. I assume you're not going at all, dressed like that?"

"I'm not here for the wedding, no. In fact, I'm leaving

Manhattan again in a few hours. I came to see you," James said, folding his hands on the table. He didn't want to have to ask Haruki for help. Not again. But he had to have a backup plan if he failed.

James continued. "There may come a time—in the next few weeks, maybe—that I need your help. And I may not be able to come to you to ask, or even make a telephone call, so I'm asking in advance."

Haruki raised one eyebrow.

James knew he had to tell him some details of the situation, otherwise there wasn't even a chance that Haruki would help him.

"Mak's husband—Eric—disappeared thirteen years ago. In that time, he's become the leader of a radical, religious cult that is very wealthy and very far-reaching. But that's not the whole problem... This same man, as it turns out, is the man that has been hunting me for the past several years."

James gave it a minute to sink in.

Haruki didn't try and hide his shock.

"I don't exactly know why they're hunting me, but it has something to do with my family. Family that I've never met. Eric is about as insane as they come, and he's been able to form an alliance with the Russians—with whom you know I have a troubled relationship. I've countered this by creating a relationship with one of Eric's enemies: Alexandr Biskup."

Haruki whistled, shaking his head. "You've started a war. A war that I will not get involved in."

"I'm not asking you to get involved in that. I need something else," James said, his abdomen contracting with unease. "I want to make provisions for Mak if Deacon and I don't walk out of this alive."

Haruki narrowed his eyes. "What do you mean, exactly?"

James took a deep breath. "If Samuel loses contact with us, I'm asking you to help Cami to protect Mak. It will be best if she's taken out of New York for a while—hidden—to buy Cami some time to devise Mak's security plan going forward."

James wanted to hide her somewhere they'd never think to look, and somewhere that was highly guarded. Haruki's compound on the outskirts of Tokyo.

"I'm not in the business of babysitting, James," Haruki said.

"I'm asking you to potentially get in that business...as a once-off."

The men locked eyes, and James was glad Haruki couldn't see his inner turmoil.

Finally, Haruki said, "I would want something in return."

James exhaled. Haruki would consider it.

"I'm aware of your current problems with the rivals. I have some information that would help," James said.

Haruki cast a challenging stare. "And how do you know about such things?"

"Just because I don't live there anymore doesn't mean I'm not watching what's going on. I have eyes everywhere. It's in my best interests to keep up to date with international affairs."

Haruki held the rim of his glass with his fingertips, turning it slowly. "How long would you expect me to guard your girlfriend? I will not have this war brought onto my ground."

"A maximum of six months. That will give Cami and Samuel sufficient time to make preparations. Cami may need to come and go, and when she is gone, I request Haruto be with Mak—in addition to her security teams. You will also be housing them. There will be no reason for Eric or Biskup to look for her in Tokyo, especially since Samuel will lead them elsewhere."

"And her family?"

"I'm making alternate arrangements for them. I don't want them all together, for many reasons—primarily that it's easier to find a group than to find one person. And they are a large family."

"Mak doesn't know about this, does she?" Haruki asked.

"Not yet, no. I'm trying not to worry her at this stage."

"Is there a chance you'll get out of this alive?"

"There's always a chance," James said, leaving it at that.

Haruki looked thoughtful and James made a conscious effort to keep his body relaxed even though the tension was making his temple pulse.

"The information isn't enough. I want something else," Haruki said, clasping his hands together.

"Name your price," James said. He was ready to do anything to make this deal.

"There is a man I want taken care of—Nao Tanaka. If you're sticking your nose in my business, then you probably know why. I can't have it linked back to me, so I want you to take care of it—once you've cleaned up your own mess."

James did know why, and he also knew the extent of Tanaka's security. It wouldn't be an easy task, but compared with what James was currently facing, it was doable. James held out his hand. "You have my word."

Haruki gave a cunning smile and shook James' hand.

Another deal. Another devil.

James sat on Mak's couch, waiting patiently for her to get home. With his worst-case scenario sorted, he felt like he could breathe again. He'd used the hours since his meeting with Haruki to catch up with Samuel and Deacon, check in with Biskup, and create training drills for his men to practice tomorrow until he returned. He'd not wasted a minute, but there was one more thing left to do tonight.

Mak was on her way home now and James had been watching the time. She'd arrive any minute and for the next few hours he could allow himself to be James Thomas. His body was aching with exhaustion, aching from the tension coiled inside it, and all he wanted was her.

He heard movement in the foyer and then the door opened. Cami walked in first, giving him a smile, and Mak followed in behind. She took a moment to see him and then blinked twice, as if she were seeing things.

He smiled the first true smile he had in weeks. "Hey," he said, getting up and walking across the room.

"Hi," she said. He detected an icy edge to her voice. He didn't know if it was surprise, irritation, or both.

Cami nodded and then ushered the security team outside.

James stopped in front of Mak, taking her hands. "I'm sorry I didn't make it to the wedding. And I'm sorry I haven't called."

"But you had time to call Jayce this morning," Mak said.

Irritation, James decided. "That was business, not personal. You're the only one I make personal calls to, Mak, and it's hard to make personal calls right now."

"Why is it hard?" she asked, searching his eyes.

James squeezed her hands. "I haven't called you because I can't risk the distraction. Jayce doesn't distract me, but you do. You make me want to be somewhere else, to pretend that our problems don't exist and that everything will work itself out. I need to be focused when I'm working. You're my motivation, but I can't be wishing I was with you and not paying attention to what I'm doing."

He wove his fingers between hers and brought them to his chest, forcing her to take a step closer.

"When did you get here?"

"A few hours ago—I had a business meeting," James said. "I can't stay long."

She pressed her lips together, nodding. She looked him over.

"No more injuries," James said, giving her a small smile.

Mak sighed. "If I hear your voice, I know you're okay," she said, tilting her chin up to look at him. "When I don't hear from you, I'm left wondering—and worrying. You could send a text message, at least," Mak said.

"I'll try, I promise," James said, meaning every word. "You have no idea how much I miss you." He drew her in.

She inhaled deeply, her chest pressing against his. The heat of her body, wrapped tight in his arms, released a sense of happiness in him that he'd forgotten in the dark days of the past few weeks.

"I love you, Mak," he whispered, kissing the crown of her head.

"I love you, too. That's what makes this so hard... I'm scared of losing you," she said, and James lifted her chin.

"We're going to get through this," he said, determination rippling through him.

She nodded, but James wasn't sure if she believed him. He wasn't confident in his own words, but he was confident he'd never give up —not when he had her to come home to.

He looked her up and down, getting a better look. "You look beautiful," James said. "I like this dress...a lot."

Mak finally cracked a grin. "Thank you."

She stood up on tiptoes and wrapped her arms around his neck. He lifted her into his arms, bringing her lips to his. Her kiss was slow and tender and made his head spin.

James moaned. "Mak, I'm only here for a few hours." He didn't want to walk in the door, have sex, and then walk out the door again.

"I want you," she whispered, and James' resolve wavered. He began rationalizing the time in his mind. Half an hour for sex, one-and-a-half hours to talk.

"I want you, too. I just don't want you to feel differently when I leave."

"I miss you. I miss the intimacy. I miss everything," she said.

James lowered her to the ground and closed his eyes as her soft hands slipped underneath his sweater. His skin burned where she touched. He couldn't fight it—he didn't want to.

His hands found her zipper and began to peel her dress off. He pulled it down to her waist, ripping his lips away from hers, only to latch onto her nipples. He pushed her dress to the floor.

She tilted her head back, moaning, and James doubted they were going to make it to the bedroom with any clothes on. The kitchen table was looking incredibly appealing.

James lifted her and she tightened her legs around his waist as he carried her toward it. He sat her down on the edge of the table. He stepped between them, running his fingers along her inner thighs. As his fingers brushed over her slick folds, their eyes locked in a blazing gaze.

She reached for his sweater, tugging it up and over his head. When she went to discard it on the floor he quickly grabbed it.

"I'll be needing that," he said, watching her response.

"You will?"

James bit his lip, and in one swift move her had her pinned to the table and her arms secured over her head, her wrists bonded with his sweater.

"Do I want to know how you're so good at that?" she asked breathily.

Her breasts flattened against his chest as his teeth grazed over her collarbone.

"No."

Mak moaned, but James didn't think for a second that his answer was responsible for it.

He planted soft kisses all over her skin. When he got to her navel he noticed her body trembling and he grinned with satisfaction.

He grabbed her thighs, roughly pushing her legs apart until he felt her muscles resist. She gasped, and when she tried to lower her arms he pinched her nipple. She gasped again.

"Keep your arms there," James demanded.

He watched her until she rested them overhead once more. James lowered himself to his knees—the table was the perfect height.

She was spread before him, and even in the dim light he could see how wet she was.

"Stay still," James instructed, knowing full well she wouldn't be able to.

He ran his tongue over her clitoris and she wiggled beneath him. He pinched her nipple. "Stay still," he repeated.

A frustrated groan slipped from her lips.

James thrust two fingers deep inside her and she bucked her hips. He pinched her nipple harder and she shrieked.

"James," Mak moaned.

"Do you want me to stop?" he asked.

"No," she panted as his fingers continued to pleasure her.

He flicked his tongue again. Her toes curled and she tried to close her legs, but she stopped the moment he pinched.

He continued to pleasure her, and she continued to wriggle beneath him. His hand was coated in her wetness.

"Please, please," she begged, but James didn't relent.

He monitored the way she arched her back, the panting of her voice, the intensity of her trembling and he brought her to the edge and back again over and over. His cock was throbbing in his pants, begging to be buried inside her.

"Please," she groaned, and this time James gave in because he wasn't strong enough to deny her. Not when he was so desperate to have her.

He let go of her nipple, scraping his nails over her tight abdomen. He licked her clitoris, soft and gentle, while his fingers penetrated deep within her. Her body went rigid before she screamed so loudly James wondered if Tom heard her in the foyer. Her body quivered and he kissed her inner thighs, her soft skin silken against his cheek.

Once her body calmed, James stood, leaning over her once more. He dove his tongue into her mouth.

"You taste so damn good," he growled. His hands were rough on her skin, roaming it, creating a map of her body—one that he'd remember forever.

He was breathless, his chest burning, but still he couldn't bring himself to tear his lips away from hers. She was too tempting, too desirable. Everything about her made him want more. James pulled back, fighting to get some air into his lungs.

Naked, beneath him, her blond hair was spread over the mahogany wood, and her eyes looked translucent. And, rare for one of the moments they were together, her eyes weren't searching his. She was in the moment.

"Stay there," James said as he darted toward Mak's bedroom. He took a condom from her bedside table and ripped it open as he returned to her. He rolled it on, noticing the sexy grin on her lips.

He grabbed her hips, flipping her over. She shrieked as he steadied her onto her stomach. Her arms were stretched out in front of her—still bound—and her hips raised. James kissed the soft pads of her ass and she shuddered. He couldn't hold on any longer.

He guided his cock in, his eyes rolling back in his head as her hot, wet vagina swallowed him.

"Oh, God," James said as he pushed his hips back and forth. His nails bit into her skin, gripping her hips. Her moans sounded like whimpers and he opened his eyes. "Mak? Are you okay?" he asked, pausing.

"Don't stop," she begged.

The palm of his hand circled her warm skin, and when she pushed back into him, he slapped it hard enough to make his hand sting.

She inhaled sharply, and then let out a guttural moan.

"Does that feel good?" James said, pushing deeper inside her.

"Yes," she said. "Again."

He grinned at her instruction, and he was more than happy to oblige. He warmed up her skin, and then two cracking sounds echoed through the apartment. Mak shuddered and her hands balled into fists.

She squeezed around him and James swore as he fought to stave off his orgasm, but the red hand mark on her bare skin was distracting his mind, and it was a battle he was losing—fast. His legs felt weightless, his heart was beating rapidly, and his body was burning like he had a fever.

James leaned over her, forcing open her hands and weaving his fingers between hers. A dull throb in his arm was persistent, but not nearly powerful enough to make him stop. He leaned his elbows on the table carrying his weight and buried his face in the crook of her neck. He sucked on her skin, tantalized by the thin layer of saltiness.

"I love you," he whispered.

James thrust harder as she rocked back into him. He waited until her body trembled again and he knew she was on the brink of climax.

"Come with me," she moaned, and his last morsel of control slipped. With two hard thrusts he threw his head back as the world went black and ecstasy ripped through him.

James' chest heaved and his legs threatened to collapse beneath him. He leaned on his left shoulder, mindful of Mak and the position her arms were in. She turned her head to face him and he kissed the tip of her nose, smiling.

He gave a long, content sigh. After the past few weeks he'd needed that release. Eventually, he stood up and untied her wrists. He rubbed them, and massaged her shoulders, and she grinned the entire time.

"Come on," he said, picking her up and carrying her toward her bedroom.

24

JAMES THOMAS

James laid her on the bed and turned on the gas fireplace. He went to the bathroom, cleaned up, and then snuggled in next to her.

He swept the hair off of her cheek, tucking it behind her ear.

"I've missed you. I miss you every day," she said.

James felt a pull deep in his chest and he cupped her cheek. "I feel the same way. I don't want to leave you, but I need to."

"What time are you going?" Mak asked, and James heard the trepidation in her voice. She didn't want to hear the answer she knew was coming.

He looked at his watch. "A little over an hour," he said, wishing he could give her the answer she wanted. The answer he wanted.

Her fingertips drew circles over his bicep. Her eyes flickered to his wounded arm. "It looks better," she said, and then added, "I mean, it's not weeping—even after that."

"It's healing," James said, slipping one leg between hers and drawing her in. She'd always fit perfectly in his arms. "Did you have fun at the wedding?"

"Yes, it was a really nice day. They look very happy." She paused. "I'm certain I never looked like that on my wedding day."

As selfish as it was, James hoped she hadn't. He only wanted her to look at him that way. "Does it make you want to get married again one day?"

She pressed her lips together. "Are you asking me to marry you?"

James chuckled. "That wasn't a proposal right then, but I would marry you, some day in the future—if that's what you wanted."

"What do you want, James Thomas?"

"I don't need a piece of paper. It means little to me; perhaps that's because of my past. I don't have a birth certificate, and I don't need nor want one. The same for a marriage certificate. But I'm not opposed to it."

"Would you get married as James Thomas?" Mak asked.

"That would be a little tricky...James Thomas doesn't exist on paper." He watched her response very carefully.

"Oh. So you don't have any identification as James Thomas?"

"None," James said.

"Okay. Who owns Thomas Security?"

"Well, technically Thomas Security doesn't exist on paper, either. At least not in that company name."

Mak's lips pressed together. "You're never going to run out of secrets, are you?"

"Unlikely."

She buried her forehead into his chest, groaning. "You're lucky you're so good in bed," she said and James' chest rumbled as he laughed.

He rolled onto his back and pulled her on top of him.

"It's time for your question of the week," he said. "What do you want to know?" He'd originally dreaded this requirement, but now he was beginning to enjoy it. He hadn't anticipated how much he'd like sharing the details of his past—as much as he could.

"I'd like to know what your first job was," she said.

An easy question. "At fourteen I started washing cars to earn some pocket money," James said. "I was good at it, too."

Mak smiled. "I have no doubt you were... What was your first real job? Career job."

James made a split decision, and decided to tell her the truth. He knew she'd already made the assumption, and given it was the beginning of his career, there was little harm in sharing it. Lots of men joined the army, but not many had progressed like he had.

"I joined the military as soon as I was of legal age," James said and she gave a small nod.

"What did you do in the military?"

James grinned. "That's three questions. And I didn't come home with any fresh bullet wounds."

"You've been away a few weeks, Thomas," Mak said.

"And I've already answered two," he said, squeezing her hand until she wriggled.

"Just one more," she said. "You grew up without parents, but did you have anyone who guided you? Someone who cared for you?"

"I did," James said, thinking of the one lady who'd cared for him in his teenage years. "Sister Francine. She was good to me. She was the one who encouraged me to join the military."

James had checked on her every now and then—via Samuel—since he'd been in hiding. She'd grown old, but she was well and still working at the orphanage. She was the closest thing to a mother he'd ever had. Sister Francine might have a heart attack, though, if she ever found out about the man James had become.

James tightened his arms around Mak and buried his face in the hollow of her neck. His lips rested on her thin, delicate skin. He closed his eyes.

James didn't count the minutes that passed, but he knew when their time together was drawing near an end.

"I need to go," James said softly. He had to get back to London. To Deacon. To Maksym. To Biskup's army.

And to Eric.

He had to find Eric—soon. If he didn't fix their problems, this could be their last night together.

James tucked the sheets under Mak's chin and then went to the bathroom. He showered with lightning speed, dressed in his standard uniform and grabbed his phone and charger from her bedside table, throwing them in his overnight bag.

She went to get up, presumably to say goodbye, but James shook his head. "Stay in bed. Get some sleep," he said as he walked around to her side of the bed. He sat down on the edge, pulling her into his arms.

"I love you, James," Mak said

James wished she knew how much those words meant to him. While Deacon, Cami and Samuel had become a family, and James was sure they all loved one another, they didn't exactly go around saying it. And given his lack of biological family, Mak was the first person to ever utter those words to him and mean it, and that made them even more special.

He cupped her face. "I love you. I'll call you soon. And text even sooner, I promise."

"Be careful, please," she whispered as he gave her one final kiss.

He wasn't ready to say goodbye. And he didn't think he would be in fifty years to come, either. He hoped to grow into an old, wrinkly man with Mak by his side, but his chances of that weren't looking great.

James closed Mak's door behind him. He walked through the living room and saw Cami sitting in the security room. She looked up.

"Your car is ready and breakfast is on the passenger seat," Cami said. "Tom's going to drive you and then come back here. How are you really holding up?"

James shook his head. "I'm worried about Eric's next move..." They'd made a mockery of the worship and James knew Eric would've had to answer to that—though to whom he didn't know—but he did know that Eric would retaliate in some way. He'd have to do something drastic to regain the confidence of those he led. James couldn't possibly predict what that would be; all he could do was to have Biskup's men prepared to respond when the time came. They were getting crash courses in espionage, in hostage retrieval, in detonating weapons. They wouldn't be masters, but James hoped they would be good enough. All of that was provided they didn't find Eric first—which James fully intended to do.

She wrapped her arms around him. "Watch your back, James. And Deacon's."

James returned the embrace. "I will. Take care of her," James said.

Cami nodded. "She's been different since she's been in this apartment. It was a good idea to move her—even though her sanity wasn't the premeditator. She's happier here, in her own space. You can go away and not have to worry about her. She's handling it better than most clients."

James had thought that all through the short telephone conversations and the time they'd spent together last night, but it was nice to hear Cami confirm it. It was one less thing he had to worry about.

James slung his bag over his shoulder as he walked toward the door. It was time to get back to business.

James tried to sleep on the flight back to London but, as exhausted as he was, stress had obliterated any chance of sleep.

As soon as he landed he'd gone straight to their safe house, where the doctor was currently treating their three patients. The doctor was a contact of Samuel's: he performed charity work and was a freelance doctor for Thomas Security.

James' medical knowledge usually allowed him to keep himself—and others—alive, but he didn't have the knowledge or expertise for ongoing treatment. Especially wound management. A flesh wound—yes. But more extensive treatment required a professional. The Medical School of Life James had attended wasn't up to par.

James let himself in, finding the doctor in his brother's room.

Deacon was awake and James didn't hear his brother's comment, but it made the doctor smile.

"You're looking much better," James said, walking in as both sets of eyes turned to him.

"Hey, brother."

"How is he doing?" James asked the doctor.

"Good. The swelling has stabilized. Rest is what he needs going forward."

James nodded, sitting on the end of the bed. "And the others?"

"Maksym is stable enough to move now, so we can go ahead with the transfer."

Good, James thought. Biskup wanted Maksym transferred back to a hospital in Prague and James agreed that was the best option. He would be protected there, and they could see to the ongoing care he needed.

"Leg wound?"

The doctor shrugged his shoulders. "It'll take some time to heal, but the bone wasn't damaged, so he'll make a full recovery. You are all very lucky... you in particular," he said, looking at Deacon. "It's a miracle you're even alive, let alone recovering so well."

Deacon gave a lopsided grin. "Depends on how you define lucky, I suppose. Thanks, Doc."

The man said goodbye, presumably returning to his other patients, and James looked at his brother.

"I can't stop thinking about Eric's wife," Deacon said. "I had assumed— incorrectly—that Eric had kept her in the dark about his life in Saratani. Much like he'd done with Mak. But she's not—she's very much a part of it." He shook his head in seeming disgust. "What do you think her connection is to Carl Junez?"

James didn't have an answer, as much as he'd asked himself the same question. "I was watching her closely at the worship ceremony...she didn't show a shred of remorse for the sacrifices. She looked to enjoy it, just as much as her husband. I think Eric found his perfect match."

Deacon scrunched up his face, shaking his head. "I feel for their daughter. She's got no hope of having a normal life."

James agreed, although it wasn't a thought he'd given any consideration to before Deacon mentioned it. Children were something he tried to block from his mind—especially after Paris.

He asked himself again why Eric and Pavel had been in Angela's house. Had they found out about her pregnancy? How? The clinic details had been printed on the ultrasound image James had found, and Samuel had since destroyed all evidence. Had they been too late? Had someone else been watching her, even before James knew she was informing on him? James' stomach soured as he thought of what Mak would think of him if she knew. He blocked that thought before the shame crippled him.

"Samuel's working hard on Eric's wife, digging up whatever he can," James said. "She might be our best chance at finding him. And Carl Junez." Or whoever he was. "I keep trying to put myself in Eric's shoes, to try and predict his next move. He's going to do something big—he has to after we made a mockery of the worship. It's a sacred event—to them at least—and that can't go unpunished." James sighed. "Maksym should've shot him in the foot immediately and disabled him—instead he took a second to gloat, and it was a second too long. So now Eric knows Biskup is involved, which is something I would've preferred to keep quiet."

"Are you worried about Mak?" Deacon asked.

"I don't know... I don't know what Eric is waiting for with her. He's had thirteen years to come for her, so if that's his intention, why has it taken so long? I just don't understand it. But, I do think our assumptions were correct—the man he is now is not the same man Mak or Ben had known. Sure, his tendencies had always been there, but he's completely radicalized now. The worship ceremony was horrifying evidence of that."

Deacon's lips wiggled back and forth and then he puffed out a sigh. "I agree. And that's the problem: we're trying to understand a madman."

"If he makes any attempt to take Mak, I think it's an attempt to get to us."

"Maybe he'll retaliate against Biskup," Deacon said. "We can't rule that out. And, currently, Mak is more protected even than Biskup. It would be easier to target him, and I think Eric would know that."

"And if he gets to Biskup, or one of his guys, Eric will count on the nonexistent loyalty between us and Biskup. He'll get the information out of them. He'll get our descriptions. He'll find out who we are. And then we've got a monstrosity of a problem—one bigger than the ones we already have. The longer we can keep my identity concealed from Eric, the better. He is going to be very fucking angry when he realizes *Liam Smith* is dating his wife."

Deacon gave a chocked laugh. "The universe has a sick sense of humor."

James' phone chimed and he drew it from his pocket. He unlocked it, and a photograph flashed up. A photograph of Eric's wife kneeling on the ground, surrounded by children who looked to be of African descent. A second message came through.

Meet Marianne Schiev. On location in Nigeria as part of a humanitarian mission. It's the only thing I've found, but I'm digging.

Deacon, too, was looking at his phone. "Humanitarian mission?" Deacon scoffed. "She'd do more for humanity by putting a bullet in her husband, and refusing to participate in rituals that sacrifice the lives of unwilling participants for nonexistent gods. What a fucking joke."

"At least we've got a surname," James said.

Who are you, Marianne?

And how did you get involved?

More questions without answers. And, until he had the answers, all James could do was train the men he had at his disposal.

"How is the girl—Julia—doing?" Deacon asked.

"So far so good. She made it to Canada. She's on her own now..." James said. They'd organized papers for her, bought her a suitcase and packed it with clothes and ten thousand in cash. Samuel had wired an additional fifty thousand to a bank account in her new name and got her on a private plane to Canada.

"Okay, I'm going to head to the camp," James said. "I'll touch base with you later. Follow the doc's orders—get some rest."

～

James was merciless in his training, transferring all of his frustration into the drills that Biskup's men repeated over and over. They were improving, fast, and the new recruits seemed eager to please. Please Biskup, James assumed—not him.

Deacon was still in the safe house although the doctor had advised he was being released tomorrow, on the provision he only instructed the trainees and didn't participate himself. Maksym was with Biskup, and reports were good. He would make a fair recovery. The leg wound of the third patient had become infected but after a few days of intravenous antibiotics, it was beginning to show some signs of improvement.

Samuel had been quiet, very quiet. James knew he felt the pressure to come up with something—anything—but that one image of Marianne was all he'd been able to find in the last week. That alone told James that Marianne was perhaps even more protected than Eric. James also thought his initial assumption of Carl Junez being a member of a higher group within the organization was correct, although he had nothing to base that on other than intuition.

The lack of data wasn't unusual for such a case, but as the timeline stood, James had little more than a few weeks to find Eric before he would have to renegotiate the deal with Biskup—if it could even be renegotiated.

But with each day that morphed into the next, the clock ticked a little louder but James held onto the one slither of hope that was still in his body. And he knew, until his heart stopped beating, he'd never be able to give up. Without Eric, he couldn't get the code. Without the code, Biskup would never give up on Mak. And without eliminating Biskup and Eric as threats, James would never be free. It was a cruel cycle of life that had only one breaking point: Eric.

Where are you, Eric?

What are you doing?

~

Incoming call: Samuel.

James bolted upright, the sound of his ringing phone enhanced by his brother's, which was also singing on the makeshift bed next to him.

"Samuel?" James whispered, clearing the frogs from his throat.

"Boys, we've got a really big problem. Go somewhere you can talk," Samuel said in a rushed voice.

James was up and moving toward the door and Deacon was beside him.

James slid his pass over the lock and stepped out into the bitter cold night. Deacon closed the door behind them.

"Go ahead," James said.

"Tracker alerts have triggered for every member of Maya's security team. Security has been breached. All men down."

James felt like his heart was going to lurch out of his throat. "When?"

"Minutes ago," Samuel said.

James had to remind himself to breathe. Deacon's face was ashen-gray, reflecting how James felt.

"I should never have approved that work trip, even with the additional security team," James said. "This is my fault. Oh, God." James pinched the bridge of his nose.

"Where?" Deacon asked.

"I'm sending you the geographic location, but it's in Istanbul. No CCTV footage. We're assuming this is Eric, right? And not Biskup."

"Biskup has no reason to betray us at this point," Deacon said. "Eric is behind this."

Think, James, think.

"Mak's parents were due to leave for the cabin tomorrow morning, right?" James said.

"Yes."

"Cancel it. And get additional security teams out to every single one of Mak's family and take them all to Mak's apartment. Take Mak to Thomas Security. Say it's a precaution—I don't want this mentioned to any one of her family just yet. It is going to create hysteria and they'll want to go to the police."

They could not involve the police—for multiple reasons.

"Eric will make contact soon," James said, fearing how that contact would come. "Once we have additional information, we can make a plan, but for now..." James didn't even want to say it aloud. With his men down, and no CCTV footage, they had nothing to go on. Nothing.

"I'll call you back when I have something," Samuel said before the line went dead.

Why did I approve that trip? James had gone against his gut instincts, and this was the result. Maya had insisted on going, refusing to let her career be impacted, so after the worship ceremony James had sent an additional security team to supplement the men already with her. It wasn't enough. She should never have gone, work trip or not.

"Stop blaming yourself—it's not going to help," Deacon said. "We need to wait for Eric to make contact. This is a hostage situation now. He's going to blackmail us, and we need to be able to formulate a response."

James nodded, releasing a groaning sigh. In any hostage situation, the waiting period was always the most excruciating, and never had James felt more helpless.

James noted the time and watched every minute pass by until the call came from Samuel.

"I'm sending you a video. Activate the sound."

James tepidly pressed play. The brothers watched in horror.

Eric stood next to a bed, smiling a grin that made fear run beneath James' skin.

"Hello, James Thomas," Eric said. "As you can see, things have gotten a little complicated..."

Acid rose up to James' throat but he pushed it back down.

Eric continued. "I don't appreciate your new relationship with Alexandr Biskup. Nor do I appreciate your relationship with my wife. Because that's what she is—*my wife.* And so, unfortunately, things have come to this."

Eric tapped something against his hand, and James narrowed his eyes, squinting at the screen. It was a syringe. "I want to meet you. I want to know who you are. So, I'm going to make you a deal. I'll swap her," Eric said, nodding toward the bed, "for you. A clean trade. After all, I have no need for her. But..." Eric said, taking the needle cap off and sticking it into a vial. He drew up the liquid, and James knew what would be in the vial. It was the drug they traded, the drug they made their money from. Heroin.

Eric gave a creepy smile to the camera before he turned, sticking the needle into the catheter.

"The longer you wait, the more addicted she will become. Maya is such a good woman, and it would be a shame for her to end up a junkie. I'll give you her location details, and all you have to do is come and get her." Eric stilled, his gaze penetrating. "Oh, and one more thing, I'd like you to bring my wife with you. Our reunion is long overdue. I'll see you both soon."

The screen went blank.

"Oh, God," James said.

"Samuel, how did he send the video?" Deacon asked.

"It came up on the dark net, addressed to James Thomas."

Mak.

James couldn't take her to Eric—he couldn't—not without a guarantee of getting her out alive. But if he sacrificed Maya, Mak would never forgive him.

Eric had James right where he wanted him. What Eric didn't realize was that he'd also captured Liam Smith in the net.

"Samuel, get Mak and the team on a plane. Bring her to London," James said.

Deacon pressed his fingers to his lips. "What are you thinking?"

"I don't know," James said. "But I know that I have to get Mak close enough for Eric to believe she's with me. And then we need to go in and get Maya, while making sure Mak is safe."

The plan was forming in James' mind like dots waiting to be connected.

"What do I tell her?" Samuel asked.

"Nothing," James said, shaking his head. "I'll call her. Just get everything ready."

"Give me an hour," Samuel said.

James noted the time on his watch. "Thanks." He hung up, but as he opened his mouth to speak, a message grabbed his attention.

James knew the message was from Eric because he recognized the address.

Maya was being held in the building where the worship ceremony had taken place. James doubted she was there yet, given the time period, but she'd be transferred there soon.

Without speaking another word, James and Deacon went inside to the whiteboard markers and began to strategize. They brainstormed entry and exit points, ruling out one plan after another. When his alarm sounded an hour later, however, they were no closer to having a plan.

As James drew his phone, his hands began to tremble. Of all of the things he'd ever done, this was going to be the hardest. Mak's world was about to crumble, and he couldn't promise her he could fix it.

James stepped outside, walking away from the building, needing to move.

"Hey," Mak said, and James wondered if it was the last time he'd ever hear her voice so carefree.

"Hi…" He couldn't get the words out. They were stuck like a lump in his throat. But he had to tell her. He needed to. *This is my fault.*

"What's wrong?" she said quickly.

"There are cars waiting downstairs for you. Cami knows, and she's packed you a bag. I need you to come to London."

James came to a stop near an old tree and rested one palm against it. He felt ill.

"London? Are you okay?"

"No, but I'm not hurt." *Tell her, James.* "Samuel received a video, a video addressed to me, from Eric. Mak… Eric has Maya."

A heart-breaking silence echoed through the line.

"What did you say?" she finally asked with a trembling voice. James hoped Cami had her sitting down.

"Eric has Maya, Mak. Her security teams were breached. I'm so sorry."

Her breath became wheezy and James grimaced. "I can't... How... Can you see her? Is she okay?"

"No, she's not okay. One of Eric's business dealings is in heroin. We saw him inject a dose in the video. It could be a bluff, but I don't think it is."

"Why? Why is he doing this? This is my fault! I brought him into our lives...I married him..." Her voice was breaking with each word she spoke.

"He's willing to give Maya up, but he wants something in return. Two things, actually." James took a deep breath. "He wants me—because I gave Biskup information that resulted in an attack on him," James said, simplifying the information. He knew there was only so much Mak could absorb right now. "And...he wants you."

"I will give myself up, but you cannot. No! No one I love is going to die because of Eric. Only me."

"You're not going to give yourself up, and neither am I," James said sternly. "But I do need you in London, because I need to make him believe you are going to give yourself in. I need him to believe that while I go in and get Maya. If he doesn't see you, the plan will never work."

James said *plan* confidently, like he had crafted a faultless master-piece that would ensure everyone walked out of this alive.

"Just give me up, I don't care—"

"I will never do that, Mak," James said, his voice firm, cutting through her hysteria. "I can't make you any promises, but I've deceived men just like Eric before, and I'll do it again. I have Deacon, Cami, and Samuel, as well as a team of Biskup's men. A team I've been training for weeks—that's what I've been doing. That, combined with the fact that I used to lead a hostage retrieval team," he said, sharing information that he knew he shouldn't but he had to do something to give her hope—even it was unfounded. "Our chances are good. No one is going to sacrifice themselves—me included. We're going to figure this out, and then once we have Maya, I'm going to put an end to Eric once and for all. But I need you in London, and I need you to be strong—for Maya if nothing else. The sooner we get her, the less affected she'll by the heroin. The plane is waiting, Mak."

"What about the rest of my family? My parents are going tomorrow. I have to call Maya's fiancé..."

"Security teams are already covering them, Mak, and they're en route to your apartment. There's no point saying anything to anyone just yet—it'll only worry them. I want to get some more intel before we speak to your family about this. Let our team deal with it, please. The best thing you can do is to get on the plane. Come and meet me in London."

"Okay," she said, her tears clogging her voice.

"Good. I'll be in the hangar when you land. I'll see you soon, Mak. We're going to get her back." James said it to convince himself as much as Mak.

He hung up, tilting his head back. The sky was like a black storm and no matter how long James searched, he couldn't find any stars. Not a single one. *I hope that's not an omen.*

He looked back to the building—their makeshift camp—and thought of the men inside. They were it, his one chance.

James walked back to the building.

One chance was better than nothing, and he never backed down. *Never.*

//

ALSO BY BROOKE SIVENDRA

THE JAMES THOMAS SERIES

#1 - ESCANTA

#2 - SARATANI

#3 - SARQUIS

#4 - LUCIAN

#5 - SORIN

#0.5 - THE FAVOR

The complete James Thomas series is available now. THE FAVOR is a novella, and Brooke recommends reading it after SORIN.

THE SOUL SERIES

#1 - The Secrets of Their Souls

#2 - The Ghosts of Their Pasts

#3 - The Blood of Their Sins

A GIFT FROM BROOKE

Brooke is giving away the first book of the Soul Series, *The Secrets of Their Souls*, for **FREE**. All you need to do is sign up here:

http://brookesivendra.com/tsots-download/

Enjoy!

DID YOU ENJOY THIS BOOK?

As a writer, it is critically important to get reviews.

Why?

You probably weigh reviews highly when making a decision whether to try a new author—I definitely do.

So, if you've enjoyed this book and would love to spread the word, I would be so grateful if you could leave an honest review (as short or as long as you like) where you bought it.

Thank you so much,
Brooke

ABOUT THE AUTHOR

Brooke Sivendra lives in Adelaide, Australia with her husband and two furry children—Milly, a Rhodesian Ridgeback, and Lara, a massive Great Dane who is fifty pounds heavier than Brooke and thinks she is a lap dog!

Brooke has a degree in Nuclear Medicine and worked in the field of medical research before launching her first business at the age of twenty-six. This business grew to be Australia's premier online shopping directory, and Brooke recently sold it to focus on her writing.

You can connect with Brooke at any of the channels listed below, and she personally responds to every comment and email.

Website: www.brookesivendra.com
Email: brooke@brookesivendra.com
Facebook: http://www.facebook.com/bsivendra
Instagram: http://www.instagram.com/brookesivendra
Twitter: www.twitter.com/brookesivendra

DEDICATION

This book is dedicated to my readers.
Thank you for making this journey possible.

CPSIA information can be obtained
at www.ICGtesting.com
Printed in the USA
LVHW08s1053050718
582769LV00001B/159/P